Night Coach to Paris

BY THE SAME AUTHOR

Pirates of Samarkand

Rogue Whaler

Ice Falcon

Secret Beyond the Mountains

The Enemy at the Gate

The Golden Hawks of Genghis Khan

The Year of the Horse

RITA RITCHIE

NIGHT COACH TO PARIS

W · W · NORTON & COMPANY · INC ·
New York

First Edition

Library of Congress Catalog Card No. 70-99455

Published simultaneously in Canada by
George J. McLeod Limited, Toronto

Printed in the United States of America

1 2 3 4 5 6 7 8 9 0

In memory of Ruth Harshaw

Contents

Dark Entry

I As THE LONGBOAT pulled steadily through the night seas, Maurice Fabry gripped the edges of his thwart in a mixture of eagerness and alarm. He could feel the thrust and drop of the ocean and hear faintly the muffled oars of the sailors. Around him there was nothing but blackness, for clouds shut out the starlight. Somewhere behind in the invisible sea the barkentine *All's Well* stood off with riding lights doused. Captain Hawthorn sat beside Maurice in the longboat, which was loaded with cargo being brought secretly into France.

The warm breeze stirred restlessly this second day of July. A light gleamed on the coast. Another appeared, and then came a broad sprinkling of lamps and torches. Two ships lay alongside a quay, and numerous fishing boats were drawn up on the flats.

"That's Port Nazaire, isn't it, Captain?" Maurice's heart lunged at the dangers he knew lay concealed beneath that peaceful night scene.

"Aye, lad, 'tis Port Nazaire. We're in the river now, the Loire. The Frenchies call it the *Lwahr*." Then he chuckled dryly. "Now I'm forgetting you'd know that, being one of them."

Maurice Fabry said indignantly, "I'm a Yankee same as

you, Captain Hawthorn, born and raised in Boston. And both of us have been American citizens for just the last eleven years."

"Since 1783, when we won our Revolutionary War," the captain acknowledged. "And you French—I mean, *them* French helped us considerable. Which is why I don't mind sneaking a bit of cargo to them past the British blockade, now that they got their hands full fighting England, the Spaniards, the Belgies, and I don't know who all."

The longboat drew swiftly toward the lighted shore. Captain Hawthorn cleared his throat. "I hear in the ports now and then that things ain't too safe for Frenchmen themselves in their own land, nowadays. And with you speaking their lingo, you might get mistook for some native-born troublemaker."

"I've got papers proving I'm an American," Maurice assured him. They were locked safely in his valise along with Claude's last letter, the one with the detailed instructions on how Maurice was to act and speak in order to avoid drawing attention to himself.

Captain Hawthorn grunted approval. "But I still can't figure what your father was up to, sending you off on a holiday to the old country when you got to be smuggled into port like a sack of contraband."

Maurice grinned at this latest of many efforts to learn what the captain obviously suspected was a hidden purpose to young Fabry's trip to France. Maurice said truthfully, "I'm done with my schooling, and in a couple of months I'll be working regularly in my father's cabinetmaker's shop in Boston. This is about the only chance I'll have to visit our relatives."

Yet so urgent was this journey that whether or not the time were convenient, Maurice would still be slipping into France some night in a vessel's longboat.

The captain sucked on his unlighted pipe. "Somebody coming to meet you in port?"

"No, sir. I'm to take the night coach to Paris. It leaves the Equality Inn at ten o'clock."

"You'll do some scrambling to catch it when we land." Captain Hawthorn spoke to the sailors. "C'mon, boys, bend them oars!"

The docks loomed up rapidly. Someone hailed them, unintelligibly to Maurice, in seaman's jargon missing from the French spoken in his Boston home. But Captain Hawthorn called an answer, and soon the longboat was made fast to a pier, and men in smocks and wide trousers caught and stacked the bales and sacks the sailors tossed up to them.

"Poudre! Savon! Gunpowder! Soap!" exclaimed one of the dockworkers delightedly.

Captain Hawthorn laughed. *"Et des souliers de cuir!"* he added in a crude Yankee accent. "Leather shoes as well!" He turned to Maurice. "Up you go, lad, and hurry. It's just lacking a few minutes of ten o'clock. Now bear in mind the *All's Well* will be in Marseille just a month hence. That'll make it the second of August, give or take a day. Be there promptly, young fellow, for I'm not staying above three days."

"I'll be there, never fear, sir."

Valise in hand, Maurice Fabry crossed the quay. A man stood under a street lamp in brooding supervision of the dock workers. He wore the same smock and baggy trousers, but his shaggy hair was topped by a tailed knitted cap of red.

Maurice paused beside him. "Pardon me, *mon—*" He bit off the *monsieur* just in time, remembering Claude's warnings. "Excuse me, citizen, can you direct me to the Equality Inn?" He had spoken in French.

The man sullenly examined Maurice's watch coat and billed cap, seaman's clothing worn for the Atlantic crossing. "Has your captain given leave for you to spend the night ashore?"

"I'm not a sailor, but a passenger. I want to take the night coach to Paris."

The man's eyes hardened. "You speak French uncommonly well. Where were you born? What's your father's name? What does he do for a living?"

Maurice answered, struggling to keep his patience. Surely by now the Paris coach horses were being hitched! It was the only coach that went all the way up the Loire valley, then on to Paris, three times a month. There were so many details to his mission that if Maurice lost ten days' time just waiting for the next coach, he ran the risk of missing Captain Hawthorn's vessel in Marseille. "Please, *mon*—er, citizen! I have to—"

"You nearly called me *monsieur,*" the man accused him grimly, referring to the old style of address. "You're one of them dirty aristocrats, crawling back to the Fatherland to plot overthrowing the Revolution."

The words took Maurice's breath away. Claude's written hints were assuming an ugly reality. He was glad he had not mentioned his cousin's name.

Captain Hawthorn spoke from behind in clumsy syllables. "What goes, François?"

François poked a dirty thumb toward Maurice. "I have exposed a dangerous type here."

Captain Hawthorn shook his head in amused disbelief. Then in halting, seaport French, he managed to account for Maurice Fabry to his interrogator's satisfaction. And at last Maurice received directions to the coaching inn.

Captain Hawthorn spoke in English. "You got the directions right, lad? He talked a wadful there that I couldn't fathom. All right, now, off you go."

As Maurice started up the cobblestone street he heard the captain say to François, "No, I won't take them paper assignats. Payment got to be silver. . . ."

Once past the corner of a warehouse, Maurice broke into a run, his valise banging against his legs. As he darted around the correct turns, he thanked heaven the streets were almost deserted. If anyone else stopped him now—

The square suddenly broke open before him, a great cobbled rectangle edged with flaring street lamps. Maurice glanced hastily through the late traffic of a few pedestrians, three horsemen, a cabriolet, an oxcart. . . . There was a large vehicle at the far end, horses snorting in their traces as people climbed inside.

It was the Paris coach loading its passengers!

"Wait up!" shouted Maurice.

As he ran across the square toward the coach he heard a sudden flurry of horse's hoofs behind him. Someone called out, "You, there, stop!"

Maurice, pretending not to hear, raced over the cobbles, arriving at the coach just as the driver slammed the door shut. Maurice pulled at the man's sleeve. "Is this the night coach to Paris? I want to buy a seat."

"Hein!" exclaimed the startled driver. "You're too late. We are just going."

The horseman across the square clattered nearer and shouted again.

Maurice pulled money from his coat pocket, Yankee silver, and shoved it at the driver. "Is this enough? I'm going to Orléans."

The coachman stared greedily at the silver. "You have papers? Never mind! I'm late, so climb inside!" And scooping the coins from Maurice's hand he yanked open the door.

Maurice jumped inside, the door slammed, and the coach lurched away from the inn. As it jolted across the square, Maurice, swaying on the floor with his face against the window, saw a cloaked horseman reining to a halt. The driver whipped the coach past him and swung around a corner.

From the occasional gleam of passing lamps Maurice saw that the cross seats of the coach were crowded with men and women, two holding children on their laps. Awkwardly, he pushed and shoved to make a place for himself against the grumblings of the other passengers. As he squeezed into a hard straight-backed bench, clutching his valise on his lap, a hand felt along the sleeve of his coat. The woman next to him said, "That is stout cloth, young citizen. Where did you get it?"

Was Maurice again to be accused of aristocracy and plots? But no. From a far corner an older man hissed, "Hoarder! Our sons fighting for the Fatherland must go about in rags!"

"Fi donc, citoyen!" rebuked a young woman. "French soldiers do not go in rags, citizen. Everyone knows how well the army cares for our brave fighting men."

"Forgive me, citizeness!" exclaimed the man. "I spoke in haste."

The young woman continued. "It is unpatriotic to say such untruthful things, even in haste. And are we not all of us patriots?"

"Mais oui! C'est ça! Vrai, vrai!"

A wave of hasty agreement swept through the crowded coach, and the passengers settled down to silence and what comfort they could find on the hard board seats. The question of Maurice Fabry's good cloth coat was forgotten.

Through the window Maurice saw the last lamps of Port Nazaire drop behind. Hoofs drumming, wheels rattling, the Paris-bound coach lumbered down the dark road. The passengers wedged shoulder to shoulder swayed in unison with every jolt. The journey would go on like this, one stifled and cramped hour after another, with no relief but periodic stops to change horses and half a night's sleep some time tomorrow. Then during the second morning of travel Maurice Fabry would at last reach Orléans—and the house of his cousin Claude Donard. It was in answer to Claude's urgent plea that Maurice had hastened across the Atlantic.

Claude, living with his widowed father and his young sister Estelle, had been the letter writer of the Donard family since the beginning of the Revolution in France five years ago in 1789. As a printer working in his father's shop, he saw all the latest reports of what was happening throughout the country. Carried along with the winds of change, Claude eagerly described events for the family of his aunt, Maurice's mother. "You, dear aunt and uncle, went to America to find freedom," one of his first letters had stated. "But here in France, at last, freedom comes to us!"

The French King, Louis the Sixteenth, had called for a great meeting to take place on May 5, 1789. For the first time in nearly two hundred years the Estates-General would gather to advise the king on government matters, for problems had arisen that neither he nor his ministers could solve. Each estate, the nobles, the Church, and the commoners (sometimes called the Third Estate), would elect its own delegates to the meeting. *Cahiers*—lists of the people's complaints—were to be taken along by the delegates.

"So that everyone may discuss the coming election freely, the king has lifted censorship," Claude's letter reported. "Our printing presses run day and night, turning out handbills, newspapers, pamphlets, even entire books. Everyone is talking of what is wrong with how the country is run and how best to fix matters. Many scholars have thought out whole new systems of government and the rights due to common men. Words like these only a few weeks ago would have meant prison for author and printer alike! Now the press has actually grown into a fourth estate."

When Claude had written this, Maurice had been too young to understand it or even to care about a nation that was foreign to him. And in recent years his parents no longer talked over their nephew's letters in great detail. They were glad for news of relatives, and it was interesting to learn of general events in France. But America was their country by choice, and in this freshly independent nation many changes were taking place around them that claimed their attention first. It was left to Maurice, disturbed by the many cautions Claude had written lately, to scan through his cousin's old letters, trying to discover what had gone wrong in the country of his parents' birth.

The great meeting of the Estates-General had taken place in Versailles at the palatial residence of the king. Here dragged the endless debating over France's ills; the enormous national debt, the heavy taxes, high food prices, closing factories, and numerous other troubles. Suddenly the impatient delegates of the Third Estate, the common people, seized control of the meeting, forced King Louis to recognize them as representing the entire nation, and began to write a constitution for France, guaranteeing liberty, equality, and fraternity for all.

Claude's letters reflected the tumultuous changes during the next five years. The people ruling themselves through elected delegates decreed religious tolerance. The new government stripped nobles and clergy of their privileges and took their property away. The State now operated the Church, though this caused serious opposition, and hundreds of priests were thrown into prison and later executed. Political clubs sprang up, supporting their delegates, issuing newspapers and pamphlets to influence the people.

Mobs gathered, burning châteaux and killing nobles in various parts of the country. Those titled and moneyed who could escaped from the new nation. In Paris the people stormed the Bastille prison, destroying it and slaying the guards. Six thousand women of the city, marching to Versailles, brought King Louis back to Paris with them. A year later, the king, fleeing for his life, lost the race when arrested near the French border. He was imprisoned in Paris.

France declared war on Austria, invaded Belgium, and began losing heavily. Defeated French generals forfeited their lives on the Paris guillotine. With the city itself threatened by enemy forces, vigilante crowds broke into the prisons and executed hundreds of people awaiting trial. King Louis died on the guillotine. The Republic of France declared war against England, against Spain, and all of Europe was in arms. Sections of France rose up in revolt against their own government. Amid charges of plots and treason, the mobs of Paris poor forced their demands on the ruling delegates. Secret police scurried throughout the country to ferret out treachery. A new court, the Revolutionary Tribunal, swiftly condemned enemies of the people to the guillotine. Queen Marie Antoinette's head fell under the national blade. One political party after another rode the grim tumbrils to the scaffold until only a single faction dominated the government, the Jacobins.

Throughout the years of turmoil, printer Claude Donard's enthusiasm turned to doubt and then to regret in his letters to his aunt's family in America. Several times he wrote indignantly of some injustice, and once he stormed in angry protest over yet another repressive decree.

Suddenly Claude turned cautious, with but a single, early paragraph to foreshadow the change: "I have spoken too freely among acquaintances and customers here in Orléans. If my father were not so highly regarded by the men in power here, I tremble to think what might happen to me. One must support every aspect of the Revolution and the Republic no matter what one thinks or suffers. . . ." After this Claude wrote mostly family news. But buried in it were veiled hints of oppression which passed unnoticed or misunderstood by Maurice's parents.

When Claude's father died, there came the blunt urgent request. "I am sending this letter by friends I can trust. Come and take my sister Estelle away to America where she can be a daughter to you, dearest aunt. It is dangerous for her to remain in France. Uncle, you must travel at once, alone for the sake of speed and safety, and take Estelle abroad. . . ."

Maurice's *maman* had said, "I will take the child gladly. Claude need not frighten me with talk of danger."

And Papa had shrugged. "The young are impatient and excitable."

But Maurice's father was reluctant to shut up his shop and leave Boston. "Several important customers are waiting for me to finish some fine cabinetwork for them that only I myself can do. You shall go to France in my place, Maurice," Papa had said. "It is a simple errand to travel to Orléans, stay a week or two to make arrangements for the return journey, and then bring home your cousin Estelle. She is of your age and will present no trouble. I will write Claude of our decision."

Maman had immediately started sewing a fancy suit of silken breeches and frock coat for Maurice to wear when meeting his relatives. During the many fittings, Maurice had protested. "But, Maman! Claude says no one in France wears such clothing any more."

Maman was adamant. "Revolution or not, the French are civilized."

Claude's last letter had been addressed directly to Maurice, and his father had handed it to him unopened. Once more sent through "friends I can trust," this one had set forth the careful instructions for avoiding notice. "Because you speak French, Maurice, you had best bring papers proving your American citizenship. Even so, the easiest way to avoid trouble is to act and speak with the same care as we must here in France. There are secret police everywhere. . . ."

As he memorized Claude's detailed directions, Maurice felt the stirring of alarm, and perceived a lurking danger of which his parents seemed unaware. But still, Maurice Fabry was the only one who could rescue his young cousin Estelle Donard from whatever hazards threatened.

It was then that Maurice went through Claude's old letters, scanning rapidly through the years. From the thousands of words about politics, law, and government, which he only vaguely understood, the news of rioting and executions, and more recently the subtle warnings, Maurice sensed the first notes of hope for the Revolution turn into chords of fear. Relentlessly, then, terror mounted throughout France, and behind this oppression drummed the name of a single dreaded man, Robespierre . . . Robespierre . . . Robespierre. . . .

The Paris coach thundered rhythmically through the night. Maurice awoke, suddenly conscious of another cadence, of horses galloping up from behind. He worked his cramped limbs, aware that during the three hours he had dozed off and on the moon had climbed overhead in a clearing sky. The clatter of hoofs sounded louder.

The other passengers stirred. A child, waking, whimpered. One man peered out of the window. "There are three horsemen about to overtake us."

"They must have urgent business to travel at such an hour!" exclaimed an old woman. "It is surely past one in the morning."

Suddenly a horseman flashed by Maurice's window, spurring his mount furiously. Two shadows flitted past on the other side. The driver and the horsemen speeding together shouted back and forth in demand and denial. Then the coach rocked perilously as its horses were abruptly pulled down. They lurched to a swaying halt. Maurice heard the driver cry, "Fool, you could have killed us all!"

One of the horsemen reined near the coach door and called out. Startled, Maurice heard his own name, some indistinguishable words, then Claude's name. Had his cousin sent word of a change in plans?

The passengers muttered in speculation. "They seek a traitor, surely." "Not among us, good woman!" "Sit quietly, citizens! They will take anyone to fill out their list."

The driver, his voice muted by wood and glass, cried in exasperation, "I tell you there is no Donard. And no Fabry! I have seen their papers. Out of my way!" He clicked to his horses.

Maurice struggled out of his seat and banged on the window. "Here I am, citizen!" he shouted.

The horseman wrenched open the door. Maurice, forgetting the step had not been set up, plunged toward the road. A passenger threw his valise out after him. Before

Maurice could scramble to his feet he heard the coach door slam, heard the driver cry up his horses, heard the rattle and clatter as the night coach to Paris started off and gathered speed.

One of the men threw himself into his saddle, but another ordered sharply, "Let it go! We've got what we want." The man pulled Maurice to his feet and jerked his head around so that the moon struck him full and bright in the face. "Bah! This lad can't be Claude Donard!"

Maurice was certain there must be some error. He tried to work loose from the grip on his coat, protesting jerkily, "I'm Maurice Fabry. You called me. What do you want?"

"Bien entendu, it is the American cousin!" The hand gripped his coat tighter. "Why didn't Claude Donard come out of the coach with you?" And then the man repeated his question, very slowly and clearly.

Bewildered, Maurice stammered, "W—what do you mean? Claude wasn't in the—the coach." Maurice was the victim of a mistake after all. He wondered if he could persuade these men to help him catch up with the coach, for in less than an hour it would have to stop for a change of horses.

The three men, one holding the horses, were indistinct shadows in dark clothing, hats or caps pulled low, collars turned up. They huddled together, muttering rapidly among themselves. The one still holding Maurice's coat snarled to another, "Clumsy oaf! This is all your fault! You leaped to the wrong conclusion."

"But, Félix, how could I know Donard would let his cousin flounder around France by himself? Everything argued that he would meet him in Nazaire and ride the Paris coach with him."

The one holding the horses added, "A natural mistake, Félix, *n'est-ce-pas?* True, we find this child knows a smattering of French, but even so he stutters it badly."

Maurice spoke French as fluently as a native. Confusion and growing uneasiness had made him stammer.

The man called Félix turned his attention to him, and speaking slowly and distinctly, as one would to a small child, said, "*Allons,* young fellow, we have made a mistake that we will now correct, *comprenez vous?* Claude Donard is our friend. Tell us where he is. We will take you there at once."

Félix's heartiness rang as falsely as his words. No friends these, though they had somehow learned of Maurice's impending arrival in France. Men who would gallop at breakneck speed to stop a coach in the middle of the night were both desperate and dangerous.

And now Félix acted as though Maurice's inadvertent clumsiness in the horseman's native tongue meant a correspondingly simple mind. Needing time to devise an escape, Maurice decided to play the role of foolish innocent that had been thrust upon him. He stared vacantly at Félix's shadowed face and spoke haltingly in Captain Hawthorn's harsh accent. "I no—understand. You take me—Claude?"

"Yes, yes, *mon ami!* We take you to Claude. Where is he?" He grinned in anticipation, his teeth gleaming in the moonlight.

There was a large boulder next to a roadside hedge, just a few steps away. But Félix's hand still twisted Maurice's collar. Maurice remembered a friend's uncle who had suffered a mishap while traveling to Philadelphia. That incident would serve him now. "Claude, yes, yes!" He nodded and nodded. "But first—my valise!" He began to wave his arms. "Find my valise! Those villains threw it! Must have . . . clothes . . . everything!" Félix's hand relaxed a little, and Maurice went on in simulated anger. "My valise! I report to American minister! I complain to French government!"

"No need to shout, *mon ami,*" said Félix. "We will find your valise. You stay here, *n'est-ce-pas?*" Somewhat amused, Félix took his hand away from Maurice's collar. It was the left hand, and moonlight shone through a clear green stone ring on the middle finger. Oddly, the third finger, which should have worn the ring, was missing.

Félix and one of the men began hunting around on the road for Maurice's valise. The third, still holding the horses, yawned with boredom.

Suddenly Maurice sprang to the boulder beside the hedge. From there he vaulted over the thick growth, landing heavily in the shadows on the other side. Before him sloped a broad pasture, well lighted by the moon. He huddled indecisively under the bottom branches of the shrubs.

On the road a few hidden feet away, startled horses whinnied, and the men shouted. Soon there was a crashing of branches some distance ahead of Maurice, then Félix and the second man burst through the thick growth. Félix began running down toward a distant clump of trees while his companion groped along the hedge away from Maurice. Plainly, they reckoned on his having run off at once.

The horseholder left on the road spoke sharply to the mounts, trying to calm them. Under cover of this noise Maurice began working his way along the deeply shadowed hedge in a direction opposite that of his searchers and back toward distant Port Nazaire.

A shot rang out.

Maurice froze, staring behind. Gunpowder flared again, and he saw that a startled rabbit had fooled Félix. Relieved, Maurice resumed his stealthy progress along the hedge.

A dip in the field soon hid him from Félix and his cohorts. He pushed his way through a clump of willows, leaving the hedge to follow the fold of the land, heading now toward the Loire River a mile or two distant. He could hear and see nothing of the riders who had stopped the Paris coach.

After a while the gully he followed in the moonlight began to widen. The soil thinned and rock broke through. Then as he was working past some bushes Maurice saw the black mouth of a small cave.

Without hesitation he stooped and thrust his way inside. The bushes sprang back into place, shutting off the entrance. In darkness, on hard ground, Maurice settled himself for sleep.

Just as exhaustion was sweeping over him, his foot struck a bottle which chimed softly against another.

Secret Beneath the Water

II SUNLIGHT BURST OVER Maurice Fabry's face. He sat up with a start, blinking, and then once more shadow swept over the mouth of the small cave where he had spent the night.

In the grayness Maurice saw a youth of about his own age step toward him. The stranger said, "I wanted to see what you looked like. You came crashing in here in the middle of the night, disturbing my sleep with your kicking of bottles."

"Bottles?" Looking around Maurice saw now the deep rows and ranks of bottles stretching far back in the cave. Shoulder to shoulder they paved the stone floor, and in wooden racks they tiled the walls. Each bottle was filled and sealed. "What's in them? Are they yours?"

The youth stood over Maurice, frowning. "Will you play the fool with me?" His clothing was tattered and badly mended, but he stood straight and spoke forthrightly. "Out of charity I did not turn you out last night. So now in payment you must satisfy my curiosity. Why would a sailor hide in a cave like a rabbit going to ground?"

Maurice's mind flashed back to last night's startled rabbit and Félix's unwitting shot after it. Maurice was in fact an animal run to ground.

The youth prompted impatiently, "Did you run from your ship?"

"No." Maurice shook his head. "These clothes—I'm not a sailor. I was a passenger on a vessel, an American passenger on a Yankee barkentine."

The youth laughed scornfully. "A stupid sort of lie to tell. Show me your identity. Let me see your bread card."

"Ration card? I don't have one. I'm not French. I have papers proving I'm an American." He felt in his pockets, then remembered. "They're in my valise. It's somewhere on the high road."

"No papers, eh? If I turned you over to the authorities I could earn myself a fine reward."

"I tell you I'm not a French citizen!" Maurice exclaimed.

"How did you get here last night?" the ragged youth demanded. "We are half a mile from the nearest road, a full mile from the highway."

Maurice calculated the youth's strength and felt that his chances against him were good. Even if it did not come to a real fight, Maurice could easily rush him and get out of the cave. Yet he would have to stop long enough later on to look for his valise. The youth might well have friends he could summon against Maurice. And some strange quirk of law or custom had given the common citizen of Revolutionary France extraordinary police powers. Maurice thought he had better follow Claude's instructions.

The youth must have seen Maurice's hesitation in his eyes, for he waited while Maurice made his decision.

"Bien," said Maurice. "I'll tell you, although I can't explain it. I was on the night coach to Paris, bound for Orléans to visit relatives. Three horsemen stopped the coach. . . ." Maurice gave a bare outline of last night's

events. But each sentence opened up fresh questions, and the strange lad listened with such absorption and sympathy that before quite realizing it, Maurice had unwound the entire tale from leaving Captain Hawthorn's vessel to his discovery of the cave. But he kept his real errand in France a secret. "I—I'm sorry if I trespassed on your property. I didn't know the cave was guarded."

The youth was silent while he thought over Maurice's story. Then he said, "I believe you, Maurice Fabry, for you could not have made all this up." He chewed his lip a moment, then nodded to himself. "My name is Jules Volant. And you, for losing your coach, are draped in a pretty cloth indeed, *n'est-ce-pas?* But I will help you and be your friend."

"You—help me? But why?"

"Some time ago a stranger found me on a road and helped me. So now I repay this debt. Come, let's breakfast while we figure out a way to get you to your cousin's house in Orléans." From a cranny in the cave wall Jules took out a large drawstring bag. Rummaging, he brought forth some hard rolls, a piece of cheese, and a leather bottle of mild wine. He divided these evenly with Maurice.

As they ate, Maurice asked Jules about himself, but the youth impatiently waved aside his questions. He did explain about the cave, which he did not own. It was underneath a vineyard, and wine was stored here both in casks and bottles because of the ideal temperature and humidity. There were many such storage caves, especially farther up the Loire valley.

Jules chewed slowly while he wrestled with Maurice's predicament. "It will be ten days or so before another Paris coach sets out. Do you have any money?"

"There's money in my valise." Maurice had given all his ready cash to the coachman. "But, Jules, that's not enough for what I need. I'll have to buy food and lodging for ten days' waiting as well as two days' traveling, not to mention the coaching fare. Luckily, my passage home has already been paid for—" A new thought struck him. "But what if I miss my vessel? Jules, losing ten, twelve days altogether before reaching Orléans might cost me my rendezvous with the *All's Well*! I'd need even more money to buy another passage." Besides ordinary expense funds, the only extra sum he had in his valise was to cover Estelle's fare across the Atlantic.

"If that happens, you might ask your cousin Claude Donard for money once you reach Orléans," suggested Jules.

"American shipmasters all want good hard Yankee money," Maurice explained. "They won't take the paper assignats printed by the French government."

"*Bien,* this cousin must have some silver put away somewhere. Everyone has, though it's hoarding and might cost one's head. Still, your problem is to get to Orléans with little delay." Jules Volant tapped his teeth with the blade of his knife. "You could perhaps rent a horse and ride to Orléans. But I don't know how you'd return the animal. And it would cost too much to buy one."

"There must be some local coaches running between the cities on the Loire," Maurice said. "I could take one after the other, from city to city."

"Delays, delays! It would take you nearly two weeks." Then Jules snapped his fingers. "Ah, I have it, Maurice! There are always freight boats and barges plying the Loire. It should be easy to find someone who'll let you go along to Orléans for just a few sous—or some of your hard Yankee money. The journey would take just three days or so, surely not as long as a week."

Maurice felt hope rising. "That's a clever idea, Jules." It would be a fine adventure to go up the great river of which Maman, reared on its banks, had often spoken with nostalgia. And if it were a little unusual to travel that way —well, it was only for a few days and Maurice Fabry would be protected by his American papers. "Jules, let's find a boat right away!"

Jules pulled on a red stocking cap that narrowed to a long tasseled tail. "First we must fetch your valise from the highway. It's not easy to live in France without money. But without papers it's absolutely impossible."

Jules tied up the drawstring bag and put his arm through the loop. Then after cautiously peering through the bushes screening the cave, he pushed his way outside. Maurice scrambled after him, and they set off up the gully, which was the bed of a dried-up stream. It was still very early in the morning, and the dew sparkled on the grass of the slopes rising above them.

"Not so fast, Jules! Those men might still be around."

"That type wouldn't be prowling in the fields. But we must be careful when we reach the road."

With Jules Volant setting a rapid pace they soon came within sight of the hedge bordering the highroad. "Maurice, hide in these willows until I whistle that it's safe to join me." Jules vanished through the thick hedge with only a faint rustle. Maurice was still wondering how he managed such a feat when the whistle shrilled. His own passage through the hedge was noisy and scratchy.

The tattered youth said, "There's nothing moving on the road. But neither do I see any valise."

The road ran broad, straight, and reasonably level between hedges broken by an occasional maple or clump of poplar. On either side lay pasture, fields of wheat and barley, small orchards, and here and there a sloping vineyard. There were no houses in sight.

Maurice studied the area carefully. "The coach was

stopped farther along, I'm sure. Someone threw my bag out. Maybe it landed in the hedge." Eyes alert, the two walked a long way down the road. Maurice found the boulder that had helped him escape. Farther on they came to the break in the hedge made by Félix and his companion. But of the valise there was no sign.

Jules suggested, "Let's search along the hedge on the other side of the road."

They spent a long time probing among the bottom branches, and then Maurice thought the horsemen might have thrown his valise over the hedge.

Jules asked, "Could they have stolen it?"

"I can't think why," Maurice answered. "They weren't interested in my valise at all, and only went to look for it to quiet me."

The sun climbed higher and hotter as they prowled along the field side of the hedges on both sides of the road. Sweat ran into Maurice's eyes, and he turned hot and cold in growing anxiety. Finally Jules said, "We must quit searching. Already I see that people working in the distant fields are staring our way. Soon someone will come and ask us questions. Without papers, Maurice, you are certain to be in serious trouble."

Maurice sank down on a flat rock and put his head in his hands. His heart was pounding and panic swept over him. Never in his life had he been so helpless. "No money!" he groaned, just stifling a sob. "And what's worse—no papers!"

"Have you nothing at all to show you are from America?" asked Jules. "A letter, perhaps, or a ticket on this vessel you spoke of?"

Maurice miserably shook his head. "There was no ticket, as it's a cargo vessel, and I'm known to the captain. I had a letter from my cousin Claude Donard. And I had written out a route and timetable so I wouldn't forget the coaches, this one and the one for Marseille. There was a letter from the town clerk of Boston, certifying my American citizenship, and another letter from a judge my father knows, testifying to my identity and good character. I had American money, too, sealed in an envelope. Everything was in my valise." He swallowed hard. "Now I have nothing but the clothes I'm wearing." And they were seaman's clothes, not those of an American cabinetmaker's son going to meet his relatives. "If only I could get to Orléans!"

At Jules' sharp comment, he realized his exclamation had been in English. He translated the phrase for his companion, then jumped to his feet. "Jules, I can prove I'm an American because I speak English!"

But Jules Volant shook his head. "It proves only that you *are* English, and therefore a spy to be executed at once. Or you'd be one of the French who fled to England at the start of the Revolution, now returning to the Fatherland to stir up treasonous activities. No, no, *mon ami!* Your English language is a curse and a danger to you now."

"My cousin Claude Donard can identify me as an American, once we get to Orléans."

Jules nodded slowly. "Yes, although if men are seeking him . . . *Allons,* one problem at a time! Perhaps we can get to Orléans after all, if we are very careful. And if you are French. First, your cap—" Jules snatched off his sea cap and thrust it deep into the thick hedge. From his bag he took a red knit cap like the one he wore, though much more faded and far dirtier. "Put this on. And this." He took out a grimy rosette of stiff red, white, and blue cloth and fastened it to the lapel of Maurice's jacket. On his own ragged coat he pinned a long ribbon of the same three colors. "Usually I do not bother, as one stranger goes fairly unnoticed."

Maurice knew of the fashion to go about wearing these patriotic decorations. Claude had deemed these unnecessary for Maurice's coach trip. Now everything had changed, and safety lay in proclaiming one's patriotism.

Jules studied Maurice, tossed some dirt on his sea jacket, then nodded with satisfaction. "We're two young fellows out looking for work. We'll stop now and then to earn a meal, but what we really want is a job on some barge going up the Loire."

So they were back to Jules' original plan, only this time they would have to work their way to Orléans. Maurice had one worry. "What if a barge master asks for my papers?"

"People don't bother wandering laborers picking up small jobs here and there," Jules explained. "If you want to stay in a place for a while, or take a better paying job, or if you get into an argument, then everyone starts poking his nose into your papers."

Jules slung his bag over his shoulder and led the way back to the dry stream bed. "Ordinarily I take the highway, but if those three men are searching for you I think we should follow the peasant cart tracks nearer the river, for they are seldom traveled."

"Won't I need a bread card?" Maurice asked as they retraced their steps caveward.

"If we get any money to buy bread, I'll share my ration with you," Jules offered.

They passed the wine cave and kept on until they reached a woodlot. Jules started off through the trees. Maurice feared the peasant owner might discover them going through his property until he learned that everyone lived in villages and went out to work in his scattered fields every day. Only occasionally would one find a farm family living in an isolated home among its fields. "I seldom meet peasants out working," said Jules, "because I usually avoid those fields where anyone is likely to be according to the crop and the season. In this way I have the greatest freedom in traveling where I wish."

It was plain to Maurice that this strange youth was accustomed to living by his wits.

Some time after passing the cave they crossed a pasture and then burrowed through a hedge at some secret place of Jules'. They came out on a rough track creeping lazily over the gentle roll of the land. Poplars flashed their leaves in the sun, and through distant trees Maurice saw an occasional sparkle. "Is that the Loire?"

"Yes, we'll see it more closely soon. Come, *mon ami,* toward Nantes!" This was the next city up the valley, a good day's walk distant. Jules swung into a long loose-jointed foot-traveler's stride, which Maurice gradually adopted.

Their hike went so pleasantly that Maurice could scarcely believe he had been in France less than a day, had been shot at, and was now a fugitive in fear for his life. People worked steadily in distant fields. A peasant's cart squealed around a bend in the track, the driver making a friendly gesture as he passed them. Later two young men called a cheerful greeting as they passed them on the field side of the hedge border.

At noon, Jules said, "People will be going home to eat now. And I think a village lies not far ahead. We'll cross the Loire now, when there's no one around to see us."

"But why cross the river?" Maurice protested. "We can reach Nantes on this side. And you said we'd probably get there by nightfall."

"I cannot forget those men who went after you," replied Jules. "Perhaps it will occur to them to search along the cart tracks. And people we've met will remember us. But these three men are certain to keep on the right bank of the river. And if we cross over to the left bank, we need never think of them again."

By right and left, Maurice understood that Jules meant on which hand either river bank lay as a person faced downstream.

They tarried near a group of small poplars until Jules felt everyone would be busy with his meal. Then they entered an apple orchard by a gate set in the hedge and walked through rapidly. The ground dropped until it was quite flat and bordered with unruly growth. Maurice sensed coolness in the still air. They thrust their way through the growth to a wide path. Before them stretched the broad Loire, its extensive mudflats cracking hexagonally under a hot sun.

"But it's brown and ugly!" exclaimed Maurice. Was this the magnificent Loire of which Maman had longingly spoken? This, the shimmering crystal Loire of Orléans where she had grown up in the very house Maurice now sought?

Jules glanced at him in amusement. "It's the fine silt carried hundreds of miles from the mountains at the source. Too, the water level drops in summertime. This year it's lower than ever because of the lack of rain." He pointed upstream toward a brushy cluster in the river. "See those islands? We'll go from one to the other to get across."

"Are we to swim?" There did not seem to be much current in the sluggish brown water, but Maurice knew the perils of undertows.

"We'll throw together a raft," Jules said. "All sorts of useful junk can be found along this barge towpath. Here's something." He bent to retrieve a scrap of worn rope.

Going up the towpath, they picked up a broken oar, two

or three bent nails, a small coil of twine, a waterworn plank, and other items. By the time they reached the cluster of islets they had enough material for a crude raft.

In half an hour everything was lashed and nailed together. "A little shaky," Jules admitted. "But good enough to get us over a step at a time."

Jules produced a knife and cut two slender branches as poles. Then the youths pushed out into the river. The raft surged across to the nearest island and grounded itself in the mud. With a rope they pulled their rough craft to the other side and launched it once more, landing easily on the next islet. "Two more trips and we're across," said Jules, a little cocky about the success of his idea. "But with all these bushes and saplings about us, this would be a good place to cook a meal."

"I thought we ate everything in your bag," said Maurice.

But Jules took out a much-mended net instead. After three casts in the slow current he brought in a large flapping fish. He quickly killed it. "Maurice, while I'm cleaning our catch, go get some wood for a fire. Be sure it's dry; we don't want any smoke for people to see."

Maurice started off among the bushes. It was not hard to find plenty of dry sticks just by moving along. He tied his first bundle with a piece of twine, then soon collected another. Finally he had a whole backload of fuel which kept catching on the bushes. Maurice detoured to the muddy bank whose shallow slope was free of growth. He tied his shoes by the laces and hung them around his neck and made good progress until he rounded a sharp bend.

Ahead, the curved ribs and broken planking of a grounded vessel rose from mud and water.

There might be something worth salvaging. Maurice

dropped his firewood and ran to the find, splashing out into the shallow water toward the largest break in the timbers.

The vessel had the lines of a barge, or at least the forward part of one. It seemed to be a recent wreck, probably torn from moorings and dashed downstream during spring freshets. This bow section had driven deep into the mud, to be exposed as summer heat and drought lowered the level of the river.

Conscious of his bare feet, Maurice worked his way carefully through the yawning gap in the side of the hulk. He paused to accustom his eyes to the shadowed interior. The bulwarks reached far above his head, and over this a few remaining pieces of deck planking shut off most of the sky. But sunshine glared off the river through the splintered gaps.

Mud and water sloshed gently inside the wooden cavern. Here and there was the soft glow of ivory-colored lumps. Maurice was disappointed. There was nothing but the rocks used for ballast, or perhaps this had been a cargo of building stone.

Turning to go, Maurice stepped on a smooth round stone. His foot slipped; the "stone" slewed around, and a grinning skull stared up at him out of its hollow eyes.

He choked back a startled cry. A sailor or watchman had drowned with his vessel.

Then Maurice saw he was standing on top of the skeleton.

Recoiling, he floundered in the mud and water of the wrecked barge. Something settled about his ankle, and kicking it off he saw the object sail through the air before it struck the side and sank back in the water. It was an iron band with a chain. The chain ended in another manacle around the bones of an arm and hand.

No wonder the sailor had— But no, this was on the other side of the hulk. *This* arm . . . Maurice peered closely in the gloom and made out another heap of bones thinly covered with mud.

Stunned, unable to understand, he staggered back toward the gap in the bulwarks, looking for clear places to set his bare feet. Embedded everywhere in the mud were more bones, of arms and legs, broken ivory shards thrust up like bare sticks or piled like kindling. Chains rusted on wrists and ankles, and twisted wire hung loose in grim bracelets. Skulls were heaped up like boulders washed together by waves. Some of these were cracked, and two or three had been split as by axes.

Thrashing among these dread relics, Maurice felt his foot sink between two ribs which gripped his ankle like a trap. Shuddering, he reached down and spread the ribs apart to pull his foot out. He saw then, with horror, that the skeleton held in its arms the bones of a small child, the wrists of both hung with chains.

In rising panic, Maurice staggered through the gap in the hulk. And as he splashed toward the island bank along the outside of the wreck, he noted a cleanly sawn hole just beneath the water level.

Someone had deliberately sunk this barge.

Raid!

III

JULES CAME RUNNING along the muddy bank.

"Maurice! You were gone so long I thought you might have had an accident."

Maurice clutched his companion's arm. "Look, Jules! That vessel is full of skeletons. They're chained, they—"

"Hein!" Jules glanced sharply at the wreck, then began pulling Maurice farther up the bank. "Come along at once. This is no business of ours. Did you get wood for the fire?"

"Yes, here . . ." Maurice recovered his bundle of twigs and hoisted it on his back while Jules urged him hastily toward their camp. "Jules, what happened in that barge?"

"Pressons—hurry up!"

A bend soon hid the dread sight. Neither spoke until they came to the circle of stones Jules had constructed to prevent the fire from escaping through the dry brush. Expertly the ragged youth broke and laid sticks for the fire, striking it into flames with a flint and steel from his shoulder bag. Showing Maurice the grilling forks he had fashioned out of supple twigs, Jules speared the fish filets and handed one to him. "Pay attention, *mon ami,* or you will burn your dinner! Here is some bread to eat with it. It is our last, and we'll have to come into some for our supper."

With much prodding, Maurice cooked and ate his fish. Jules' cheer seemed forced, and he hurried through the meal. Quickly he put out the fire, burying it with mud carried from the bank, then covered the site with bunches of grass and leaves.

But Maurice could not get his discovery out of his mind. "Jules, you know what happened back there, don't you?"

"I have heard rumors, only rumors," his companion answered grimly. "The less one knows, the better. Here is your pole. Get on the raft."

But Maurice hung back. "Why were they chained? Who were those people?"

Jules Volant exclaimed in exasperation. "That was a prison barge. It sank. Now you know everything."

"There was a big hole cut in the bottom. Maybe more than one," Maurice persisted, the fresh saw marks clear in his mind's eye. "Don't you understand, Jules? Someone sank the vessel with all those people inside it!"

"Euh, they say these were corpses, victims of disease. I heard they were sunk to keep the plague from spreading."

"There's no need to chain the dead!"

Jules gazed at him intently. "Maurice Fabry, if anyone learns that we have seen that wreck, we are as good as dead. Robespierre will have his secrets kept."

"Robespierre!" Maurice remembered the name from Claude's letters. "He—he holds France in an iron fist."

"Hush!" Jules gestured fiercely. "He is our benefactor, and can do nothing wrong. Men call him the Incorruptible." Swiftly he strode toward the flimsy raft. "Come!"

Thrusting across inter-island waters in two more stages, they reached the south bank of the broad Loire. While hiding the makeshift raft in thick shrubbery, Maurice came across a sign nailed to a tree and faded by several months' weathering. It was a warning not to use the river water because of pollution. "Look at this, Jules."

"I've seen those signs before below Nantes." Jules picked up a newer strip of paper out of the deep grass where it had fallen. "They have these fastened across them now."

The paper bore the single word, "Potable."

"That barge—" Maurice broke off, realizing with sudden horror that one boatload of prisoners would not render the entire lower Loire unusable. How many barges had gone to the bottom, how many men, women, and children, alive, chained, screaming . . .

"*Hé,* Maurice, will you linger the whole day?"

Maurice scrambled up a twisting path to join Jules at a cart track.

Aspen leaves winked and twirled in the bright sun, and birds scratched under the hedges. In an upper meadow someone was scything hay. Maurice was glad to put the fateful barge out of his mind.

The cart track joined another, wider one, and this in turn led to a fairly well-used road, though it was not a highway. Jules said, "We can travel faster now and will surely come to Nantes tonight. In the morning we can seek work on the river boats."

"Will your parents mind your going off with me like this?" Maurice wondered. "Won't they worry where you are?"

"I have no parents," Jules told him. "Nor any home but the road itself. Now don't linger; we have a long walk ahead of us."

Throughout the long hot afternoon their feet wore away the miles. They carried their jackets over their shoulders, but Jules insisted on their wearing the knitted red caps of liberty. Along the way they met a boy driving a small herd of cattle into a pasture; a carter with a load of wood rumbled past in the opposite direction; three girls with hoes over their shoulders went through a gate in a hedge; a horseman trotted by, then wheeled around to ask the way to some lake, but Jules had to admit he had never heard of it.

By the time the sun stood well behind them in the west, they had walked through two villages and one very small hamlet. "Time now to look out for our supper," said Jules.

At the top of the next rise Maurice pointed to a distant valley where houses huddled under trees. "We can try our luck in that next village."

"This is closer," said Jules, gesturing to a walled square near the bottom of the hill. Above it showed several thatched roofs. "There stands a farmstead by itself. It's better to beg a meal in such a place than to arouse a whole village with knocking on doors."

They reached the farm lane quickly, but Maurice was uneasy as they approached the walled premises. He had never begged for anything in his life, and he felt there was something shameful about it. "Jules, let's offer to work for the meal."

Jules raised his eyebrows. *"Oui,* if you, or they, insist. But there is seldom any work left undone by a peasant."

The big timber gate in the wall was unlocked. Boldly Jules pushed it open, setting off a violent barking from within. Ignoring the clamor of a chained dog, Jules strode past the barn, past the dungheap, and went straight to the door of the cottage itself. He knocked, not like a ragged wanderer but like the mayor of a village.

Maurice saw movement behind the narrow darkened windows, and then the door was flung open. The man standing there was a fierce-looking fellow, not tall but very strongly built and roughly bearded. His smock, trousers, and wooden shoes had taken on the patina of his farmwork. He inspected Maurice and Jules sharply and then said with surprising amiability, *"Bien,* citizens, what would you have of me?"

Though the dog still barked furiously, Jules replied with easy grace. "A meal, citizen, if you have food to spare for my friend and me. We will gladly work—"

The man uttered a short laugh. "All work is done promptly on these my acres!" Suddenly he roared out at the dog. "Montagne! Shut up that yapping, you cur!" The animal subsided into a whine, and the man turned back to the youths. "Come in. Perhaps we can find an extra crust or two."

The inside of the cottage was shadowed, but while the host spoke with his wife, Maurice's eyes became accustomed to the dimness. The beaten earth floor was covered with pleasant clean straw. An alcove held a great bedstead piled high with quilts. There were many cabinets around the walls, and the big fireplace was well equipped with cranes and kettles. A large oak table and two benches completed the furniture. But hanging on the wall, surprisingly, were five deerheads with impressive antlers.

The woman set out bowls of thin milk and big pieces of barley bread, then went back to tend a pot simmering on the fire. The man sat opposite the youths. "Eat with good appetite." Then he chuckled and said to Maurice, "You can't take your eyes from those deer. *Oui,* I shot them myself. It was the first thing we did in this district when we heard they had destroyed the Bastille prison in Paris."

"Ah, citizen, that was a day!" said Jules, hardly pausing in his eating.

Maurice chewed on his bread. It was coarse, but he was so hungry it went down easily.

The peasant went to light a pipe from a coal at the fire.

When he settled down again he said, "It was a day to snatch our freedom! We gathered together here in my farmyard, all of us peasants, and we marched to the baron's manor house a mile or so over the hills. After calling out him and his family, we set a grand fire. Do you know, those huge glass windows of his exploded like musket shots! Later I picked up some big pieces and had Jean of the village, who knows such things, cut it straight and set it in my own open windows here." He gestured proudly at the glass, flooded with rosy light from the lowering sun.

Jules bolted the last of his bread and stood up. "Thank you for the fare, good citizen."

The peasant seemed disappointed that his reminiscence was cut short. He sucked reflectively on his pipe. "Stay a moment, citizens. Perhaps we can scrape up a bit of cheese." He called out to his wife, and soon the youths were sitting over a large piece of cheese and crusty wheat rolls. The man hesitated briefly, then brought out a jug of cider, pouring each a mugful, as well as one for himself.

He resumed his story. The baron and his family were sent out of the district in oxcarts with only the clothes they wore. His cattle and pigs were divided among the peasants, and the fields were later sold by the village council. "I added a good bit of wheatland and orchard to my holdings," said the man contentedly. "And I have many years in which to pay for this, at low interest."

Maurice picked up his last crumb of cheese. "You were going to tell us about the deer."

Jules stirred restlessly. "We have taken up enough of our good host's time. . . ."

The man plainly hated to lose his audience. "One moment. My wife might find a scrap of meat for you."

In a short time Maurice and Jules were devouring thick

ham sandwiches while generous wedges of cherry pie stood at their elbows. The mugs foamed with good grape wine, and a pair of candles lifted the gloom stealing into the cottage from the courtyard.

The peasant once more picked up his tale. "With the baron gone we could at last wreak our vengeance on his accursed game animals! A sound beating made his gamekeeper lead us to the lairs and burrows. With one of the baron's own guns I shot these deer. Hundreds of quail, partridge, and rabbit were slaughtered during the next weeks. Entire herds and covies were wiped out."

Maurice nearly choked from astonishment. Coming from a country whose population still fed itself from uplands and forest, the deliberate waste shocked him. "Game is food! You could have managed those hunting preserves for your own benefit!"

The peasant spat contemptuously on the floor. "Are you from the city, then, not to know of such things?" And out poured the memory of pent-up suffering. Deer browsed on the peasants' vines and fruit trees. Rabbits nibbled the green shoots of crops. Wild boars rooted in the vegetables. Partridges and pigeons ate the wheat, the rye, the barley. "And can one fight back at such marauders?" demanded the peasant. "No! For only the lord may kill any game. A peasant could be shut in a dungeon, or even executed, for setting a snare! Can we build fences, then? Bah! That's not allowed, for that would interfere with the movements of the game. May I weed my crops or grub out brush? *Non, non,* we must not destroy the cover for game!" The man pounded angrily on the table. "The gamekeeper on his rounds and the noble hunters themselves ride their horses through my crops, trampling, destroying!" He shook a wrathful finger under Maurice's nose. "And what does this continual waste and destruction mean—a few sous out of my pocket? Child, you cannot imagine the suffering! It means food out of our mouths and clothes off our backs, and even scant fuel for a winter fire."

From the fire came the anguished voice of the wife. "There was that winter our Remi died."

The peasant's head sank briefly to his chest. "*Oui,* a bad winter, that. There was little fuel, almost no food, and scarcely a rag among us all to keep warm. Remi, our four year old, took sick." He shrugged hopelessly. "Could one send two villages away for a physician, or pay for what medicine he might order? Remi burned with fever, wasted away, and died." He raised his head, and Maurice saw the tortured look in this man's eyes. "And only that summer we had the best weather and the finest crops."

The wife's bitter voice reached them from the fireplace. "That autumn our baron held a hunting party every single week."

The peasant nodded. "My fine crops were trampled before my eyes. And the game, so plentiful that year, ate what was left." His huge fist thundered on the table. "And do you know, citizens, after harvest, the baron sent for his usual rates and taxes, based on the crops I could not harvest!"

The wife added, "That wasn't the only winter we suffered through on watery soup. Tell them of the fees, Pierre." She left the fireplace and came to the table. "The baron owned the flour mill, the baking oven, and the winepress, and we must all use them and none other, not even make do with our own skill! *Oui,* we paid for using these facilities, either in coin, or in half the flour, bread, or wine. There was a great tax on salt, and we had to buy a certain quantity each year whether we wished to or not."

The peasant drank down the rest of his wine. "Tax on this, tax on that—on land, on produce, on wine and tobacco and income! *Euh,* there's little enough money coming in anyway, and half of that went each year for taxes! There was hardly a sou left to buy nails and rope and things we cannot make ourselves, things we need to farm or to live. A man could never get ahead."

The wife added, "I don't know how it went with you in the city, and you lads are too young to remember. But here, if the taxman came and found hen's feathers in the courtyard, your taxes were raised. And if there were another beehive in the orchard or jugs of new cider, again the taxman demanded more. Anything you did to try to raise yourself out of poverty was at once seized upon through taxes!"

"They used to force their way into a man's house," growled the peasant, splashing more wine into his cup. "They would seize furniture or clothing, anything, to sell for one's taxes if a man fell behind through bad luck. Sometimes the house itself was pulled down, the bricks and timber being sold to satisfy the debt. Women and children slept in ditches. And if you protested, you were thrown into prison at the pleasure of the baron."

Maurice ventured a question. "What happened to all this tax money, and to the fees for flour mills and so on?"

Both the peasant and his wife exclaimed over Maurice's ignorance. The man declared, "It all went into the baron's pocket. Some, I suppose, eventually trickled into the royal treasury when these rich nobles bought favors in the king's court. But to what use was this money put? Bah, it went for jewels and wigs and fancy silk clothes and fine prancing horses not fit for any real work. A noble might own half a dozen huge manors and never live in them but continue to collect the fees and taxes from each estate. Men in office were likewise bought, to favor the noble and squeeze the peasant!"

"Things were bad in the cities, too. I know!" said Jules Volant with feeling. "Every mouthful of food that came in was taxed, and the poor went hungry."

The peasant's eyes glowed in the light of the candles. The courtyard through the windows appeared quite dark. "But in the city you did not have to give your labor up free," said their host. "Whenever the baron beckoned, I had to go off and work on the local roads or in his fields, even though my own needed attention urgently. And if the royal army needed transport, the soldiers came and dragged me, my carts, and my oxen away to abuse as they wished! Once they broke a leg of one of my oxen, and it had to be slaughtered. They allowed me the injured leg to take home for food, and they ate the rest themselves. Payment? *Non,* there was no payment." His angry excitement ebbing, the peasant sat back. "Now it is better in France, citizens. What matter now a few sacrifices when all will be well once the wars are won?"

"Our son, the one born after Remi died, is fighting in the Netherlands," put in his wife proudly. "He has merited the rank of sergeant through hard work and study."

"In the old days," mused the peasant, "no amount of hard work or ability would advance one anywhere. Now, one may benefit from one's own labor and thrift. We peasants can have pride and self-respect."

Suddenly a heavy pounding started up on the door. The stout oak planks shuddered under a barrage of thumping from outside.

The peasant sprang up, and his wife shrank against the wall. Jules glanced around, perhaps seeking an exit. Maurice sat as nailed to the bench while the marauding thunder reverberated through the cottage.

The latch burst, and the door crashed against the wall. From the dusk of the courtyard surged a squad of men in blue uniforms, white belts crossing their chests, sabres held at the ready.

The wife whispered, "Soldiers!"

The peasant gurgled in his throat, his face gray with fear.

The corporal in charge stepped forward and commanded in a ringing voice, "Back against the wall, all of you!"

Someone prodded Maurice in the back with a sabre. He rose hastily, knocking over the bench, and was pushed along with the others. Two soldiers crowded them up against the cottage wall and stood guard over them. The rest of the squad under the eye of their corporal ransacked each cupboard and pried into every corner. One soldier found the pantry door and broke through it. The corporal took a candle and went to investigate, returning with a gleeful smile to stand before the peasant.

"The rafters are heavy with hams and flitches of bacon, citizen. There are sacks of onions and potatoes as well, too much for your family. And I counted six large casks of well-rendered fat. Thought we'd overlook you because you live off by yourself, did you? *Bien,* citizen, this hoarding can cost you your head."

The peasant, as strongly built as one of his oxen, trembled, and his voice was as small as his courage. "Citizen Corporal, I am only about to take these things to sell."

"At the maximum price set by law," said the corporal.

"*Certainement,* citizen! I would never sell above the maximum."

"Would you believe it, citizen?" asked the corporal in seeming wonder. "There are those who sell secretly, on the black market, to evade the law and charge more for scarce goods. What was your income last year?"

The peasant named a sum and the corporal laughed derisively. "Listen, citizen peasant, you're in enough trouble without lying! What about the wheat in your granary? Yes, we went through your buildings before calling upon you. There was a fine pile of hides, too, badly needed by the army. These goods should have been sold months ago, unless you are hoarding."

"No, no, citizen!" cried the wretched peasant as his wife began sobbing. "First my carts broke down, it took a while to mend them. And then my draft oxen became ill, they have only just recovered. And there was still the farm work to be done, and with this I have not yet taken these things to market."

"We'll save you the trouble, good citizen," snapped the corporal. "We'll load up your carts and take everything with us. Sometime in the future you will get your money from the army." He paused and added, "If you still have your head."

The peasant and his wife burst into tearful pleading. From Jules' expression, Maurice guessed that the corporal was playing some grim game of his own.

The corporal faced the youths, his eyes raking over them like the points of a bayonet. "You don't seem worried over the fate of your parents."

"Citizen Corporal," said Jules, "we are strangers to these people and only stayed to eat a meal."

The soldier glanced triumphantly at the couple. "So you are well enough off to feed two wayfarers!"

The wife wrung her hands. "Just a bit of skim milk and some barley bread."

The corporal looked around at the scraps on the table and sneered scornfully. Then turning to Jules he demanded, "Let's see your papers, citizen."

From somewhere within his layers of torn garments, Jules produced a slender canvas wallet. The corporal brought this collection of various cards and permits closer to the candles, slowly turning them over in his fingers. He asked several sharp questions which Jules answered without quaver or hesitation. The two of them were looking for work, Jules explained, preferably in Nantes where the pay would be higher. Yes, he'd worked steadily, at various farms and in small towns. Jules named some of these and gave names of employers. The corporal could see from his papers he was just a little too young to be conscripted into the army. He and his companion had stopped here and asked for work, and the peasant had invited them in to eat.

The corporal did not write down any of Jules' replies but appeared to be satisfied. He returned the canvas wallet.

Jules stuffed it inside his clothing, asking casually, "We may go, then?"

The corporal nodded. *"Oui."*

Jules sauntered leisurely across the room. Maurice, suppressing a wild desire to run, followed him, pausing briefly at the table to pick up both their jackets. They were just three steps from freedom when the corporal's voice struck like a dagger.

"Un moment! I haven't seen your identity. Yes, you there! Give me your papers."

Maurice looked over his shoulder.

The corporal was pointing at him.

A Band of Horsemen

IV MAURICE'S MOUTH WENT DRY. "Citizen Corporal, I—"

Jules said swiftly, "He had lost his papers traveling up the Loire valley from Nazaire. We met this morning and decided to travel together, looking for work."

While Jules explained, one of the guards herded them back against the wall. The corporal now spoke with far more seriousness than before. *"Alors,* citizen peasant, by harboring someone without papers, you and your wife have truly put your heads under the knife."

The peasant's eyes widened in terror, and he babbled, "I swear I didn't know, Citizen Corporal! They knocked on my door, they—"

But the wife suddenly collected herself, and, gesturing her husband into silence, she pulled at the corporal's sleeve. "Citizen, please, there is something . . ." She glanced meaningfully at the guards.

The corporal jerked his head at them. *"Bien,* soldiers, you can go help the others now." When the guards joined the men still rummaging through the cottage, the corporal bent his head to the wife's whispering.

At the end, he nodded. *"Soit!* It is done, citizeness! Go

fetch them at once. Henri!" He beckoned one of the soldiers toward him. "Go with this woman and assist. Discreetly, now."

While the soldier followed the peasant's wife into the pantry, the corporal ordered the rest of his men into the courtyard to begin loading the wheat and hides. To the peasant he said, "A clever wife is often what one's life is worth, *n'est-ce-pas?* You're lucky, citizen, for I will not report you for hoarding this time, nor for harboring criminals."

The peasant's gratitude was a sob of relief. "*Merci,* Citizen Corporal!"

"Shut up!" hissed the corporal fiercely, glancing at his men as they filed out of the door. "Be careful after this, for your name is now on the list." He turned to Maurice and Jules. "You two lads, come with me."

He marched them ahead of him into the dusk-filled courtyard. Detailing a soldier to stand over them, the corporal went off to supervise the loading of grain. Maurice saw the dog Montagne with a strap around its muzzle, the remains of some joint on the ground. He nudged Jules. "That's why the dog didn't bark a warning."

But Jules was not listening. He spoke to their guard. "*Allons,* citizen, we're just two fellows trying to get along."

The soldier was unmoved by this covert plea. "I'm just a private doing my duty, citizens."

Maurice and Jules dispiritedly watched two soldiers bringing the squad's horses into the dark courtyard where the others were harnessing the oxen to both the peasant's carts.

The cottage door opened, and Henri put out his head. "Bring the corporal's mount," he ordered. One of the horse tenders led up a fine bay, holding it while Henri swiftly put into the saddlebags two new pairs of boots. He added three bottles of very old wine, to judge from the dust, and a small ham together with a flitch of bacon. Lastly he dropped in a tiny leather bag that chinked softly as it struck the bottles inside.

"No assignats in that bag," muttered Jules, referring to the paper money everyone scorned. "Citizen Private, do you think you'll share in that loot?"

The soldier guarding them grinned. "I will when I make corporal, young citizens."

When the carts were loaded with sacks of grain and bundles of hides, the corporal detailed a man to stay in the cottage until the squad returned to load the fats and meats from the pantry. There was also homemade soap that Henri had discovered in the same hideaway that had held the other treasures. Some bars of it had already found their way into various saddlebags. Maurice and Jules were placed on two horses, their hands tied behind their backs while the reins were taken by soldiers on either side of them. The mounted squad and the oxcarts started out of the courtyard, moving through the violet twilight toward the village two miles distant.

Maurice pulled furiously against his bonds until a soldier riding behind him jabbed him with his sabre. Jules rode with his head slumped against his chest, and Maurice watched carefully to see if the road-clever youth were going to make a sudden break for freedom. But Jules was sunk in his private misery and did not rouse himself until they arrived in the village.

The soldiers kicked up their horses, scattering chickens and pigs. Children darted back into dark doorways while their elders peered out curiously. They rode past a small tumbledown church, its great broken windows agape, and past the boarded-up school next to it. Lanterns lighted the interiors of two or three tiny shops. Finally the horses were halted before a large stone building. The youths were pulled from their horses and taken inside the dark hall. Someone led the way with a lantern as Maurice and Jules stumbled along a hallway ahead of three soldiers. They went through a door, down steep brick steps, and along a short passage where the stone walls were scaly with lichen. The man with the lantern unlocked a great iron-bound oak door and pulled it open. One of the soldiers cut their bonds with his sabre, then pushed them into the small cold dungeon. The door thundered shut, and the lock creaked into place. Silence fell as thick as the darkness.

Jules groaned aloud. "We are dead!"

Maurice felt his way along the rough stone wall and found his companion. He sat next to him on the straw-strewn floor, drawing his watch coat close against the chill already striking into his bones. "We'll straighten this out somehow in the morning."

"Maurice, Maurice, in the morning we will die!"

"Don't talk that way!" Maurice said sharply. "We have done nothing. Pull yourself together, Jules!"

But Jules went on in a hopeless tone. "You are without papers, and that is a crime. The only punishment for crime is execution. And my crime is that I was with you."

Maurice stood up and began pacing. "They have to give us a trial first."

Jules laughed hollowly, but Maurice continued. "I must prove that I'm an American. They can send for my cousin Claude Donard. This will show you are innocent also."

"And why should this wretched village spend money trying to prove our innocence?"

"It's our guilt they have to prove, not our innocence," replied Maurice.

"Maurice, do you really believe anyone cares about truth or justice? Such luxuries take time and money and are useless except to the victim."

"But what purpose is there in executing us?" demanded Maurice challengingly.

"When the good citizens watch us die, they will be afraid to hoard their boots and soap. The men won't try to hide when called up for military service. The peasants will sell their grain and meat at the official price. And no one will dare complain, no matter what Robespierre does in Paris or his cohorts do in the provinces."

Maurice felt a chill of fear. Jules' expectation of death was entirely real. And he recalled the terror of the peasants caught sheltering a paperless person.

It could not be true; he, Maurice Fabry, merely traveling to Orléans, was now in a dank dungeon awaiting execution. And no one knew, no one cared. . . .

"Jules, those peasants bought their lives! Why can't we?"

"With what?" Jules asked tonelessly. A while later he muttered, "*Euh,* had I thought quickly enough . . . Never mind, it is too late!" And he sank into a brooding silence from which Maurice could not rouse him.

A long time later, after Maurice had grown almost insensible from the cold, the dark, and the silence, metal screeched on metal and the heavy oak door swung open. The lantern light bursting inward nearly blinded him. Beyond the brilliance Maurice made out two armed men blocking the doorway. The lantern advanced into the dungeon and swung over him and Jules.

"Get up, scum!" the man ordered. "I am the mayor of the village."

Maurice forced his stiff limbs into action. He and Jules stood swaying against the stone wall. The man did not look like a mayor, as his clothing was the plain peasant garb, only dirtier. He did wear a red sash across his chest, and it had embroidered on it in silver a bundle of rods topped by an ax blade. Maurice recalled that this device was the fasces, a symbol of the Revolution taken from old Roman authority.

The mayor said, "I need your names for the execution list. That stupid corporal failed to write them down, and he's ridden off somewhere. You, there." He pointed a thumb at Jules.

"Jules Volant, Citizen Mayor." He held his head up as he spoke, and though his voice was low there was a new vibrance to it. "This is my companion, Maurice Fabry. We only met this morning, after midnight, quite by chance. He came from a ship, but lost his papers."

The mayor grunted. "You didn't think it was dangerous to take up with him?"

Out of the corner of his eye, Maurice saw Jules' expression turn sly. "Citizen Mayor," the wanderer said, "if one wishes to gain, one must take risks."

A moment of silence stretched out tensely. Then Jules added, "I believed he was from a ship as he said, because of his clothing. You can see he still wears a sailor's coat."

His attention directed, the mayor stared at Maurice with unblinking eyes. Then he said ponderously, "Ah, but such a one as he would have papers of some sort."

Jules shrugged. "When one travels quickly by night, things can get lost. And what does it matter to such a one as my friend here? All would have been well had we but reached Nantes tonight as we planned."

Maurice fought his urge to blurt out his American citizenship and beg that word be sent to Claude, to Captain Hawthorn circuitously en route for Marseille, to the American minister in Paris. It was obvious that Jules was working on some plan, and perhaps one extraneous word would ruin it.

The mayor said, "Nantes, eh? I suppose you have friends there." He jerked his head toward Maurice. "Or *he* does."

Jules folded his arms and actually swaggered. "Citizen Mayor, my companion and I are worth more alive than dead."

The mayor brooded on this and at last nodded. Turning, he shouted to the guard, and when the heavy door was swung shut against them he placed his lamp on the floor. "Let's get down to business then."

But Jules feigned surprise. It took a few seconds for the village dignitary to fall in with this new tack, but then the two spoke together in lengthy, round-about sentences, so heavily weighted with innuendo that Maurice could scarcely follow. Neither one, he noted, actually said or promised anything at all. And yet, by the time Jules gave a final nod, there was the sense of a bargain having been concluded.

The mayor rubbed his hands. "I can see you are just two harmless lads who shouldn't be locked up at all. That corporal is nothing but a fool, and if he isn't careful I'll report him. But I can't just let you go. It would look bad to the village. As mayor, I must set an example of Republican zeal." Then he tapped his temple. "An idea comes to me. In the cell next to this are four suspected persons. Tomorrow morning they will be taken to the next village, which has a guillotine, where they will be executed. Now, you can sleep in here tonight as a charity. And tomorrow you'll show your loyalty to everyone by being the ones who cut off the heads of the condemned. Then you can go on to Nantes, eh?"

Maurice could not believe his ears.

But Jules said calmly, "Agreed!"

Speechless with shock, Maurice stared at his friend.

The mayor picked up his lantern and banged on the door. When he left, the dungeon was once more plunged into darkness.

Maurice managed to find his voice. "Jules, what have you promised?"

Jules sat down in the straw. "I promised nothing. The greedy fellow thought you were a smuggler, and I did not enlighten him. Nantes is a port, and he's going to let us go there with the idea that you'll send him things like shoes, a couple of good muskets, some powder and bullets, and a few sacks of wheat. In truth, he'll never see either of us again after tomorrow."

"Tomorrow!" Maurice sank to the floor. "And we're supposed to—to execute four people? Jules, I can't do anything like that! Not even to criminals."

"Had I not used my wits, Maurice, our names would be on that execution list. Do you want to pull the cord that drops the knife or be the one on whose neck the knife drops?" After a while Jules said more kindly, "I can't do it either, Maurice. But we must get out of this dungeon. And then be ready to seize the first chance for escape."

With this crumb of cold comfort, Maurice huddled in the filthy straw and fell into exhausted sleep.

Hours later the oak door thundered open. A rough-looking man brought them a lantern and bowls of lentil soup. When they had eaten he led them up steps and through passages until they stumbled out into the square before the village hall.

The sky was pink with dawn. Men and horses stood about. Within a stake-sided, two-wheeled cart shivered four people with hands bound behind them. A group of children were laughing and calling out insults while their parents waited patiently. More villagers collected, housewives with their knitting, men with scythes over their shoulders, girls carrying hay rakes, boys leading cattle. From the talk, Maurice learned that the soldiers who were supposed to escort the prisoners were instead out searching for an army deserter. Jules muttered, "Lucky for us, that."

At last the mayor arrived and joined Maurice and Jules. Taking a piece of paper from his pocket, he said to the crowd, "Citizens! These two valiant youths have eagerly volunteered for the privilege of beheading the four desperate criminals we found in our midst. Let such zeal inspire all of us to greater Republicanism! The condemned are . . ." He read out their names and crimes. The middle-aged village schoolteacher, working as a stable hand, was caught reading books with pictures of the dead king in them, evidence of royalist feelings. The ex-maid to the baron's wife, of late working for the grocer, had said her life was better under the old system. An old man was chronically drunk and a burden to his hard-working Republican family. The blacksmith's assistant, in the village just three years, gambled successfully at cards like an aristocrat, proof that he was indeed one.

When the list ended, the villagers cheered. Maurice and Jules, as befitted their new status of executioners, were given two fine horses to ride, doubtless from the former baron's stable. The rude escort formed, and a tricolor banner led them out of the village to cries of, *"Vive la République!"*

The road stretched over gentle slopes, and poplars twirled their leaves in a light breeze. Jules and Maurice rode behind the mayor and the flagbearer and just in front of the tumbril and its four criminals numb with despair. The cart was well guarded by riders on all sides, and two men frequently rode up beside the honorary executioners.

Jules called out ahead, "Citizen Mayor, how far is this village with the guillotine?"

"Patience, *mon ami*. It is a two hour ride."

The cortège went slowly because of the tumbril, the creaking of its wheels mingling with morning birdsong. Jules leaned close to Maurice. "Watch me closely. When we get well away from their neighborhood, I'll make a sudden break off the road."

The day's heat made itself felt as the sun climbed, and the horses' hoofs began churning dust from the road. The wretches jolting in the tumbril began coughing and then begged for water. One of their civilian guards silenced them by beating a stout rod in warning against the vertical rails of the cart. Two men argued about the identity of some ruined walls beyond the fields. Ahead, the road led into thick woods. Jules glanced at Maurice and tightened his reins.

Hoofs drummed behind the execution party. Twisting in the saddle, Maurice saw a company of men and women trotting briskly on horses. The group came up rapidly, and a bearded man in the lead shouted, "Ahead, there! Make way, make way!"

The mayor turned on his plodding horse. "This is official business! Keep back!"

But the troop surged toward them with much talk and laughter among its members, most of them wearing red liberty caps and a great many patriotic decorations.

The road was too narrow to allow the execution party to turn aside. Quickly overtaking the cortège, the cheerful troop skillfully parted its ranks, and the individual riders slipped easily around the tumbril and between the mayor's escorts. Then both groups mingled, the mayor's indignant shouts overwhelmed by the loud chatter of the strangers. They all entered the woods together.

Maurice found himself separated from Jules, for a stout woman rode on one side of him and an old man on the other. These two talked to each other as if Maurice were not there, and they chattered on about the weather, about crops and cattle and each other's relatives. The dappled shadows of the woods confused Maurice completely. The horses jostled one another, the strangers pressed close, there was an abrupt turn in the road. Somewhere behind him he heard shouts and the rumble of creaking wheels. Suddenly Maurice was clinging to the mane of his racing horse, plunging heedlessly over a rough path, following the mount ahead. Behind panted another animal, and trees whipped past on both sides.

Maurice burst into a small sunlit clearing where the strangers milled on their horses, their talk now subdued. Someone snatched the reins out of his hands. "Change horses—quickly!" commanded the leader with the black pointed beard and flashing eyes.

Maurice gaped in bewilderment. A huge fellow reached up and locked his hairy arms around his waist, pulling Maurice out of the saddle. The black-bearded man sent Maurice's mount off with a slap on the rump, back the way he had come. The one with hairy arms lifted Maurice onto another horse, and then the group spurted out of the clearing and along a narrow twisting path through the woods at a reckless pace. There was no laughter this time, only the rattle of hoofs. Somewhere up ahead Maurice caught a glimpse of Jules Volant.

They rode out onto a stony field and picked their way more carefully down the slope to a brush-grown creek at the bottom. There, three men rode out of some willows and trotted along with them. The black-bearded man asked them tersely, "Were you followed?"

One shook his head. "No, we doubled back after tipping the tumbril into a quarry." He pointed. "There's a small bridge over this stream."

At a nod from the black-bearded one, the group of men and women swerved toward the creek. Maurice glanced at each in turn but could not find any of the three men who had taken him two nights before from the coach to Paris. The stout woman riding on one side of him smiled agreeably, and the old man on the other offered a friendly opinion of their pleasant ride.

The horses stepped slowly and carefully along the rough log bridge, and when Maurice came to the other side of the creek he suddenly kicked up his mount. His horse lunged past the company and Maurice called to Jules ahead of him.

Abruptly, Jules turned his mount deliberately across Maurice's path, forcing him to a rearing halt.

"What's the matter with you?" cried Maurice angrily, striving to rein in his horse. "We could have escaped!"

"It's all right," said Jules. "We've just been rescued."

"How can you say that?" Maurice demanded, gripping the reins tightly. "Who would want to rescue us?"

A hand on his arm made him turn toward the black-bearded leader who had ridden up beside him.

"I would rescue you," declaimed the man with flashing dark eyes. "I, Sebastien Brillon."

The man faced Jules, his neatly trimmed beard jutting like a sword point. "*Eh bien,* Jules Volant, I have not seen you since Chartres. And how have you been keeping, young vagabond?"

Jules grinned. "Well enough, Sebastien Brillon. Well enough."

Jules' Nightmare

V

THE COMPANY RODE at good pace along a wide straight road toward Nantes. Maurice Fabry glanced around to make certain no one could overhear him before bringing his horse closer to the one Jules Volant was riding. "Jules, who are these people?"

"They are players of Sebastien Brillon's traveling theater," Jules explained. "Didn't you understand that while we stopped at that little stream back there?"

The halt they had made when Jules had prevented Maurice from galloping away had been brief. The flamboyant Sebastien Brillon had issued decisive orders. Maurice had found his sturdy sea jacket whisked away. "Far too conspicuous," Sebastien had declared, replacing it with one badly patched. Sebastien had then thrust a battered wallet crammed with papers into Maurice's hand. "Bread card, identity, character, employment," Sebastien had stated. "Show upon demand, but don't lose them!" Maurice had been allowed to keep his red liberty cap, and someone had draped a huge red-white-and-blue ribbon across his chest. Sebastien had boosted him into the saddle. "You are now working for me, and this is your horse. Now, everyone, *pressez-vous!*"

The thirteen riders had cantered away from the rude little bridge. Rapidly they had threaded their way through a maze of intersecting cart roads to come out, at last, on a good highway. Only then had the players clumped into small groups, laughing and talking though they kept their horses at a brisk pace.

Maurice was still bewildered by the rapid turn of events. "Jules, how do you know if this Brillon fellow can be trusted?"

"Bien, he won't throw you into prison for a slip of the tongue. And in his company you don't have to mouth patriotic phrases every time you speak."

A sudden new worry gnawed at Maurice. "Do you mean we'll be imprisoned if we're caught associating with him?"

"No, he's not a suspect," said Jules, using the word which designated any undesirable liable to imprisonment. "Sebastien's a good sort, Maurice. I have worked for him several times, for our paths often cross. I spend the winter in the south of France, and when spring comes I travel north up the Rhône valley. During the summer I go back and forth along the Loire valley and sometimes get as far as Paris."

Citizen Brillon's voice rose from behind. "Never mind Paris, *mon ami!* We'll take you on a rapid journey throughout France, a new place every day." He eased his horse up beside theirs. "We are luckily met, for now you may ride at your ease."

Maurice could not rid himself of the last trace of suspicion. "It's lucky you had two extra horses for us, Citizen Brillon."

"Indeed it is," Sebastien agreed easily. "Otherwise you might have had to ride with the wagons. But they took another route. We will meet them in Nantes, and Jules can teach you your duties."

"But I'm not a player!" Maurice protested.

"Of course not, imbecile!" Sebastien said scornfully. "Yet even a dullard can be of use to me. You shall help Jules look after the animals and properties."

Jules explained. "Properties are the things Sebastien uses in his plays, Maurice. The costumes, equipment, and the background flats and drops."

Sebastien expanded with pride. "We travel about, giving patriotic plays in towns and villages, spreading the spirit of the Revolution among the peasants and provincials. I, myself, have written nearly all our scripts, and I might say modestly that they are enthusiastically received by many of our audiences."

A tender contradiction was voiced from Maurice's other side. *"Non, non, chéri!* By *all* our audiences." The woman who had ridden up beside Maurice was so very pretty with dark brown hair and dimpled pink cheeks that one quickly forgave the bulging figure straining within dust-covered silk clothes. Smiling at him, she said, "You are the lad Maurice Fabry, *oui?* I am Yvette Brillon. My husband, I fear, is too reticent about his attainments. Yet none has so quick a wit as he! Ah, *chéri,* how cleverly you dealt with that party barring the road."

Sebastien's stark bearded features assumed a pleased, if rather haughty, air. "Eh, Yvette, I seized the moment, did I not? There was this self-important idiot with his grand banner and magnificent escort. A mayor, was he, purifying his village of anti-Revolutionary taint. *Alors,* I could not resist sweeping through his column, and what a stroke of luck to find my friend Jules! And a grand joke, too, to take him and his companion Maurice along with us, leaving the good mayor to shake his fist, his tumbril lying smashed at the bottom of a quarry!"

"And the prisoners?" asked Maurice. "Are they too smashed?"

Sebastien shrugged. "I think they ran off in the underbrush. They may fend for themselves or not as they desire."

"How can they with their hands bound?" Maurice retorted.

Citizeness Brillon laid a pudgy hand on his arm. "It is possible they were freed in some fashion or other. Eh, Maurice, do not borrow trouble! Let the mayor do his own worrying."

Sebastien turned to Jules. "And what were you doing in the mayor's illustrious company?"

Jules waved a hand in dismissal. "Oh, we were going in the same direction. He let us ride his horses."

Sebastien laughed. "*Allons,* you will work for your ride this time."

Maurice spoke to Sebastien's wife. "Mada—I mean, Citizeness Brillon, who has cared for the troupe's equipment up to now?"

"Call me Yvette, *chéri.* We are theater people, and there is no formality among us, not even in the old days when one used the formal courtesies. And there is always room for workers in our troupe, for people come and go. Some don't care for this wandering life, others find better paying jobs, for while we are paid by the Republic, and the sale of tickets brings something, the sum is unfortunately small as it must also cover all supplies, costumes, and travel expenses."

Sebastien had been listening, and now he said with passion, "I tell you, young Maurice, there is no more glorious occupation than the theater! Think of it—to stride in lonely splendor into the magnificent amphitheater of men's souls, to breathe the fire of life into a playwright's imagined characters! All eyes are upon the actor, each ear is strained to catch his every nuance. To act, Maurice, is to be larger than life, it is to be immortal!" Carried away by his own words, Sebastien struck a pose, his eyes gleaming with an inner fire as his mount trotted on indifferently.

Maurice could not resist adding, "But someone must care for the wagons, the animals, and the properties."

Sebastien's expression mirrored his journey from a flight of fancy to the everyday world. He said with a sigh, "That is true. And all I can get are idlers and wretches interested only in filling their stomachs and pockets."

Yvette added, "Sebastien is brilliant, hard working, patriotic, and generous to a fault. His sole failing is that he can not stand stupidity."

Her words soothed her husband's temperament until his beard jutted at a jaunty angle. He flicked his reins on his horse's flanks and called out, "Let us not linger! Press on to Nantes!"

When the towers and bridges of Nantes came into view hours later in the early afternoon, Maurice was surprised to find it a large city sprawling over both banks of the Loire and the islands between. The broad river was crowded with many different kinds of boats, barges, and ocean vessels, for as Jules pointed out, the city was actually an inland port. "We could still seek work on the barges going upstream," he said, "but if we stay with Sebastien's troupe we'll come to Orléans more quickly."

The horses slowed to a walk as they followed the city's cobbled streets, winding their way along the riverfront past warehouses and over bridges. Tall narrow houses overshadowed the crooked streets, relieved from time to time by large open areas where many streets joined. Entering one great square, the troupe was nearly overwhelmed by a raw stench hanging in the still hot air. A group of laborers was scrubbing the street around a high wooden platform that bore two tall timbers connected by a crosspiece. Jules answered the question poised unvoiced on Maurice's lips, "A guillotine, that."

As the troupe went through the square the horses trembled at the smell of the blood staining the cobbles, rolling their eyes and stumbling in their eagerness to be gone from it. The reins cut into Maurice's hands as he steadied his mount, and he overheard one laborer order his young assistant, "You, Étienne, fetch more water and another scrubbing brush."

The young man picked up a bucket, grumbling, "We didn't lack for water last winter when we sent the rogues downriver." He kicked a starved-looking dog licking the cobblestones out of his way.

Cool shadows fell over Maurice once more as the troupe left the sunny square. The horses walked along in calm obedience. The players talked and joked among themselves as if they had seen and heard nothing at all unusual. Even Jules was deep in conversation with the kindly old man whose face was inhabited by a constant though vague smile. A few streets later they arrived at a large park where orderly trees drooped darkly with heat and the vast level lawns and thick shrubbery bore a coating of dust.

As they dismounted in the shade of the trees, Sebastien cried out, "Where are the men with the wagons? Can't they travel alone on the other side of the river and still meet us in Nantes at the right place, the correct hour? Jules, Maurice! Ride out of the city along the right bank, and look for them."

Just then a man came striding through the trees, hailing Sebastien. Jules nudged Maurice. "That's the rider who asked his way of us yesterday, long before we came to that farmstead!"

Sebastien nodded. "He is my outrider, the man who goes ahead to attend to the troupe's various arrangements.

He is new to the troupe since you were last with us, Jules. Now I shall learn about the wagons." He went forward to meet the new arrival.

The other members of the troupe settled themselves in the shade. Yvette called Jules and Maurice to sit beside her and share a bottle of cool wine. They had hardly joined her when shouts attracted their attention.

Sebastien was gesticulating wildly, his voice raised in violent protest while the outrider drooped unhappily. Sebastien pulled his hair and strode up and down in a frenzy. Then he ran toward Yvette and posed tragically before her. "Yvette, Yvette, a great calamity! The wagons have not arrived. They are still ten miles below Nantes, one with a broken axle, another without a wheel, the rest remaining to attempt repairs!"

Yvette was instantly alert. "What happened, *chéri?*"

He flung his arms wide. "Something frightened the horses. They bolted and overturned the wagons. There they are, the costumes, the properties, the scenic drops—miles away and unusable!" He strode about in agony. "And we have a play to put on in two hours! It is all planned—" He broke off and flung himself down before her. "Yvette, I am destroyed!"

"But *non, chéri!*" She stroked his thick black hair soothingly. "True, we can not give *The Storming of the Bastille,* but perhaps we can present something that needs only what we have here." She glanced around the park. "This makes a fine country setting. We could have the play here, instead of in the hall. See, those bushes set off a space like a stage. . . ."

Sebastien raised his suffering face and gazed over the park. "Yes, yes, I see it now!" Joyfully he arose, his imagination moving like quicksilver. "We will have something very simple, the patriotic peasants searching the countryside for men evading military conscription. We can use our own clothes, and do not even need a regular script. We will have patriotic speeches and the audience can join in the singing." He threw himself on his knees and grasped Yvette's hand, kissing it ardently. *"Chérie,* you are my salvation!"

She said gently, "Remember, the presentation must first be approved by the Jacobin censors."

He waved an impatient hand. *"Certainement!* I go to them immediately. The speeches will be the standard Jacobin ones already memorized from other plays, and of course everybody knows the songs."

"Shall we eat while waiting for you?" Yvette asked. "It is well past lunchtime."

The tall lean figure was already striding away. "Go ahead, and don't bother to save anything for me."

Yvette shook her head. "He misses too many meals, that man! Jules, you and Maurice can help me pass out the food."

From the various saddlebags they took hard rolls, cheese, some dry spicy sausages, and more bottles of wine. When this was distributed among the troupers, Jules and Maurice found a place by themselves.

Their simple meal was soon finished. As they waited for Sebastien's return, Maurice asked, "Jules, what are Jacobins?"

"They are the politicians who rule France," his companion explained. "At first there were many political parties, but now there is only the Jacobin Club. Each commune, or town, elects its officials and makes public appointments, but the local Jacobin Club must approve of everything. If you go against them in any way, it means prison, death."

Claude Donard's letters had mentioned the Jacobins and some other political parties. But Maurice had skipped over the dull politics, as he had the diplomatic affairs, in favor of the more interesting news about daily living conditions. Now for the first time he began to understand that national and international events determined exactly what kind of daily life one could lead. And in France, today, perhaps it was safest to keep moving, as did Jules, as did Sebastien Brillon's troupe. "Jules, how did you come to know Sebastien and his players?"

Jules gazed over the dusty park. "I met them nearly two years ago, about the time of the September Massacres in 1792." And his features puckered as if someone had drawn the hand of pain across his face.

I was in Paris then (said Jules Volant). I grew up in an orphanage there, and when I was twelve I was sent out as an apprentice to a mason. But I had consumption, the coughing sickness, and could not work as hard as the master wished me to. After six months he turned me back. I was put in an institution for paupers and the chronically ill. It was like a prison and a hospital both, with bars on the windows but a clean cot for each soul and wholesome food. We were confined to prevent begging, stealing, and the spread of disease. Half the building was for women, who sometimes worked in the quarters where we older children lived.

Rumors were thick in the streets of Paris that summer, and anyone sent out on an errand returned laden with them as with mud on his shoes. It was true France was losing battle after battle ever since declaring war on Austria and Prussia that April. Now the talk of the streets had it that our defeats were caused by spies and traitors, by those who hated the Revolution, who were plotting to restore King Louis to his old royal authority. But loyal Parisians would put a stop to that!

We heard a great crowd gathering in the streets one day in early August. They began marching, their ranks swelling as they sang the *Marseillaise,* shouldering their muskets and pikes, and dragging their cannon. The news burst into our hospital—the people of Paris had seized the city government, the Commune! Now they were advancing on the Tuileries where the Royal Family lived.

That night the crowds surged back through the streets, shouting with victory, bearing torches and pikes tipped with the heads of the king's Swiss Guards. The king and queen had escaped through the gardens to take refuge in the Assembly, the parliament which ruled the nation. (This was soon replaced by the National Convention, which rules the country now.) But the Assembly was afraid of the Commune, the nation trembled before the city, and the Royal Family was imprisoned.

That did not stop the enemy invading France! Foreign troops captured Thionville. And then Longwy. At the end of August Verdun fell. In Paris everyone was put to work digging trenches and throwing up barricades. We children in our hospital were busy tearing cloths into strips, while the women in their half of the building rolled bandages for our troops. The Commune of Paris ordered a house to house search for aristocrats and spies. Some newspapers were foolish enough to protest, and they were closed down. Relatives of emigrants were arrested as hostages, to save Paris from destruction. Traitors were seized in the streets and either hanged at once by the crowd, or thrown into one of the prisons. Then a great plot was uncovered: when the first enemy troops arrived, the prisoners would break out and seize Paris from within!

The enemy was to reach the gates of Paris on Sunday, the third of September.

Even through the thick walls of our hospital we heard

the bells ringing the tocsin, and the cannon booming the alarm. Drums rattled in the streets to summon the National Guard of the various Sections of the city. All that day there was a continual running of people through the streets, with news shouted up to us who stood before open windows. Death to the spies and traitors!

Vigilante mobs broke into the prisons and set up tribunals where the suspects were identified and condemned to death. Each traitor was executed then and there. The job was a long one—it took days.

The workers in our hospital, who went home each night, told of meeting groups of *les tueurs,* the killers, going out for wine or food. They carried their red knives and bloody cutlasses with them. Our cook recognized among them two of her neighbors, a locksmith and a cobbler, decent family men.

People were continually shouting in the streets around our hospital, and we quickly grew accustomed to the sight of bloody heads carried on pikes. But two days after the slaughter in the prisons began, a vast crowd of screaming, howling men surged through the streets and surrounded our building.

They broke into the women's section first, and through those stone walls we could hear their shrieking as they fell before the blades of *les tueurs* who had come to do justice. We children, orphaned, crippled, ill, we piled furniture in front of our doors. We took the cooks' knives out of the kitchen.

Did you ever try to stop a river? They burst through our flimsy barricades and laughed at our feeble blades. They were covered with blood, drunk on it. They fell on the first group huddling behind a door. The boys fought with their fingernails but *les tueurs* cut them up quickly.

The rest of us turned and ran. I plunged through the

cold gray bare corridors, I whose lungs burned with sickness. Some darted into other wardrooms and hid under beds. Even as I raced away I could hear them screaming as *les tueurs* dragged them out. Some of my friends jumped out of windows to escape, and died on the cobblestones below. I hurtled up steps, climbing ever higher, forcing air into my fiery lungs, and my heart begged to stop.

Always I was just ahead of them, by one corridor, one flight of stairs, one corner. Behind me footsteps thundered, blades thudded, boys screamed and corpses fell. I climbed higher, higher! I was in the bell tower. I scrambled up a rope ladder that led to the bell cradles, and I pulled it up after me.

Footsteps scampered below and a boy's head appeared. But before I could throw the rope down or shout a warning, I saw a cutlass swing through the air. The boy fell back dead. His killer bounded up the steps, glanced around the dark timbers of the bell tower, and ran back down without seeing me.

The shadows grew long and cold, and I clung to my perch, ignoring hunger and fatigue. From outside a new burst of noise swelled and died away. Had *les tueurs* left? I dared not see. I tied myself to the timbers with the rope ladder and spent the night, not sleeping, but fainting from time to time from pain and fear. I thought my lungs would finish me.

At dawn I climbed down to the floor of the bell tower and peered out of the open window. I could see here and there through the bare streets little knots of men trooping wearily, dragging their reddened swords. Torches flared in some prison courtyards. Now and then National Guardsmen trotted along on horses or marched briskly through the streets, their white belts making an X over their blue coats. This made me remember the enemy near the city walls, and I looked over the country outside Paris.

Strange! There were no troops at all!

Then I saw how beautiful and peaceful it was with the Seine winding through the rolling fields and orderly woods. I determined then and there to leave Paris and somehow shift for myself in the country.

Very slowly and in great fear I crept down the stairs. I went through the gray corridors and many of the rooms, now stained with red. In all that hospital not a soul was alive, except for me.

The murdered lay just as they had fallen, in hallways, dormitories, dining rooms, the kitchens, and even in classrooms where they had wedged themselves under the benches.

The doors leading to the women's section hung open. I looked through, and it was too horrible so I did not go in. The street doors were broken down, but my strength was utterly gone. I was coughing up gouts of blood, and I could scarcely stand. Leaving was out of the question until I grew stronger.

For sleeping, I dragged a mattress all the way up to the bell tower. It took a long time and caused me much pain and blood. I wondered now where I had gotten the strength to outrun *les tueurs.*

I stayed in the bell tower from which I could observe the progress of the slaughter by the rushing crowds of killers, by the pike-borne heads, and the drunken laughter. But I had to go down to the hospital kitchens several times to forage for food. I lived on some raw vegetables and dried bread. The rats had gotten the meat.

They were everywhere, those rats! I would pick my way down through the hospital very carefully, stepping between corpses so as not to disturb those vile pests. But they would dart up anyway and try to bite me. I got a piece of broken chair in order to club them off. Then on Thursday night, two days after the hospital had been stormed, the rats started overrunning the bell tower.

They drove me out of the tower and through the hospital thick with rot and stench. I stumbled out into the night among the people, the carts, the horses, the National Guard, the dogs, and the killers roaming the streets.

In spite of my weakness I set out toward the edge of the city. I walked and walked without resting, for to stop was to be questioned, and I had no papers.

At last I passed through the gates. Outside the walls great fires threw orange and yellow light over men digging huge trenches. Carts came up loaded with cruelly hacked corpses, and these were dumped into the trenches and buried. But more carts came, and more, and men dug frantically. *"Hé, gamin!"* somebody yelled at me. He was a great fellow with his shirt open on his sweaty, hairy chest, his trousers crusted with blood, and his arms loaded with spades. He thrust a shovel toward me. "Get in there and dig for the Fatherland! Don't worry, brat, you'll be paid for it."

Glancing around I saw other men and boys eagerly joining in the work, so I was afraid to refuse. I got into a crowded trench, and we shoveled dirt out, then shoveled it back in again on top of the bodies. We toiled at this all night long, with a short rest now and then for the passing of a wine bottle.

At dawn I recognized the contents of the latest cartload. They were some of the boys from my hospital.

Sick and exhausted, I threw down my shovel and started away.

But another man stopped me. "Here is your night's pay, good citizen," he said, and handed me an assignat worth one louis d'or. "What is your name?" he demanded, and he wrote it down in a ledger he had, for he was keeping the accounts of those heroes who assisted with these executions and the cleaning up.

I did not go back into Paris, though I needed food and clothing, but just struck off on a country road. Exhaustion sapped me of all reason and I plodded on without awareness. The sky darkened. It rained. Soaked and shivering I fell, coughed blood, got up, fell. I lay beneath the roadside hedge, dying.

That's where Sebastien Brillon found me.

"What happened then?" Maurice Fabry prompted as his companion fell silent.

Jules Volant's forehead shone with fine sweat, and his face was taut as a drum as he gazed down the dread corridor of the past. Maurice's question brought him to the present, and his features relaxed. He said, "Why, he brought me back to life, did Sebastien! And he gave me papers of my own. I traveled with the troupe for many months, though I was too ill at first to do any work. Sebastien insisted that living in the outdoors would cure my lungs, and it did. That and plenty of fresh food."

Maurice asked, "Did the enemy troops ever come to Paris?" From Cousin Claude's letters he knew of the war in a general way, but he had not taken note of particular battles.

Jules Volant shook his head. "No, they didn't. I found out much later that there were no foreign troops within hundreds of miles. Someone must have made a mistake. But Frenchmen rallied to the danger, for only two weeks after the September Massacres we earned a victory at Valmy."

Maurice nodded, remembering now that the very next day the monarchy was abolished and the French Republic was proclaimed. And four months later King Louis XVI was guillotined.

Jules continued his story. "I traveled with Sebastien's troupe for nearly a year, and then went off on my own. Now I wander where I will and work when I must. Occasionally the troupe and I cross paths, and sometimes I travel along for a few weeks. But then it seems I feel walls closing in on me, and since those nights in a building full of dead I cannot bear sameness for long. I must strike out on my own again. Sebastien has often said he would help me apprentice myself to some trade with friends of his, but I know I could not settle down in one place."

Sebastien Brillon returned to his troupe, calling out triumphantly that everything was arranged. He moved among them, issuing rapid orders, urging haste, his features alight and his pointed beard bristling with *joie de vivre.* Rapidly Sebastien assigned parts, moving the chosen players among the shrubbery, roughing out the action, and setting the remainder of his troupe to various tasks.

After a hectic hour they were nearly ready with their presentation. Lemonade sellers arrived, tinkling their bells and pushing their carts up and down the paths. A group from the local Jacobin Club came and set up a gigantic red-white-and-blue banner with *Vive la République* sewed on the white middle stripe. People began gathering, wandering through the space Sebastien had selected for the stage. He shouted, he fumed, then at last he ordered rope to cordon off the area.

Jules and Maurice helped the other workers lay out the rope, tying it waist-high to trees. The rapidly growing audience pressed close, and the youths had to force their way through the crowd.

Maurice was just finishing a tight knot when a hand fell roughly on his arm. A man shoved him aside to make way as he strode past. Maurice saw the flash of a green stone on the wrong finger, the blur of a crippled hand. . . . Then the man was gone, swallowed up by the moving throng before the startled youth could catch a glimpse of his face.

Jules joined him, and asked sharply, "What's happened? You're as pale as a ghost."

Maurice whispered, "I saw one of the men who stopped the night coach to Paris. He was the one they called Félix. Jules, they've followed us!"

The Face of an Enemy

VI SEBASTIEN BRILLON'S IMPROVISED presentation was a great success. The audience cheered the players, applauded the speeches, and lustily joined in the singing. Maurice stayed near the troupe's horses, finding enough work to keep him busy until the audience, after one final burst of applause, broke up and drifted out of the park. Then Sebastien went rapidly among his players, giving the order to pack up and get moving. "Repairs have been made and the wagons have passed Nantes, according to the instructions I sent earlier today. An hour's riding should bring us all together again."

The troupe was soon riding through the streets of Nantes. After crossing several bridges the players finally emerged from the town on the right bank of the Loire. "Back on the side the night coach to Paris travels," Maurice said to Jules. "And the men who stopped it."

"Forget them," Jules advised. "If Félix is in Nantes the other two must be with him."

The sun was just marking the supper hour when the troupe came to the end of its long hard ride. Five wagons stood on a scrub heath, their horses already turned out to graze. Maurice and Jules were set to work unsaddling the animals used as mounts. "No wonder the vans traveled so slowly," said Maurice. As he worked, he studied the high-roofed wooden wagons painted in gaudy colors with lettering announcing Sebastien Brillon's Patriotic Players and giving a summary of the presentations in the repertoire. "They are so heavy, and each is pulled by only a pair of horses."

"Tomorrow we'll be hitching four to a van in the usual way," said Jules. "The players ordinarily travel in the wagons, but if they must go quickly they ride the dray horses as well as the two or three extra mounts. That's why these saddles are only the roughest sort of leather or sheepskin."

By the time Maurice and Jules finished their task, red sunlight spilled across the heath, and good cooking smells wafted from the supper fires. The kind old man with the vague smile appeared beside them. "My name is Timothée," he said. "You won't remember me, Jules Volant, for I joined the troupe just this spring, and two weeks later you left it."

"But I do remember you, Timothée," replied Jules.

The kind old man, only as tall as Maurice, told them, "You lads have been assigned to our wagon. Now come and eat."

He led them to one of the fires where a younger man was broiling fish on a grate. Jules and the man greeted one another as old friends. Timothée said to Maurice, "This is Guy. I see Jules already knows him."

Guy's smile was light and as lively as his thick curly brown hair. With lithe movements he snatched the fish from the fire, forked potatoes from a pan, and served up supper on wooden plates. "I apologize for the wine. I much prefer white, but we have only some full-bodied red." He set the bottle where they could all reach it.

Maurice hesitated, holding his plate. "We've been working with the horses. Where can I wash my hands?"

The three stared at him, their forks between plate and chin. "Wash?" repeated Guy. "But this is incredible! Only aristocrats wash."

Timothée gestured with his fork. "Maurice is making a joke. He knows we're all patriotic sans-culottes."

"Ha ha," said Guy without amusement. "He will jest our heads into the basket."

Bewildered, Maurice could only heed the warning in Jules' eyes. Still begrimed from the horses, he began to eat.

Afterwards Guy fetched six wooden balls from the wagon behind them and began tossing them in a whirling circle as he walked among the campfires. Timothée wiped their plates with a rag. "I am only an old fool fit for crowd scenes and some tableaux. But that Guy is a genuine artist, a real professional. He can act nearly as well as Sebastien, and he is an acrobat and juggler besides." Finished with his sketchy dish cleaning, Timothée took Maurice and Jules up the narrow steps at the back of their van and through the small door. After some fumbling in the dusk, he lighted a lantern and hung it on a hook.

Maurice exclaimed, "Why, it's like a ship's cabin!"

Of similar size and shape the van had a great deal of supplies and fixtures ingeniously stowed. Shelves let down on chains to make bunks. This left space in front for a hinged table top, two or three chairs and an iron brazier for inside cooking in case of rain. There was a window in each door and on either side. The roofed driving platform was just outside the tiny front entrance.

Timothée pointed to some chests. "There are blankets and straw pallets stored behind those. You can make up the top bunks for yourselves." He went out of the wagon, leaving them to their task.

As they worked, Maurice said, "Jules, I made a *faux pas*

over washing my hands. But I don't understand why it was a mistake."

Jules smiled thinly. "I had almost forgotten how they made us scrub ourselves back in my hospital. It is different now that everyone is a sans-culotte."

Maurice nodded to show he knew this meant the common people who did not wear the knee breeches and stockings of pre-Revolutionary high fashion. "What has this to do with not washing before eating?"

"No longer does one strive to imitate the upper classes," Jules told him. "Anything aristocratic is dangerous to the Republic and to oneself. All aristo customs are wrong: washing, polite speech, neatness. It is fashionable, and far safer, to scratch your dirty hide, gobble your meals, and dress in worn garments."

"The people in the Paris coach were suspicious of my good jacket," Maurice recalled.

"Sebastien took it from you to avoid arrest," Jules said. "And that probably saved you from Félix's attention this afternoon. He would be looking for a youth in a sea cap and jacket. But do you think he might recognize your face if he saw you directly?"

Maurice thought back to the moonlight of two nights before. "It was light enough then, but he was expecting to see my cousin, Claude Donard, not me. And he had only a brief look at my face before I got away from him. His own features were in shadow, and all I saw was his hand." Maurice described the missing finger and the ring. "That's how I knew he was in Nantes. I didn't see the other two riders that night except as shadows."

"Perhaps they have given up the search for you," suggested Jules. "If Félix lives in Nantes he would naturally go to see the patriotic play."

"Men desperate enough to stop a public coach wouldn't

give up the search for me," Maurice replied. "They want me to lead them to Claude. I wish I knew why they were after him."

"Alors, it must be some personal matter," said Jules. "Or, as they don't know where he lives, some business affair. If it were an official grievance, Claude would simply be condemned and guillotined. It looks to me as though Félix and his friends have something of their own to hide while they are seeking Claude Donard. You're lucky to be in Sebastien's troupe, Maurice. You can now travel to Orléans without fear of discovery."

"How long will it take for us to get there?"

"Sebastien usually lingers a good month in the Loire valley," answered Jules. "Let me see . . . Angers . . . Saumur . . . Tours . . . It will take perhaps ten days or two weeks, depending on how quickly Sebastien wishes to travel."

"That leaves very little extra time," said Maurice. "I will just barely meet my vessel in Marseille." A new thought struck him. "Jules, should we tell Sebastien of Félix and his men searching for me?"

Jules shook his head decisively. "You can not be certain that they still are. And even so, no one in France wishes to be burdened by the secrets of another. What one does not know, the police cannot make one tell."

Maurice, remembering the pathetic guillotine-bound victims of yesterday's village, exclaimed, "Secrecy isn't enough to keep some people off the scaffold!"

"Oui, true enough. One must also have friends."

There was a knock on the back door and Timothée apologetically put his head in. "Sebastien is calling a rehearsal, Maurice. And you are to be in his new play."

Jules, laughing, pushed Maurice toward the door. "That's what comes of looking like a clever fellow. All I have to do is take care of the horses."

Timothée led Maurice to a group standing between two campfires, for by now the sun had set. Sebastien handed him a scrap of paper. "These are your lines. Memorize them until I call your cue."

"But I'm not an actor!"

Yvette gently took Maurice aside. "It's not difficult, *chéri*. And Sebastien badly needs someone like you for the part. Won't you help us?"

It would have been churlish to refuse the charming Yvette with her plump dimpled cheeks and soft eyes. "I don't know what to do," Maurice said, protest slipping away from him.

Yvette reached for Maurice's paper. "Let me show you how simple it is."

The isolated lines did not make much sense, but Maurice faithfully imitated Yvette's enunciation and emphasis. Then Sebastien, all business, called for him, and Maurice spent an hour being pulled and pushed here and there, faced in front of other people and poked in the ribs to make him say his lines. Sebastien called him seven different kinds of a fool, but Maurice soon noticed he did this to everyone and nobody seemed to mind.

When the group was dismissed, Maurice walked back to their wagon with Guy, who was playing the aristocratic villain in the new play. "Guy, aren't you afraid to be an aristo on the stage?"

Guy laughed. "I'm safe as long as I behave nastily enough. But you must act much angrier when you discover my identity, Maurice. Denounce me like a true patriot."

"I'm not really an actor."

"Only three or four of us actually are. But we'll have plenty of rehearsal during the three days' travel to Angers."

The last throb of campfire light hissed out as someone

threw water over glowing coals. Jules and Timothée were already asleep when Maurice and Guy reached their van.

Climbing into his upper bunk, Maurice realized that this was only his third night in his parents' homeland. And already he had slept in a coach, a cave, a dungeon, and now a traveling theater wagon.

The players roused at dawn and immediately after breakfast Sebastien held another rehearsal, this time concentrating on the stage directions.

"Look where I am directing you, dolt!" he shouted to Maurice who had lost his place while reading from his paper. "You can memorize your lines as we travel, but staging needs a solid piece of earth. Therefore, observe the direction of my pointing finger."

Maurice endured an hour of Sebastien's temperament, and when the order was given to board the wagons, he whooped with joy and ran across the camp where Jules was already sitting on the driving platform with the reins in his hands.

The troupe moved out into the road, heading east up the Loire valley toward distant Angers. Everyone rode in the wagons except for Sebastien who was on horseback.

The sun climbed higher and grew hotter. Dust plumed up from the horses' feet. In midmorning Sebastien ordered a rest beside a small, clear stream. They had another, longer rest at noon, lingering over their bread and cheese. Yvette helped Maurice with the lines he must speak in the play. During a midafternoon halt, Guy sketched out Maurice's stage movements on a piece of paper. "This will help you know your place."

Sebastien collected their ration cards and rode ahead of the caravan to buy provisions and arrange a place to spend the night. He was successful, for when they met up with him two hours later he pointed out the lush meadow he had chosen with a running stream and plenty of cool shade.

Hardly allowing time for supper, Sebastien put the players through another strenuous rehearsal. Maurice, to his own surprise, found he was actually learning his part. Sebastien seemed to read his thoughts. "The brain is beginning to function, yes?" He waggled a finger under Maurice's nose. "Still *far* from perfect! I only beg that you do not disgrace me in public." He drew a sigh out of the depths of despair. "Perhaps we may yet survive." From Sebastien, this was encouragement.

The next day, though the road continued to swing away from the Loire, the ground swelled into hills so that Maurice, sitting beside Jules on the driver's bench, could catch an occasional glimpse of the great river and its web of tributaries beyond sloping vineyards and through distant orchards.

Timothée, inside the wagon, patched a pair of worn trousers while Guy, singing lustily, worked out the makeup for his villainous part. The wheels creaked lazily under the hot sun, birds darted among the beech trees, and the smell of earth was agreeable to Maurice's nostrils. "I can see why you like this kind of life," he said to Jules. "I could ride along like this forever."

"Have you ever driven a team?" asked Jules.

"Just the pair that pulls my father's freight wagon. I've never had a four-in-hand."

"Then take the reins for a while."

Under Jules' instructions, Maurice soon had the knack of controlling the four horses. "Of course, they know what to do anyway," he admitted to his friend.

"Right now you must stir them up," Jules pointed out. "We're falling behind the other four wagons."

The van just ahead curved up over a hill and disappeared from view. Maurice slapped the reins on the horses' backs to make them hurry. They leaned into the traces at a half trot. As they turned the curve near the crest of the hill, Maurice concentrated so much on keeping the reins untangled that he let the animals swerve into the middle of the road.

Suddenly Jules cried, "I hear a horse coming this way!"

At that instant a horseman charged over the crown of the hill.

Maurice's animals shied, whinnying and crowding one another against the dense roadside hedge while the rider's mount reared and pawed the air. Maurice sawed the reins as his plunging horses entangled their traces. Standing in the stirrups of his prancing mount, the rider bellowed, "Pull your horses down! Get that van out of my way!"

Maurice braced his feet on the raised edge of the platform and pulled with all his might to get the horses under control while Jules uttered terse directions. The animals lunged out of the way of the rider, but the heavy wagon still blocked the thickly hedged road.

The horseman began edging his tightly-reined mount past the wheeling draft animals, pressing closer to the driving platform. "Did you hear me?" he roared in fury. "Get that wagon to one side!"

Maurice felt Jules' capable hands close over the reins. Relinquishing them, he slid over to the passenger's side. Now he was face to face with the horseman, who shouted, "Make way!"

Maurice retorted angrily, "If you'd just stop scaring our horses—" He broke off, staring at the rider's hands clenching the reins of his pawing mount.

Guy's head thrust out of the little window behind Maurice. "What's the trouble here? Do you need help?"

But Jules was too busy controlling the horses to answer

him. The rider and his capering mount poised tensely to pass. And Maurice was hypnotized by the green stone on the horseman's left hand next to the place where the third finger should be.

Tearing his gaze away from the crippled hand, Maurice surveyed Félix's face, burning into his memory the pinched nostrils, square jaw, and ruthless mouth.

Félix's eyes narrowed as they locked with Maurice's in a long steady stare.

Then the wagon jolted under way, moving slowly to the side. A space opened between vehicle and hedge, and Félix, loosening his horse's head, lunged past and vanished downhill in a burst of speed.

Jules stopped the van, and Guy jumped down to untangle the harness. Timothée put his gray head out and offered to help. Guy nodded, and Maurice moved over so the old man had room to clamber down the iron staples on the side.

Maurice spoke in a guarded voice. "Jules, that was Félix!"

Jules glanced at him sharply. "Take care, Maurice! You are seeing villains everywhere."

"It was Félix!" Maurice insisted. "I know by his hand and the ring he wears. How did he get here? Why is he riding toward Nantes, instead of away from it?"

"Are you sure of this?" At Maurice's nod, Jules suggested, "You must have been mistaken the other time, then."

"There's no mistake! It was the same hand, the same ring, the same missing finger."

They looked at one another, each struggling for comprehension.

Then Maurice said, "He stared at me, Jules. He must realize now who I am!"

"Did you look at him?"

"Yes, I studied his face well. I would know him anywhere now."

After a thoughtful moment Jules said, *"Bien,* he stared at you because you stared at him."

Guy and Timothée climbed aboard the wagon, and Jules clucked to the horses. They topped the hill and started down. The other four wagons were far down the road ahead. They could see Sebastien turn his horse out of the line and start riding back to them. When he saw they were all right, he waved and returned to the caravan.

Jules shrugged. "Eh, Maurice, this Félix has business that takes him back and forth from one town to another. It's nothing more than that."

"But why . . . ?" Why did Félix and his henchmen stop the night coach to Paris? Why did they believe Claude Donard would be on it? Why were they searching for Maurice's cousin? There were other "whys," all equally unanswerable.

Shortly before noon the next day the roofs and towers of Angers appeared ahead. It was not long before the theater caravan came to the city astride the Maine River which flowed several miles south to join the mighty Loire. Waiting for them just outside Angers was Hugo, the outrider. He led the wagons to a field that had been set aside for their use. When the horses were unharnessed Jules and Maurice started them toward a creek for watering. Hugo went along to show the way.

Maurice stumbled over a low grassy ridge. A few more steps brought him to another awkward rise.

"Take care," warned Hugo. "There are three or four more of these mounds."

Maurice noticed that Jules was leading his string of horses carefully around these obstructions. He asked

Hugo, "Why is the ground so rough?"

"These are mass graves of counter-revolutionaries," explained Hugo. "The local patriots won a fine victory over enemies of the people during the rebel uprising some months ago."

Hugo left them at the creek, watering the horses.

Maurice's foot grated against something embedded in the mud. He kicked it free. It was a little tin rattle. Some of the cold horror he had felt at the broken barge below Nantes swept over him. "Jules, did that baby's toy belong to an enemy of the people?"

"Alors, one naturally slays the families of the victims as well," said Jules factually. After a moment he added in a swift, hard voice, "The same is done by the rebels wherever civil war breaks out, in the southeast, the west, the north. They bayonet with pitchforks; they club; they slit throats; and they bury alive."

Was this the France of Maurice Fabry's ancestry? From king to dictator, from repression to terror. Turmoil, civil war, death! Maurice groaned, "Oh, God, a nation of savages!" But the same blood flowed in him, and he knew he was not a monster. "Why, Jules?" he asked hoarsely. "How can this be?"

"Someone wants something—power, wealth, revenge. And he uses the fears and sufferings of others to win it for himself." Jules lifted his shoulders negligently. *"Eh bien,* it is a feat to merely remain alive!"

After the troupe's noon meal in the field, Sebastien and the actors of his new play walked to the theater through the streets of Angers between rough-faced buildings of local black stone. Inside the playhouse a group from the town's Jacobin Club was mounting tricolor banners on the walls. On the stage Sebastien began a long, merciless rehearsal. He was so particular about every detail that

Maurice despaired of doing anything right. Yet when it was over Sebastien surprised him by saying, "You did well, Maurice. You have nothing to fear tonight. Remember only one thing: do not look out over the audience. That alone will give you stage fright."

There was nothing else to do but wait. Maurice stood around, aware of increasing hunger, but Guy told him actors almost never ate just before a performance. The Angers censor came, glanced through Sebastien's script, and wrote out a certificate of approval. The rest of the troupe arrived bringing a vanload of costumes and scenic drops. The men quickly set the stage for the new play. People began hurrying about in subdued tension.

Yvette, dimples vanished in her concentration, sat backstage in a corner near a flickering lamp, stitching furiously in a flurry of last-minute costume fittings. Beckoning to Maurice, she thrust a bundle into his hands. "Here, dress quickly."

It took a while for Maurice to figure out exactly how to present himself, but with Jules' help he finally emerged from a flimsy dressing booth with ragged sans-culotte trousers over a pillow paunch, a dirty shirt with a huge red-white-and-blue rosette pinned to it, and a wig of straggly gray hair.

Guy took him off to another corner, daubing and lining his face with the effects of age and hard toil. "A true sans-culotte patriot," he pronounced, pleased with his handiwork. "The audience is already filling up the seats."

Maurice seized Guy's arm in panic. "I—I can't!"

"You'll be all right, but don't let your eyes wander out from the stage," said Guy.

Sebastien hurried by, hissing, "Places!" He paused before Maurice. "Hmm, a fair make-up job, Guy. Now, Maurice, no matter what happens, you must never—"

"—never look out into the audience," Maurice finished for him.

"It may bring on an attack of stage fright," Sebastien added before hastening away.

Maurice went toward the wings. In the dimness he saw Timothée coming toward him. Suddenly he blundered straight into a full length mirror. "Timothée" was actually his own reflection! "Guy did a fine job of making-up," he muttered, readjusting his wig.

The stage, still curtained, was full of people whose costumes and make-up turned them into strangers. Someone shoved Maurice into place, and then they stood taut and waiting. Beyond the curtain local musicians struck up the *Marseillaise,* and the audience sang fervently. Then the curtain parted. Maurice stared out over the brightly burning footlights at the softly lighted seating area.

A woman playing a fish seller turned to him and spoke. Maurice answered without thinking, and the play was on.

He was soon very much in his part, striding about the stage the way Sebastien had drilled him, gesturing and throwing out his lines clearly, leaving and entering on cue. Even the sight of Guy did not put him off stride, though Guy was resplendent in velvet and silk and lacy ruffles, with huge imitation jewels glittering at every move. The audience loved Guy; it hissed and booed and howled for his aristocratic head.

Waiting in the wings for his last cue, Maurice was joined by Sebastien who had changed into tight-fitting green breeches and tailed coat, accented by the snowy white of silk stockings, ruffled shirt, cravat, and curled white wig. He had even powdered his beard white.

Maurice exclaimed in a whisper, "I thought there was only one aristocrat in the play!"

Sebastien struck a pose. "I am Robespierre, man of the

people. After Guy is guillotined, I give one of my speeches against treason."

Maurice stared. Was this how the ruler of France looked?

Sebastien nudged Maurice. "There is your cue."

Maurice went out for the last time, and when Guy was exposed as an aristocrat to the astonished characters (the audience had never been in doubt), he launched into a scathing denunciation.

At that moment a door opened in the back of the theater. Uniformed gendarmes trooped down the aisles. The officer in charge pointed to someone in the audience. "There she is—arrest her!"

Maurice's mouth hung open. People in the audience stood up and craned their necks. A young woman screamed as the gendarmes dragged her up the aisle. The officer called an explanation to the audience, "Someone watched her secretly taking food to prisoners."

An excited murmur ran through the audience as the theater door closed behind gendarmes and captive.

Sebastien hissed from the wings, "Maurice, on with the play!"

And then Maurice saw Félix.

But only yesterday Félix was riding westward at high speed, away from Angers, toward Nantes.

"Maurice!" It was Guy this time. "Your lines!"

The trouper playing a blacksmith repeated the speech that cued Maurice's denunciation of the aristocrat. But Maurice stood there with frozen tongue, staring at the insolent eyes of Félix, the pinched nostrils, the square jaw, and ruthless mouth.

The audience stirred restlessly.

Maurice looked at his fellow actors, and grinned foolishly. For the life of him he could not remember a single word. Yvette, below the footlights, prompted in a whisper, but the words meant nothing.

People in the audience began laughing and calling out.

The blacksmith took over, speaking Maurice's lines, fitting them to his own part, while the woman fish seller firmly grasped Maurice and led him into the wings, pushing him straight into the angry arms of Sebastien Brillon.

Eyes blazing, Sebastien seized his shirt and dragged him into a far corner. "Assassin!" he raged. "Destroyer! You have completely demolished my magnificent new play! The great Sebastien Brillon plucked you out of the dirt, and now you have ruined him! Fool! Imbecile! Villain!"

Maurice tried to apologize, but it seemed that every half-hearted word of his provoked a new storm of abuse.

Timothée came, hovering fearfully on the edge of Sebastien's wrath. "Er—Sebastien—your cue . . . They are just cutting off Guy's head." He referred to the stage guillotine, an illusion invented by Guy himself who had once worked for a magician.

A sudden silence fell. Sebastien drew himself up haughtily, poised for a moment, then added icily to Maurice, "I will deal with you later." And off he strode, beard jutting, implacable in the simulated power of an imitation Robespierre.

Night in the Forest

VII

"It is only his nerves," said Yvette soothingly to Maurice.

They were crowded together on the bench of a tiny dressing booth. Maurice had already changed back to his everyday garments, though they were nearly as shabby as the ones he had worn onstage. Sebastien's troupers hurried around busily, taking down the drops, packing up costumes. Outside the heavy stage curtain the singing audience was well into its third round of *Ça ira*.

Yvette patted Maurice's hand with her plump one. "So you must not speak of leaving the troupe. Indeed, Maurice, you do us a great service by playing your part."

He had not really meant it when he had declared he was leaving. That had been a burst of defiance and self-pity to Yvette, who had come backstage looking for him immediately at the end of the play. Maurice needed the troupe; it was his sole safe passage to Orléans. Alone, without money and proof of his American citizenship, Maurice stood slim chance of surviving in this strange and terrifying France.

"He is like that during a play," explained Yvette. "Very taut and quick to anger. His curse is that he seeks perfection, and there is no longer any place for that. Poor Sebastien was never meant to drag his genius through the rutted roads of the provinces! In the old days . . ." She looked into the distance, then sighed heavily. "Ah, but one does not speak of the old days when Sebastien Brillon played the first theaters of Paris. And I—you may not believe it, Maurice, but I was for years a prima ballerina, dancing for those with the wit and culture to applaud. Then came the Revolution . . . the theaters closed down. . . ." She shook her head sadly. "*Allons,* it is something, at least, these performances we give among the provincials, though often this idiocy rankles Sebastien. Yet it is his hope that from his ordeal will emerge a new theater for France as little by little the sans-culotte comes to understand and desire good drama."

Sebastien appeared suddenly in the doorway of the little dressing booth. He had changed from his costume though his black beard was still streaked with powder. He leveled an accusing finger at Maurice. "Aha!"

Maurice, unable to explain about Félix, said swiftly, "The gendarmes came barging in. That would put anyone off, wouldn't it? And that woman screamed. They're going to kill her, aren't they?"

Sebastien nodded. "Someone saw her throwing dry bread between the window bars of the prison. She will be guillotined tomorrow for consorting with the enemies of the people. But this shouldn't put you off your stride! It happens all the time, as we Frenchmen know, eh?"

Yvette spoke to Sebastien. "Be kind to him, *chéri. Vrai,* he made a mistake, but he is so young."

Sebastien struck his chest dramatically. "I was *never* that young!" He strode away, shouting orders.

Maurice drew a breath of relief. Yvette was right; now that the play was over, Sebastien was nearly back to his normal jaunty self.

That night the troupe camped in the field where they

had left horses and wagons. Dawn was just struggling over the horizon when Sebastien routed them out and hurried them through breakfast. Day had scarcely begun as the wagons took the road leading south toward the Loire. An hour's travel brought them to a bridge spanning the river, and they crossed to the left side.

Maurice had had no chance to tell Jules of seeing Félix in the audience last night as someone was always close by. But now as the caravan turned east toward distant Saumur, Timothée went to visit in some other wagon. Then Guy, who had been driving, gave the reins to Jules and went inside the van to rest.

Sitting beside Jules on the driver's bench, Maurice at last told him the reason for his attack of stage fright.

For a long time Jules said nothing, then finally he shook his head in bafflement. "Maurice, Maurice! You are seeing this Félix everywhere. Surely he cannot *be* everywhere!"

"He must still be searching for me," Maurice insisted, irritated by Jules' skepticism. "It's a good thing we crossed the river once more. I feel safer on the south bank. But perhaps Félix has sent his two companions to search along this side."

"The other two didn't get as good a look at you as did Félix, did they? *Alors,* you need fear only one man." Jules shook his head regretfully. "It's a pity I can't recognize the villain."

"You'd know him by his hand, Jules. There is no other with the left ring finger missing and a large green stone on the middle digit."

Jules squinted down the dusty road thoughtfully, then nodded. *"Bien,* at our next performance I'll volunteer for the job of taking tickets at the door."

By midmorning the troupe ran into a road block. Soldiers out on a routine check were stopping all traffic passing in either direction and making a thorough search. Sebastien's vans halted behind a long line of hay carts, freight wagons, a drove of lambs, a load of pigs, and people traveling ahorse or afoot.

"What are the soldiers looking for?" asked Maurice.

Jules shrugged. "Leather, suspects, gunpowder, runaway conscripts . . . what does it matter? But this will make us too late to give tonight's performance at Saumur. You can see how methodical *les bleus* are today."

Blue-uniformed soldiers, sweating under the hot sun, inspected every vehicle and person carefully, driving bayonets into hay or sacks of grain while animals milled nervously, whinnying, bleating, squealing, and lowing. The humans, when not tending their beasts, stood or sat in patient submission. But not Sebastien Brillon.

"Impossible!" he roared to the sky. "This delay is intolerable. I won't have it!" Eyes flashing, beard bristling, he spurred his horse toward the captain in charge.

Two heads bent together in consultation, the shiny black leather of the officer's shako and Sebastien's grimy red knit cap. Then Sebastien came riding back, stopping at each of his vans to collect the papers of his players. Maurice handed over his worn wallet, as he had done before when someone needed the ration cards to buy food for the troupe. He had never bothered to examine the papers Sebastien had given him the day they had met, and now he stirred anxiously as he watched the captain rapidly going through them all.

In a surprisingly short time the officer handed all the papers back to Sebastien, nodding and gesturing so that even Maurice could understand that the troupe was being allowed to pass on. "How has Sebastien done it?" he exclaimed. "He did not even bribe the captain!"

Suddenly there was a commotion at the head of the line.

One of the soldiers had found some guns concealed in a load of hay. The peasant began protesting his innocence. The captain uttered a sharp order. Two soldiers dragged the peasant to a clear place in the road while a third, standing away, leveled his musket and shot him. They threw the body under a hedge.

Maurice started up, but Jules seized his arm and fiercely held him to his seat. "Eh, you wish to join him under the hedge?" he muttered. "Look how the others turn their faces away. Now if ever someone should ask questions they can say they have seen nothing. It will be the same with you, *oui?*"

And a moment later Sebastien came and handed back their wallets. Then the players' caravan pulled out of line and resumed its plodding journey toward Saumur. Maurice kept his eyes resolutely ahead as they passed the hedge sheltering the corpse.

It was night when they reached Saumur with its towered château brooding high over the town. Tired and hungry, for Sebastien had driven them all day with little rest, the troupe went directly to the hall that Hugo, traveling ahead, had arranged for their use.

The troupers set to work immediately, preparing the stage, changing into costumes, applying make-up. Jules stationed himself outside the main entrance to receive the tickets sold in advance by the local Jacobin Club. Saumur musicians arrived, launched into loud patriotic airs, and were joined by the voices of the growing audience. At curtain time, Sebastien laid a hand on Maurice's shoulder. "You will do well, I know. But do *not* look at the audience!"

As once before, the curtain parted, the woman fish seller spoke, and Maurice was caught up in his role. Guy overplayed his part, to the raucous name-calling delight of the crowd. So contagious was the audience's hatred of the aristocrat that in the end Maurice's denunciation of the exposed traitor rang with genuine passion.

But to Maurice's surprise and disappointment, Sebastien was not waiting backstage and had missed the successful scene. Maurice discovered the other troupers busy dressing in costumes. He found Timothée putting on make-up. "Where's Sebastien, Timothée? He'll miss his cue."

The old man carefully stroked in some additional wrinkles. "There's to be no Robespierre tonight, Maurice. Instead we're presenting four tableaux. You're to be in two of them."

"I—in a tableau? But—we've had no rehearsal!"

"It's quite simple," Timothée reassured him. "Even I can do it. One need only stand still."

Yvette came by, whispering breathlessly, "There you are, Maurice! Quickly, put on this uniform, leave your make-up as it is. Take this musket." She pressed a bundle and a wooden stage musket into his arms.

After Guy "died" on the guillotine, the stage was swiftly cleared and the tableau actors positioned themselves while the curtains opened and closed, the audience clapping and showing its approval. Maurice was in two of these living pictures; in the first he held his musket up in surrender while another French soldier, clutching the national tricolor to his chest, cowered beneath the bayonets of a booted British redcoat and a grinning Belgian soldier. In the second scene, Maurice was poised in the act of bayoneting the redcoat as the other French soldier held the flag triumphantly aloft while resting his foot on the chest of the dead Belgian. The audience, deeply moved, applauded for so long that the curtains parted for a second viewing of that same scene. At last Maurice was free to go backstage.

Guy caught him up in the wings. "Pack up at once. We're leaving town right after the other two tableaux."

"Why—has something gone wrong?"

Guy shook his head. "Nothing at all except that it's a day and a half of travel to Tours, so by starting now and going through the night we'll arrive by sundown tomorrow."

The moon had been up only two hours when the caravan once more crept along the base of the château ramparts, then turned east toward Tours, trundling alongside the Loire.

The players ate a cold supper as they rode, and then one by one the lamps in each wagon went out as members of the troupe retired for the night.

Guy was driving, and Timothée slumbered amid gentle snores. From his upper bunk, Jules whispered across to Maurice, "I watched for Félix's hand as I took the tickets tonight, but I didn't see it. I even stood on the left side of the entrance so that the fingerless hand wouldn't be hidden from me."

"I didn't expect Félix on this side of the river anyway," Maurice murmured. "He seems to keep along the right bank. Perhaps he thinks a foreigner—he doesn't know I speak French fluently—would go along the more heavily traveled roads."

"If that is true," Jules replied, "you won't see Félix in Tours, as it is on this side of the river." A moment later he added, "It may be he won't search this far east, Maurice. By tomorrow we will be better than halfway to Orléans."

Halfway to Orléans! And this in only four days of travel with the theater caravan. Maurice was glad that Sebastien Brillon's need for haste coincided with his own.

Jules, experienced trouper that he was, fell asleep readily. But Maurice was kept awake by the wagon's jolting and the axles squealing in the wheels. Lying on his side he gazed through the open window at the moon plating the broad Loire with silver and at the shadowed trees, black as carbon, arching across the sky. A chance breeze wafted inside the van and stroked his cheek warmly. Maurice recalled the increasing numbers of vineyards they had passed in the last two days, the orchards heavy with swelling fruit, and the thick fields of lush hay and ripening grain. He felt he could remain forever in such a beautiful and fruitful land. And then he remembered the foul deeds of men that had cursed this lovely Val de Loire.

Wondering when it would be that Frenchmen could once more live openly and proudly, Maurice Fabry fell asleep.

He awoke to a strange silence. The wagon still swayed in the rhythm of movement, shadows fled across the open windows, and the hoofs of the horses thudded steadily. But the wheels no longer squealed advance notice of the caravan's coming.

Craning his neck for a look at the moon, Maurice estimated that it was four hours since they had left Saumur. Somewhere during that time, the troupe must have stopped to grease the axles.

Then he noticed that the trees and hedges pressed much closer along the side of the road. Hitching himself forward on his bunk for a better look, Maurice saw that instead of the broad highway leading out of Saumur, the wagons were winding more slowly along curving backroads. Trees massed thickly into real woods through which he could catch an occasional glimpse of small streams and placid ponds. Then on a hill, through the leaves, Maurice saw a tall stone tower, its roof caved in, the broken windows staring blankly. Later as the caravan went through a crossing, Maurice saw far down the side road a huge clearing in the woods, and rising from a welter of scrub bushes and rank weeds were the jagged scorched ruins of a château. Many of the nobles who had inhabited these magnificent dwellings, Maurice realized, had brought about their own destruction. But he wondered what had happened to the children, the gardeners, the cooks, stableboys, huntsmen. . . .

The wagon lurched, then slowed. The train was turning into another road, much narrower, more rutted. An owl hooted; a fox darted away from beneath the muted wagon wheels; a rabbit cried out. Moonlight blurred through interlaced treetops.

Maurice stirred uneasily. Surely this could not be the road to Tours!

The wagon stopped. Through the window of the front door he saw Guy leap to the ground. Then the van moved again, Guy leading the horses. Maurice saw that the wagons ahead were also being led. Now they turned off even this narrow road into the very woods, lurching slowly over a crooked track. They soon came to a natural glen, where the trees stood farther apart. The vans were parked in a rough circle, separated by only a few clumps of trees.

Maurice sensed rather than saw movement of men among trees. Guy did not come back to his wagon, but soon a light sprang up behind the shutters of Sebastien's van. Maurice recalled now that he had not seen Sebastien since the beginning of the play in Saumur.

Were those hoofbeats? Yes, a rider was going farther along the rough track through the woods, hoofs muffled on the forest mold.

Silence descended and deepened. Nothing moved. Maurice dozed.

He awoke with the moon shining on his face and the conviction that something was wrong. He sat up, straining his ears, but heard nothing beyond the steady breathing of Jules and Timothée.

It was the moon—its position showed that the wagons had been parked in these woods for about an hour. The horses still stood in their traces, not unharnessed as they would be if the troupe were camping. From a chink in the shutters of Sebastien's wagon came the faintest red glimmer, a heartthrob of lantern light. Had there been an accident of some kind?

Slipping out of his bunk, Maurice crept to the front door and glanced out of the open window. There was no sign of Guy. Pulling on shirt and trousers, he quietly climbed through the window to the driver's bench, then let himself down the side to the ground. The shadows had shifted with the passage of the moon, but Maurice stumbled onto a clear path that ran crookedly behind his wagon to Sebastien's on the other side of the wooded glen. His bare feet were soundless on the springy woods duff as he slowly made his way between bushes and trees.

Suddenly something snatched his ankle and jerked him to the ground. His side struck painfully. Maurice tried to wrench his foot free, but it was held fast.

Then a shadow loomed above him. Moonlight glinted on a knife blade.

A cry of horror gurgled in his throat.

The knife fell away. A hand pulled him up. "*Hein!* It's you, Maurice!" exclaimed Guy in a whisper. "One moment, I'll cut you out of that snare. What are you doing out of the wagon?"

"I—I woke up. We've been here an hour. I thought something was wrong." He rubbed his sore ankle.

Guy chuckled. It sounded dry and a little forced to Maurice. The actor said, "The horses are resting. These snares? *Bien,* there's no one to stop us from catching a few rabbits for the pot, eh?" He grasped Maurice's arm, walking him along to Sebastien's wagon, pushing him up the back steps. "A warm drink will help you sleep better, Maurice."

Yvette opened to Guy's knock. "Eh, it's Maurice!" When Guy explained how he had found him, Yvette said, "Come in, then. There is hot coffee on the coals."

Guy left as Maurice went inside and sidled past the empty bunks to the front where an old woman sat at a folding table, carefully laying out cards from a greasy pack in her hands.

Yvette poured coffee into a cracked cup. "Sit here. There is sugar in that jam pot. You know Tante, don't you?"

It was a title, not a name, but whose aunt she was, Maurice never did find out. Tante was a member of the troupe, traveling in Sebastien's wagon, busying herself with making and mending both costumes and clothing. Now she hunched over her cards, a shawl snug over her gray hair and shoulders despite the closeness of the van. Her bright eyes darted toward him in recognition that took the place of welcome.

Yvette picked up some knitting. Maurice sipped the hot bitter coffee as needles clicked and cards whispered. Yvette spoke of the performance in Saumur, how well everything had gone. She talked on in a detailed triviality that was unlike her. He wondered if her mind were really on something else.

Finishing his hot coffee, he stood up. "Thank you. I think I can sleep now."

Yvette smiled, her dimples winking in her full rosy cheeks. "But I cannot, and you must keep us company a while, Maurice."

"And where is Sebastien?" he asked.

"Outside," Yvette answered. "There is yet time for a good visit. Sit down, Maurice."

He obeyed reluctantly, feeling less like a guest than a prisoner.

Perhaps his uneasiness showed on his face, for suddenly Tante scooped up her cards with clawlike hands and said, "You would like to see how cards can tell one's fortune? Now, observe!" She spoke French fluently, but with an accent that rang of some distant mountainous corner, and it was hard for Maurice to follow her. Tante laid the cards out slowly, explaining their meaning, but the scheme soon grew so complicated that Maurice lost track of it. He longed impatiently for her rambling discourse to end so he could leave the wagon.

After what seemed a long time, Tante at last ran out of words. Maurice sprang to his feet. "I must go. I can scarcely keep awake—"

Yvette said, "You're lucky Tante thinks well of you, Maurice, for I can see she intends to tell your fortune. It is not for everyone she does this." Gently she pushed him back to his seat and refilled his cup while Tante shuffled the cards and began setting them out in a pattern.

Maurice heard that he would visit a famous city and take a trip over water and a few other things that seemed quite likely to happen sometime during his life. Tante said, "Beware of blades," and Maurice smiled, remembering his many cuts before he had mastered the wood chisels of his father's shop.

Tante turned over another card. "Danger here! It pursues you. A dark stranger—" Breathing shakily, she turned over cards very rapidly, mumbling to herself. "Night . . . a hand . . . it moves. . . . Look out! He—"

She broke off suddenly, staring at the cards before her.

"What is it?" Maurice cried in alarm. "What do you see?"

"Voilà tout!" exclaimed Tante. "Enough!" She clawed the cards toward her.

A knock came from the back door.

The three froze in position as if in a tableau. Then Yvette took Maurice's arm, facing him to the front. "These fortunes are only for amusement, Maurice. Do not let this game give you nightmares." She opened the front door and gently propelled him out on the driving platform. "Guy will help you find your way back. Guy!"

And Guy was there, helping him down to the ground, piloting him around some bushes toward his own wagon.

But Maurice said, "One moment, Guy! My foot—" He bent as if to examine his bare foot and peered through the bushes at the wagon he had just left. The back door was wide open, lamplight glowing full on Sebastien's face as he pushed a smaller figure inside before him. Standing nearby, Hugo held the reins of two horses.

Then Guy stepped around Maurice, blocking the view. "If you've hurt your foot, I can carry you."

"It's all right," said Maurice, and he willingly returned to his van with his escort.

He went inside to his bunk while Guy climbed into the driver's seat. Maurice could see nothing out of the window, but after a time there was stirring around each wagon, and the caravan began to move, circling back the way it had come to the rough side road.

Maurice dozed fitfully the rest of the night, aware from his many awakenings that they were traveling ever better roads, that forest gave way to cultivated fields and orchards, that they were crossing a bridge over a wide slow river. . . .

Now the wagons were heading east along an excellent highway, stars fading before the blue of unborn dawn. This must be the main road along the right bank, thought Maurice. Would Félix be watching, not for Claude Donard's cousin from America but for Sebastien Brillon's theater troupe? Even easier would it be for Félix to just visit the large cities up the Loire, watching for the advertisements of the performances Hugo rode ahead to arrange, as the patriots needed only a day or two of notice for their entertainment.

When Jules shook Maurice awake, the sun stood midmorning high. Timothée was driving the horses, and Guy sat inside at the folding table, eating with gusto a meal of bread, cold pork, and salad. Jules said, "Hurry and eat, Maurice, or Guy will leave you nothing."

"Where are we?" Maurice asked, pulling on his ragged clothes.

Guy paused in his eating to answer. "On the right bank. We'll reach Tours tonight in time for our performance."

Jules put Maurice's wooden plate on the table. "Guy says we have a new member in the troupe. Last night when Sebastien decided to stop long enough to trap some rabbits, they picked up some half-starved urchin. His name is André."

Maurice asked Guy, "Did you catch any rabbits?"

Guy shrugged. "Only one. But anyway the horses got a good rest."

The troupe did not stop for its usual midmorning break but pressed on until noon when Hugo met them to point out an excellent place to rest. While cooking fires were lighted and the horses led to a pond, Sebastien ruthlessly drilled the actors of his latest play. Maurice suffered both heat and hunger as delicious roasting smells wound their way under a hot sun to his nostrils. He was wet with perspiration when Sebastien finally released the players for their meal.

Jules and Timothée had already eaten. Guy took his plate in search of some shade. Maurice, too hungry to wait, began eating at once.

Jules started putting out the fire carefully. "I met this André. He is about our age and travels in Sebastien's wagon. He was supposed to help me water the horses, but he just huddled on a stone, wrapped up to the eyebrows in garments as if he had a chill. *Bien entendu,* it's like Sebastien to pick up sick strays. He took me in when I was dying."

Maurice's eye fell on a small newcomer. "Is that André? There's nothing wrong with his appetite."

Wrapped in a variety of torn and dirty garments topped with a large stocking cap pulled over the ears, a grimy youth sat on the ground with Yvette, Sebastien, and Tante, eating hurriedly out of a battered tin plate.

Maurice said, "He's probably thin underneath all those clothes."

"Yvette will soon fatten him, and Sebastien will give him plenty of work to do for exercise. He's pale, as if he had been shut up somewhere."

From the pity in Jules Volant's voice, Maurice guessed he was thinking of when he had been penned in the hospital during the September Massacres. But in Jules' tone also was the natural contempt the robust feel for the weak.

Maurice said, "If André has escaped from some prison, won't we all get into trouble?" This might well be the reason for the clandestine activity last night. Knowing that Jules did not like to be burdened by another's secrets, Maurice said nothing about it.

Jules said, "Sebastien is too clever to get into trouble, especially over someone else. He'll give André papers and employment, as he has done for us. And as for questions, no Frenchman who values his head dares ask any these days!"

They reached Tours at six o'clock that evening. Sebastien allowed the actors a light supper, and then they went to the theater. André shuffled around backstage, getting into everyone's way until Sebastien, driven frantic, ordered him to stay in a corner. André sat hunched on a stool, wiping his nose on his sleeve.

During this performance, Maurice actually enjoyed striding about the stage, declaiming to an audience that murmured sympathy and roared approval. When he finished his great denunciation speech, the applause left him dizzy with triumph.

Sebastien, waiting in the wings as Robespierre, met him with a grin, whispering, "*This* is the actor's pay! We work to exhaustion for the plaudits of strangers."

While Maurice did not want to devote his life to acting, he began to understand the fascination the theater held for others.

His elation was short-lived.

Jules was waiting for him near his dressing booth. His news tumbled out in a jerky whisper. "Tonight while I was taking tickets, I saw the fingerless hand. And the green stone ring. I got a good look at his face, too. Maurice, I saw Félix!"

A Bullet for Maurice

VIII THEY CAMPED JUST OUTSIDE TOURS, cooking a late meal over small fires and glowing coals. The waif André, set to work gathering twigs and carrying water, distinguished himself by upsetting a pail over Sebastien's meal, then cringing under the inevitable storm of abuse. A shove, meant to send him back to work, sprawled him on the ground.

Maurice, sitting on the back steps of his wagon with his plate balanced on his knees, said to Jules, "André doesn't seem strong enough for any work yet."

Jules tossed some more sticks on the fire. "It's more stupidity than weakness. This André seems dull-witted, and I wonder if Sebastien will regret his kindness." He glanced up at the shadowed steps. "You don't have to hide, Maurice. Félix wouldn't dare creep into our camp. Guy is wandering around with his juggling. Timothée and some others are checking on the horses, so an intruder would be noticed immediately."

"I used to think I was safe on this side of the Loire," Maurice said. "But with Félix turning up in Tours I am certain now he is following the theater troupe because of me. In spite of all that makeup I wear onstage, he is bound to recognize me sooner or later."

"Even if he does, it'll take him some time to devise a plan for you," said Jules. "By then you'll be safe with your cousin, for after Blois comes Orléans."

At dawn the next day the troupe traveled along the right bank toward Blois. They met little traffic, but Maurice was edgy all the way, keeping an eye out for Félix. Jules told him he was wasting his efforts. "If Félix knows you are with the troupe, Maurice, he has only to wait in the next town for us to come to him." But Maurice was distracted enough at rehearsal during the noon break to earn Sebastien's wrath and André's ill-concealed mirth. Even Guy was impatient with his fumbling, and later kind old Timothée asked if he were getting ill. Yvette sent him an extra sausage, but whether for nourishment or apology for Sebastien's abuse he could not guess.

That afternoon the caravan met with another military road block. As before, the officer waved them through after a cursory glance at their papers. Maurice, sitting inside the wagon with Guy, remarked, "Sebastien must know some important people if army officers are impressed with him."

"It's the theater that's important," explained Guy. "It is through troupes like ours that the National Convention instructs people in the glories of the Revolution."

Maurice could not resist saying, "It's lucky Sebastien agrees with the National Convention's views. Traveling around the country like this, he must see many things that would disturb another."

"If Sebastien didn't agree with national policies, he would lose his commission, his theater, and his head," Guy replied coolly. "Besides, under the king, one did not have to travel to see suffering."

The Val de Loire grew yet richer as the caravan approached Blois. The sloping land was a patchwork of uncountable vineyards, and wine caves riddled the cliffs. Some of these even had front entrances built into them, for often a vintner lived with his produce. In the afternoon the traveling theater train entered the cool dark forests near the town, pausing long enough to snare a quantity of rabbits for the late supper after the night's performance.

Hugo was waiting for them in the town's central square. "We have permission to keep our wagons overnight in the theater's enclosed courtyard," he told Sebastien.

"We'll go there now, but not to stay for the night," said Sebastien. "Hugo, ride out and find us a good place along the road to Orléans. I want to get away early tomorrow."

But Hugo hesitated. "There is something else. I showed the censor the paper you got in Angers that certified the play for performance, but he said it wasn't enough. He wants to read the script for himself before he allows tonight's presentation."

Sebastien Brillon's black beard bristled, and his lip curled. "So, the imbecile does not trust the judgment of his peers? Where is this exalted pouter pigeon?"

"At the Jacobin Club. He said he would be there until he had the script in hand."

"*Alors,* let's hope he can read."

Sebastien took the troupe to the theater. In the courtyard the players unhitched and stabled the horses. When they began unloading the backdrops and costumes, Sebastien turned into his nervous, restless before-the-play self, darting everywhere, hurling orders and advice. He forgot about the Blois censor until Yvette reminded him, then he struck a despairing blow on his chest, cried out that he was ruined, and catching sight of Jules and Maurice, shouted for them.

"Here is the script," he said tensely, handing Jules a thick wad of scribbled sheets. "Go to the Jacobin Club—

Jules, you know where? Good! Discover this semiliterate malefactor, explain the play to him, and bring back—" he emphasized each word clearly with his finger "—the censor's stamp right on this front page. *Comprenez-vous?*"

"Mais oui!" cried Jules. "Come on, Maurice!"

They rushed out of the backstage door and through the courtyard, then jogged along sunset-splashed streets twisting beneath high-storied steep-roofed houses. Traffic was light during this supper hour as Jules led the way to an impressive house fronting a small square. Maurice noticed that a stone fleur-de-lis, a decoration of royalty, had been chiseled off above the entrance.

Jules explained their errand to the unshaven and sweat-stained sans-culotte guarding the entrance. He took them inside to a small, dark, paneled sideroom, then fetched the censor.

This man, Citizen Pintade, was dressed only slightly better than the worthy guardian of the Club entrance. Strutting up to the youths, he said, "The script at last, eh? Citizen Brillon took his time about it." And when Jules asked him if he could hurry, he glared angrily. "I won't slight my duty for mere convenience. Stay here." He swaggered out of the room with the script in his hand.

They settled down to wait on hard straight-backed chairs. Maurice soon felt time weighing heavily. Outside the watery glass of the leaded window, he saw that the slanting sunshine had already changed to a deep orange as blue dusk crept along the feet of the houses in the square. Through this passed cabriolets, horsemen, and pedestrians. "Traffic is thickening," he told Jules. "There goes a musician with his instrument case! The audience will be gathering soon for the play. Jules, we must hurry!"

Jules shrugged helplessly. "This Pintade was offended by Sebastien's tardiness in sending the script. I suppose he isn't reading it at all but just holding it back long enough to teach us all a good lesson."

Maurice roamed restlessly around the small room, then stopped before a full-length oil portrait catching the last of the bright sunlight. "Who is this, Jules? Why, he's wearing the kind of breeches and ruffles Sebastien puts on for playing Robespierre."

"And that is who it is," Jules told him. "Maximilien Robespierre."

So this was the tyrant of France! Maurice was surprised to find under the curled, powdered hair, a soft-looking face with a delicate nose, sloping forehead, and small chin. Only the tight little mouth hinted at the zealot. "What is he exactly—a president, a prime minister?"

Jules counted on his fingers. "He is head of the Jacobin political club, the only organized party left after he had the others guillotined on one pretext or another. He is president of the National Convention, which rules France. His friends run the Paris Commune, which dominates the other cities and towns. The same comrades also run the Revolutionary Tribunal, the court dedicated to beheading enemies of the state. But the main thing, Maurice, is that Maximilien Robespierre is president of the Committee of Public Safety. The Committee has police powers, and Robespierre can do absolutely anything he wants to if he claims it's for the greater good of the Fatherland. Robespierre's word is law."

Maurice studied the portrait, trying to visualize the vast power residing in this unimpressive person. "What happened to his beard?"

"Robespierre never had one. And Sebastien won't shave his own off, not even for a role. *Allons,* it's Robespierre's words that are important, not his features."

The door opened and the pompous Pintade entered. "I

have been unable to find anything unsanitary in this play," he announced with a trace of regret, handing the script back to Jules. There was a bright red wax mark on the title page. "I've passed it, but I fear you will be late." And on this tiny note of triumph, Citizen Pintade led them to the entrance.

As soon as the door closed behind them they took off as if they had springs on their feet, but very quickly they were slowed by the increasing crowds flocking in the streets. "It must be nearly curtain time," complained Jules as he tried to slip through a group in front of him.

Maurice felt his stomach sink. "I have to get my make-up and costume on. Sebastien will be furious!"

"Let's try the back streets. They won't be so crowded."

"Do you know the way?"

Jules shook his head and grinned. "But one need only keep to a general direction. Hurry!"

They darted down the narrow cobbled streets, Jules choosing another as soon as he encountered a crossing or a wrong curve. There were few people about, old women carrying bundles, a man with an empty barrow, children hauling water from courtyard wells.

Suddenly not far ahead, a face lifted up to be lighted briefly by the late sun and then quickly lowered.

Maurice gasped. Seizing Jules, he pulled him into a deeply shadowed doorway. "That's Félix up ahead," he whispered into his friend's ear.

Jules studied the two men talking before a shop. After a moment he grunted agreement. "*Oui,* that's the one. Is the other one of his companions who stopped the coach?"

"I don't know. He could be." Maurice's chest ached with fear. "Let's go around the long way. I don't care how late we are."

Looking back the way they had come, Jules uttered a

sharp, "Hsst!" and froze within the dark shadows.

A steady clopping came from that direction, and soon a man leading three horses passed the dark doorway and went directly to Félix and his companion. Then the three mounted and rode down the street together.

When the horsemen went around a corner, Jules sprang out of the hiding place. "Now let us run as if all the devils in France are on our trail!"

After one block, Maurice gasped, "Not . . . so . . . fast! Have to . . . say my lines . . . tonight."

Reluctantly Jules slowed down. When they neared the theater they could hear the Blois band playing for the audience. Backstage Sebastien was frantically pulling his hair, and Yvette alternately wrung her hands and attempted to soothe him. André saw the youths first and piped up, "Here they are, Citizen Brillon!" Pulling his dirty red cap farther down over his ears, the urchin giggled. "You're in for it," he told them.

Sebastien strode over with such fire in his eyes that Maurice trembled. But Jules quickly distracted him with the approved script while Yvette pulled Maurice into a dressing booth. "Guy will help you change."

Guy, already costumed for his role, grumbled as he pushed and pulled Maurice's clothing, then swiftly greased and powdered his face. "Take your place onstage, quickly!"

In the wings Maurice blundered into Timothée. The old man sighed with relief. "Ah, I'm glad you're here! Sebastien said I must take your place if you didn't come soon. *Vrai,* I know the lines from listening to you rehearse, but I am not certain of the movements. I stood here afraid I might have to go out on the stage."

An idea began glimmering in Maurice's mind. He put a hand on Timothée's shoulder, as they were the same height. "Watch me well tonight, Timothée. We do look alike when I am made up for my role, and perhaps some day I may fall ill and you will have to take my part."

Timothée nodded a little unhappily. "*Soit,* I will attend closely."

After his haste and excitement, Maurice's performance lacked force, though only once did he stumble badly, in the second act. But the audience seemed pleased by the play, and backstage after Sebastien's ringing Robespierre speech, no one criticized Maurice's mistake. Everyone was busy packing up and moving the wagons east of the city to spend the night in a meadow Hugo had found for them.

Just before he fell asleep after a late supper, Maurice remembered that Jules had been too late to take the theater tickets at the door. For all they knew, Félix and his two companions might well have been in that night's audience.

"But it doesn't matter," Jules pointed out the next morning as they took their turn driving the horses. The theater caravan plodded along the right bank of the Loire. "We will be at Orléans tonight. Only one more performance, Maurice, and then you will go to your cousin's house. As for me, it's time I struck out again on my own, for this settled life grows confining. Sebastien will be in a temper over our leaving, but he has survived many a crisis before."

Maurice glanced back into the van through the open window. Guy, whistling between his teeth, was nailing patches on the soles of his shoes. Timothée, far back, was rearranging some supplies that had shifted loose. Maurice leaned close to Jules. "I'm not going to risk Félix seeing me again, Jules. I plan to leave before tonight's performance. Timothée can take my place. He knows the lines and he looks like my stage character."

Jules reflected a moment, then nodded. "*Alors,* I will leave then too. And that lackwit André can start earning his meals by taking over my job with the horses. Do you remember your cousin's address? One never knows the danger of asking a question or admitting a fact."

"*Oui,* but I also know the way to the Donard house. Maman gave me exact directions, for it's her childhood home. Come with me, Jules. Stay for supper and a night's lodging. I owe you that much, and I'm sure Claude would be glad to put you up."

That noon Maurice had no heart for the daily rehearsal, and Sebastien became exasperated. André, snickering on the sidelines, made rude remarks in his shrill voice until Guy cuffed him on the side of the head.

Sebastien cried, "*J'en ai assez!* I've had enough!" He glared at his players in disgust. "You can all spend the rest of the time learning your lines for the new play I have just finished. André, fetch—*non, non,* I am mad to trust my script to the little idiot. You, Timothée, bring the script from my wagon."

During that afternoon's journey, Maurice made excuses when Guy offered to help him learn his new lines. And when at last the towers and roofs of Orléans gleamed in the evening sunshine, Maurice felt a surge of relief at thus being so close to the end of the imposture Sebastien had unwittingly thrust upon him.

The theater lacked a courtyard, but Hugo, who met them there, held in his hand written permission to close off the short street behind the building for the use of their horses and wagons. Jules and Maurice invented various tasks to keep them busy and together until just before the make-up call. Then in the gathering dusk they slipped between the vans and out into the cross street. Jules had his wanderer's bag over his shoulder. Maurice had nothing of his own to take along. "We must begin at the square," he said.

Jules knew how to reach it. When they came out at the vast central square, Maurice paused only to get his bearings, then chose the street leading directly north. Counting the blocks, turning left or right, Maurice carefully noted the landmarks, though the statue of Louis XV Maman had spoken of had been torn from its base, and one particular baker's shop was empty and shut. "Now," he said eagerly to Jules, "just down this street. It's the fourth house on the right, a printer's shop."

Safety and comfort lay just a few hundred feet away. Claude and Estelle would marvel over his adventures. Then Estelle and Maurice, his American citizenship confirmed to the authorities, would travel by coach to Marseille in plenty of time to board the *All's Well* and set sail for Boston.

There was a gap between the third and fourth houses of Claude Donard's street, a space filled with rubble. But the fourth house was not a printer's; it was a tailor shop, shuttered and dark for the night.

"I don't understand," said Maurice, puzzled. "I followed the directions. . . . Perhaps we should ask someone."

A shadow detached itself from a nearby doorway and approached, long tattered skirts dragging in the dust. The woman was as old as Tante, but busied her fingers with knitting instead of with cards. "Eh, you look for Claude Donard?"

Jules avoided answering by shrugging carelessly. "Why should we seek someone we've never met? But tell me, citizeness, how we might find the theater. They say there's a good antiaristo play being given tonight."

"I know nothing of such pleasures," she replied, her fingers manipulating needles and yarn. "I've worked hard all my life and had time only for scant meals and exhausted sleep."

Fearing the long complaining harangue of the very old, Maurice began sidling away, but the ancient's hand whipped out and caught his arm in a surprisingly strong grip. "*Tout doux!* Listen to my story. I saw it all out of my window high under the eaves of that house. Young Donard's father was a good man, but when he died Claude's secret counter-Revolutionary feelings came out. A word now and then, a gesture, a criticism. How dare he speak against Robespierre? Bah!" She spat in the street. "But now look what's happened to him and his print shop!" Gleefully she pointed to the space between houses that was choked with broken beams and torn masonry. Only the ragged finger of a chimney struggled upright from these ruins that were the goal toward which Maurice Fabry had labored.

Gone! Destroyed!

Where was Claude? And Estelle?

In the gloom the old woman peered closely at the horror Maurice felt etched on his face. She cackled in vicious mirth. "There's a good lesson for you, citizen, and you don't even have to pay for it."

Jules, his face a mask against his feelings, asked, "And did this Donard rascal lose his head?"

The crone's voice held regret. "*Non pas,* the dirty aristo wasn't home when the police came after him. But they had a grand time smashing his presses and burning his papers. The next day a work gang came and scraped down all the walls to make saltpeter for gunpowder. Then they tore the whole house down. What a crashing! A week after that another gang went picking through the ruins to rescue the metal for guns. They forgot to look for food—I swear the *cochon* was a hoarder as well. This happened a month ago, and by now the rats have gotten it all. Donard must have heard what happened, or else they caught him in some distant place, for there's been no word about him in Orléans, *non,* nor of the girl either."

"The—girl?" That would be Estelle, Maurice thought. How real was Claude's fear! How wise to arrange for her escape! And how tragically futile.

The hag shook her head. "Oh, she pretended to be one of the people, all right! Couldn't do enough for me, fetching my bread ration when my legs ached from the damp, reading me the latest issue of her brother's newspaper. . . . *Allons,* one doesn't know where evil lies, eh, citizens? Then I had to spend all those hours explaining to the police how that sneaky brat had deceived me!" She muttered reflectively, defending herself, as if to the police.

Jules said heartily, "A tale well told, good citizeness! Better entertainment than the theater, and we bid you a happy farewell."

Before the ancient could think of any way to detain them, Jules pulled Maurice away, striding rapidly and turning a corner. Maurice walked numbly, letting his friend lead him among the twisting streets. "Jules, what will I do? Where can I go now?"

There were no answers, and they wandered aimlessly through the town for a long time, drifting along the better, lamplighted, streets when night blackened the crooked cobbled ways. At last they came to the vast central square and roamed around its great edges, refusing the importuning licorice-water vendors and chestnut roasters.

Finally Jules said, "We must spend the night somewhere, Maurice. Where better than with our friends, the players?"

"You mean go back to Sebastien's troupe? But, Jules, I have to stay in Orléans and find out what happened to Claude and Estelle. Perhaps they're hiding with friends."

"And you think you could find them when the police could not?"

"Claude knows of my coming," Maurice said stubbornly. "Somehow he'll get word to me."

"Where will you stay?" Jules demanded. "In the ruins of Donard's printing shop? The police will seize you within the hour. You are a relative of a suspect, and you'd be lucky indeed if you were allowed to spend a few months in some damp filthy dungeon instead of being guillotined immediately."

Maurice knew Jules was right. But perhaps the morning would bring fresh ideas. "All right, let's go back to the theater."

A few blocks down lighted streets brought them to the front of the theater. The horses and cabs still hitched outside, watched by old men and young boys earning a few sous, indicated that the play was not yet over. Anxious to delay the wrath of Sebastien that surely awaited them backstage, Maurice suggested joining the audience. "There'll be no one at the entrance this late hour."

Slipping through the door, they stood in the shadows behind the last row of seats. Onstage, the play had just reached the exposure of Guy, the aristocrat. Timothée, playing Maurice's part as he had planned, launched into the great denunciation speech, word perfect though uncertain of his gestures. Jules dug his elbow into Maurice's ribs and whispered, "He could be your twin, Maurice, when you're made up."

"Yes—oh, look, he's turning the wrong way. He should go to the—"

Suddenly a shot rang out.

Timothée froze with a look of astonishment on his face; a rapidly swelling trickle of blood ran down his chest. Then he crumpled up and pitched forward on the stage.

Maurice cried out.

A shadow, black and swift, whirled along the far wall of the theater to the entrance. The door opened, banged shut.

Jules yelled, "There he goes! After him!"

Sebastien leaped onstage, crying, "Curtain, curtain!" The audience, suddenly aware of the truth, began rising and shouting. Maurice and Jules plunged through the door into the dark lobby. One of the outer doors was still swinging. They burst out into the street, making horses whinny and pull their tethers. "A man came out!" Jules yelled at the horse tenders. "Where'd he go?"

Fingers pointed uncertainly, but Maurice heard the clop of hoofs around a corner. "Come on, Jules!"

They raced to the corner in time to see a silhouetted horseman recklessly cantering down the street. At the far crossing he was suddenly joined by two other men on horses, and the three swiftly twisted out of sight along the crooked ways.

Maurice slowed, stopped, and sagged against a house, gasping for breath. "Did you see him, Jules? His face—in lamplight."

"We'll never catch them now!" Jules cried in frustration. "No, I didn't see his face, as he was riding away from us."

"I mean, one of the men that joined him. He—they both were the ones we saw a while ago, talking with Félix. It was Félix himself who fired that shot!"

They stared at each other in the glimmering lamplight. Maurice licked his lips. "If I had been onstage tonight, I would have been murdered. But instead, kind old Timothée . . ."

"He may only be wounded. Let's go and see."

They were close to the short street where the vans were

parked. Finding their way among them, they entered the theater through the backstage door. The entire playing troupe was on the stage, grouped around Timothée, and beyond the closed heavy curtains the audience muttered and buzzed, and the doors banged and banged as gradually the people began leaving the theater. The local band ran some idle scales, then abruptly swung into the *Marseillaise*.

Timothée's head slowly turned and his eyes opened. Lips moved, a harsh whisper dragged from the torn lungs; "Sebastien."

"Yes, old friend." Tears ran unheeded down Sebastien's cheeks, washing through his careful make-up, and staining the silken Robespierre costume. Yvette, her face wet, kneeled on the other side, stroking Timothée's white-haired temples.

"Mistake . . ." muttered the old voice with great effort. "No . . . one . . . could . . . know. . . ." The last, undecipherable word was lost in a grating rattle. Timothée's eyes stared unseeing. Yvette gently closed the lids and kissed the dead hand.

Lights and figures ran into a blur as hot tears scalded Maurice's eyes. He turned away, fumbling through the backdrop curtains and staggering blindly until his hands scraped on the rough brick back wall. His throat was a knot of grief.

Jules shook him. "Don't blame yourself, Maurice."

"He's—he's right. It was a mistake. It—it should've been me!" Sorrow choked off Maurice's words.

"That wasn't what Timothée meant," said Jules in a low guarded voice. "He was saying no one could know that he was one of the very few who escaped the mass drownings at Nantes last winter. I overheard him telling Sebastien about it shortly after he joined the troupe. The barges were packed with men, women, and children, tied with rope to each other and to irons inside the vessel. They were towed down the river at night, then the executioners in rowboats tore off the hatches made below the water line. When the river rushed inside, the captives screamed and tore and clawed, and some broke free of their rope bonds. Timothée and a few others managed to hide in the reeds and get away, but others were clubbed or shot as they swam for their lives. After that, the executioners of Nantes used only chains on their victims." Jules' eyes were fires of anger when he finished. "Tonight, Timothée thought he must have been shot by mistake. And so he was. But at least he died a quicker, neater death than the one first planned for him in the Loire." He gripped Maurice's shoulder. "Now we must think about safety for you."

Maurice said slowly, "The bullet was meant . . . for me. Félix . . ." For the first time since the shot had rung out in the theater, he felt the stirrings of fear.

Jules said, "Félix will shoot again when he finds out you're still alive. The troupe is no longer a refuge. You must flee tonight—right now!"

Maurice nodded. "Let's go."

Quietly they slipped outside, Jules with his bag still slung over his shoulder. Guided by the faint light of a moon not yet risen above the houses, they wound among the tethered horses and vans. Maurice sensed movement in the darkness behind them. It was probably a prowling rat, or perhaps one of the many homeless dogs roaming the city. Though it made Maurice uneasy, it was not worth bothering Jules about.

They slipped down deserted streets whose darkness was only faintly relieved by the glow of an occasional lamp through an upper window. There was no sound beyond their own mute tread.

Yet Maurice could not rid himself of the sensation that they were being followed.

The Ruined Château

IX

THE MOON WAS SHROUDED in vaporous clouds as Jules turned down a rutted cart track closely set with trees and shrubs. Maurice hung back a moment, glancing down the broad smooth road they had just left. "Jules, someone's following us."

They had left Orléans behind, crossing the bridge spanning the Loire by falling in behind theater patrons straggling home to the scattered houses of the left bank. Anyone watching would have thought they were part of the group instead of two youths fleeing an assassin. Once or twice Maurice had glanced back at the city, only to see similar groups trudging home. But on the other bank, when the road finally emptied of pedestrians, there had still been a persistent shadow flitting along the hedges. It was then Maurice had warned his companion.

Now Jules strained his eyes and ears while the moon waned and brightened as the clouds scudded across its scarred face. Then he grunted impatient agreement. *"Oui,* there is some life slinking in the dark there, but it can only be an animal. A fox, perhaps. Maurice, we have a long walk ahead, and there's no time to wonder over stray shadows. Come!"

After a last anxious look down the broad road, Maurice

fell into step. "Where are we going?"

"Deep into the thick forest, where there are no villages. Nobles used to hunt there, and we can live off the land. Now be quiet or we may attract some late homecomer!"

The abrupt order struck resentment from Maurice's heart, but he forced back a retort. Jules was risking his life to help him, for even now Félix and his henchmen might be trailing after them. Half expecting the crash of a bullet, Maurice matched his step with Jules' long-legged distance-gulping stride.

After a quarter hour, Maurice's muscles were protesting in painful throbs. But Jules, refusing to stop for a rest, struck off on a smaller and rougher track. The woods thickened, shattering the moonglow into sharp splinters of light. Glancing behind, Maurice saw a slithering shadow. Startled, he tripped over a rut and blundered into Jules. "Pick up your feet!" his companion snapped in exasperation. "Don't linger, there are still wolves and boar in these parts."

The land gradually seemed to flatten, then lower. Maurice smelled moist earth. His muscles had at last worked into hiking rhythm, and he knew he could trudge for hours if he had to.

Jules chose another trail, this one a mere path running through thick forest which forced them to go single file. Moonlight fell in scattered patches, and between these they walked through great halls of darkness. Now and then something started up and away from their steps, soft though these were on the springy forest mold. Things rustled and crept through undergrowth or in the leafy treetops lacing over the trail. A brook chuckled from the blackness, and once Maurice saw a shine as of still water reflecting moonlight.

Cold seeped through Maurice's shoes, and he realized

they were wet. Jules stopped abruptly. "We're getting into a bog. Turn back."

They made several false starts trying to find a way around the bog, stumbling into trees, scratching their hands on shrubs. "There must be a path!" Jules insisted, casting about in the fragmented moonlight. "Ah, here's a game trail. It'll do."

The game track wandered aimlessly in great loops and curves. Once in a while Maurice could hear animal life bounding away, either in front or behind him. At last moonlight broke through thinning trees, and they came out on a meadow. Carefully skirting its margin, they plunged into a more regular path on the far side.

Now they could move rapidly along smooth dry ground. Meeting another, even wider, path, Jules turned down it with all the instinct of a hunting hound closing with its prey. Trees fell back from shrubbery, some bearing scented blossoms, and then Maurice and Jules burst out into a vast neglected park. Before them reared the broken towers of a ruined château.

Bone white under the merciless moon, the walls were stained with fingers of soot where rebel flames had leaped. The roof of one entire wing had been burned, leaving but the ribs of a few surviving timbers. Open windows gaped with mouths full of splintered glass. A corner tower, heat-exploded, staggered on a drunken foundation amid the tangle of its fallen weed-crept stone. Statues torn from their plinths lay in the clutches of wild growth along the edge of the terrace, and many of the tiles from the château's forecourt had been ripped out.

Maurice and Jules approached slowly, seeking to avoid pieces of broken columns and smashed fountains concealed by the overgrown grass. The sound of steady washing drew Maurice's attention beyond one of the château's many wings where black water winked steadily as it streamed away into the forest. "Look, Jules, a creek."

"*Bien,* there'll be good fishing," responded Jules happily. "We can stay here, but first let me find a safe corner. In many of these châteaux, the flooring has collapsed during the assault."

"Were all the nobles' homes destroyed?"

Jules shook his head. "I have seen many fine ones still standing in places where the lord and his peasants got along fairly well. Wait here for me."

Jules blended with the shadows, and Maurice, prodding the rank grass with his foot, found an old stone column to sit upon in the shadow of a large bush. He studied the great park with interest, discovering in its neglected growth the traces of stone paths, old flower beds and, perhaps, reflecting pools where goldfish flashed for the pleasure of richly clad ladies. The lord's children might have played here, boating on the creek or riding their ponies along the forest paths. Barred by status and inclination from developing a skill or learning a trade, what did they do when they reached manhood?

They became officers in the army, or high-ranking clerics in the Church. Maurice was not Catholic, yet he had heard that its ministers were subjected to a strict set of rules. Military life demanded rigid discipline too. The foot soldiers and the village priests, drawn from the common people, had carried out their tasks in hardship and poverty. But how fared these youths raised in idle luxury and thrust into command? It would not matter that they neglected their duties and abused their positions, for their noble rank protected them from consequences, and their wealth, wrung from peasant labor, bought friends and favors at the king's court. Maurice would have hated to trust his life to such officers, his soul to such clerics.

A statue moved in the park.

Maurice started, thought he had been dozing, and instantly knew he had not. A figure was moving uncertainly among the bushes and overturned stone ornaments, as if it had lost its way. Maurice suppressed an exclamation. The prowling shadow was André.

Anger raced along his limbs, and he leaned back in the shadows, waiting. That wretched gamin had followed them all the way from Orléans, in hopes, no doubt, of being paid for silence, or of getting a reward by telling Sebastien where they—

André was quite close now, still casting around in a puzzled way. He would soon discover the value of minding his own business.

Maurice leaped up. André, untouched, shrieked and staggered backwards in his fright. Maurice rammed his shoulder into the waif and was both surprised and disappointed when the lad easily gave way and fell down. "Get up, you coward!" he commanded.

A sudden blow struck his knee and pain lanced through his leg, bringing him low. André was on him like a cat, and like a furious cat indeed he pummeled and scratched while sobbing through clenched teeth. Maurice, hurting in a dozen places at once, managed to twist around and deliver a solid punch on André's back. Instantly teeth clamped on his ear, tearing a howl of rage from him that echoed among the ruined battlements. Blindly he struck out, the teeth unclamped, and quickly Maurice squirmed out from under. Springing up, he stood over André who was sprawled on the ground holding the side of his face while tears washed a path down grimy cheeks.

Fury corded Maurice's right arm as with his left he reached down and jerked André upright. The dirty red stocking cap flew off, and long dark hair swung free. Astonishment sapped the tension of Maurice's arm and his blow went wild, striking only a lilac bush. "You—you're a girl!" he gasped. He leaned closer in the moonlight, adding, "You are, aren't you?"

"Of course I am!" cried an indignant female voice. "How dare you come at me in the dark like that!"

"No wonder you fight like a girl," said Maurice, still caught in amazement. He fingered his bitten ear and winced.

Jules came running up. "What's this—who are you?" Then, like Maurice, he gasped. "A girl! You look like— No, it's impossible."

"She's André," said Maurice. "He, I mean, she followed us."

"Followed!" exclaimed Jules. "You! I ought to—" But then he hit his fists together in frustration. "I wish you were a boy for five minutes. Why have you come here? You must go back at once!"

She shook her head, the long black hair catching the moonlight. "I must stay with Maurice."

Jules' eyes sent a piercing inquiry to Maurice, who could only gape.

"Because," said the girl with maddening deliberation, "I am his cousin Estelle Donard."

Maurice, struck numb from shock, cried, "I don't believe it!"

"Mon dieu!" breathed Jules. "Where—how—? But not here. Come with me, for I've found a shelter for us." He led the way through the scrubby park toward the sound of rushing water. Rounding the corner of a wing, he took them in back of the château where a low stone extension of the huge building reached along the margin of a black pool that spilled slowly over a rough rock dam.

"This is the boathouse," explained Jules. "It's completely ruined inside, but it connects with the rest of the château. Just beyond the servants' quarters, which are a shambles, there are a few small bedrooms with fireplaces."

"Where the noble's sons lived," Maurice guessed. He would live near the boats, too.

Jules led them through a gaping oaken door. Holding hands, they felt their way through the devastated rubble-filled servants' quarters into one of the small rooms. Moonlight poured in through an intact window showing a small neat bed with an embroidered cover and carved posts. A huge fireplace yawned along one stone wall, but rich-looking tapestries covered the other three. Dusty toy soldiers and carved horses lined two shelves, and a small cabinet held tattered and scribbled copybooks. Dainty chairs stood about and except for a thick coating of dirt, it seemed as if their young master had just left the room.

Jules fetched flint and steel from his shoulder bag and lighted the candle in its stand on a small table. "The stable and other outbuildings have been burned. Don't wander around the château carelessly. The floor is broken in many places, especially over the dungeon. And now, Citizeness Donard . . ." He bowed mockingly.

Candlelight danced in Estelle's black hair as Jules' derision provoked a furious toss of her head. "I *had* to catch up with Maurice tonight because I'm traveling to America with him. My brother Claude arranged it. Now I'm not going to tell you any more, Jules Volant!"

"You can trust Jules," said Maurice. "He's risking his neck to help me—us. Now, where is Claude? Why are you posing as a boy? Please, Estelle, we have to know what's happening!"

She gazed at Jules with a thoughtful little frown, then nodded. "Very well, since Maurice trusts you. . . . I don't know where Claude is. I haven't seen him since the men came to the printing shop after him three weeks ago."

"What men?" Maurice asked sharply. "Were there three, and one of them—"

But Estelle impatiently shook her head. *"Non, non!* Half a dozen, perhaps more. Who were they—Jacobins, secret police? I don't know. But Claude had been warned that very morning. He came into the kitchen from the shop to tell me a friend had sent word that within a few hours men hostile to Claude would be coming after him. Now that our father was dead, and his influence in Orléans gone, my brother would have to pay for having criticized the Revolution some years ago. Claude decided he must go into hiding, but first he had to ride out to stop someone who was journeying to Orléans to see him. Otherwise the visitor would be swept into the trap when he arrived at the shop. Claude and I both felt that I would be safe while he went to warn this expected visitor. I had many friends among the neighbors and was known as a good sans-culotte."

Maurice thought of the vicious-tongued old crone blackening Estelle's name. Perhaps there were others, too, the butcher on the corner, the lemonade seller down the street, a dressmaker, the lamplighter . . . all seizing this chance to demonstrate Republican loyalty, buying their own safety with another's life.

Estelle continued. "When Claude rode off I locked all the doors and windows and went on with my housework. Early that afternoon I heard someone banging loudly on the shop door, and I came out into the hallway to answer."

"Madness!" cried Jules, springing up from the floor. "Didn't you think of your brother's enemies?"

"Mais oui," answered Estelle. "And I wanted to see if I knew any of them."

Maurice groaned aloud at this courageous stupidity.

"Before I could get there," said Estelle, "I heard them battering down the door, and I became frightened."

"At last!" exclaimed Jules. "So you crept out the back way?"

She shook her head. "I slipped into Claude's office—it's a little cubicle shut off from the printing shop—and went through the trapdoor into the cellar below, where Claude stores many things for the printing presses. I heard the men break into the shop—their heavy feet trampling as they searched the place. After a long time they began smashing the presses. I squeezed into a small closet in the corner of the cellar, and I could still hear the thumps and crashes as they ravaged the printing shop. Then they found the trapdoor in the office floor and came down. I was terrified!"

Estelle's blue eyes were wide with remembered fear.

"The closet where I hid was small and stuffy, and I had left the door open a little for air. Now I didn't dare close it for fear of attracting attention. The men brought down lighted lamps, and they searched the cellar, hurling pieces of press machinery off the shelves, throwing down large boxes of type. I saw shadows looming, and sometimes a back or an arm, but no faces. They cursed Claude and swore over missing us, for they thought we had both gone off. The man in charge of this gang finally ordered them to stop. He said there was nothing here any more and they must get on Claude's trail. They would look for clues in the private letters in Claude's office. Then they went up and kicked the trapdoor shut."

Estelle's hands were trembling as she picked on her ragged coat. "I don't know how they missed seeing the little cupboard where I hid, except that it's built right into the foundation, and the door is so old and worn it looks like part of the walls. The leader of the gang even stood directly in front of it, so close that I could see the large green stone ring on his left hand. It was on the middle finger, because the ring finger was missing from some old accident."

Maurice cried out, "Félix! You saw Félix!" He turned to Jules excitedly. "They went through Claude's letters. That's how they knew I was coming to Nazaire, for I'd written my entire schedule out for Claude. They must have thought Claude arranged to meet me in the port."

Jules' eyes narrowed thoughfully. *"Soit!* And when Claude was not on the night coach to Paris with you, they thought you would know where he was hiding. *Eh bien,* no wonder Félix has ridden up and down the Val de Loire after you! You are his only link with Claude Donard."

This puzzled Estelle, and she asked many questions. But Maurice insisted that she finish her story first.

Estelle continued. "I stayed in the cupboard a long time until I heard the men upstairs leaving the shop. Then I came out, but stayed down in the cellar for hours. That's where Claude found me when he came back that night. He had learned of the assault on the printing shop from his friend who had lingered on the bridge to meet him that afternoon and who insisted on hiding him until it was dark. Claude thought I might be with neighbors and was surprised to find me in the ruined shop. We hastily packed a few things. Claude found a box of old worn type, the only set that had somehow escaped the raid. His friend gave us an extra horse, and we rode half the night to a distant town. Here we met with the man Claude had ridden out to warn away. My brother had also made arrangements for me to live with this man's family. That was the last time I saw Claude, though he said he would somehow see to it that I travel to America with our cousin Maurice Fabry."

Estelle journeyed to a distant province with her new protector, whose wife gladly took her in. They lived apart from their local village, tucked behind some hills, and Estelle went unnoticed in the neighborhood. "Three days ago Sebastien Brillon brought me into his troupe. I had to dress as a boy, a stupid obnoxious boy." Estelle's eyes sparkled mischievously. "Sebastien introduced himself as a friend of Claude's, and said he was to take me to Marseille. I was to go in disguise, and we acted out scenes together so no one would suspect that he and Yvette were actually being kind to me. And he pointed you out to me, Maurice, as my cousin."

"Me?" cried Maurice in surprise. "Sebastien knew I was your cousin? But he never asked—I never said—Jules, did you tell—?"

"But I knew nothing about a girl cousin until tonight!" Jules protested. "You have spoken only of your cousin Claude to me. Perhaps you let out more than you intended to old Timothée or to Guy."

Estelle frowned. "The way Sebastien spoke, everything was arranged. Except that Maurice was not to know I was disguised as André. I had the idea everything would be made known in Marseille when we boarded the vessel for America."

"How did Sebastien know me?" puzzled Maurice. "The only person in France who can recognize me, besides you two, is Félix." He thought back to the day a week ago (only a week!) when he and Jules had been the reluctant escorts of a cartload of condemned and when Sebastien's laughing, talking troupe had swooped down upon the cortège, absorbing him and Jules and, bursting into a gallop, had twisted away through the woods with them. Maurice said, "I gave Sebastien my name when he offered me a job, but he made no sign of recognizing it. Perhaps he did not realize who I was until he heard later on from Claude. What a coincidence!"

"Nothing is a coincidence," Jules said flatly. He paced up and down the room, his shadow looming and vanishing on the tapestried walls, the candle flame leaping wildly every time he passed. "Try as I will, I can make nothing of it," he confessed at last. *"N'importe!* We are no longer with the troupe, no one can guess where we are, so it does not matter. We are entirely on our own now."

"Now tell me why you ran away from Sebastien's troupe," pleaded Estelle. "And what of this man Félix?"

Maurice began the long story with his landing at Port Nazaire. Jules took his turn, too, in describing their adventures, ending with the bullet that had struck down kind old Timothée instead of Maurice Fabry.

Maurice said, "I'm glad you followed us from Orléans, Estelle, for that solves my first problem of finding you. But how are we to contact Claude? Did Sebastien intend to meet your brother somewhere?"

She shook her head. "Sebastien said nothing about that at all. My trip to America was already entirely arranged." She wrinkled her forehead in thought. "Claude did say, that night we parted, that it was time to tumble Robespierre from his mountain of power."

"That means little," said Jules, "except that Claude was complaining against the man who dictates everything in our lives."

Maurice said slowly as an idea unfolded, "There's only one way Claude could get word to me in his crisis. He could have left a message with the American minister in Paris."

Estelle caught her breath as hope danced in her eyes. But Jules snorted in derision. "Why risk discovery to leave a message? Sebastien was right—Estelle's journey was already arranged. Our task is not to find Claude, but to reach Marseille before your Yankee vessel arrives and departs. How much time remains—three weeks, a little more?"

Three and a half weeks in which to reach Marseille, five hundred miles away! And they must do this without money, transportation, or the protection of Sebastien Brillon's traveling players. Even at a brisk hiking pace they would need over a month to arrive at that distant port.

And something else had to be done, which would add two more weeks of foot travel. "We must first go to Paris," said Maurice. "I need to get a new passport from the American minister to replace the one in my lost valise. Then I can travel safely through France, protected by my American citizenship. And if we miss my vessel, I'll need the passport to get aboard another." As he talked, Maurice began to see other possibilities. "The American minister may even lend us money to take the coach to Marseille. And he might help arrange passage on another vessel if need be."

"But what of me, Maurice Fabry?" demanded Estelle. "I, too, need safe conduct through France."

Jules said, "If everything was arranged through Sebastien, perhaps he acquired papers and permits for you, Estelle."

She shook her head. "Being a member of the troupe was all the protection I needed. Maurice had written Claude that one does not require papers to enter the United States."

"*Alors,* we can't rejoin Sebastien," said Jules. "Félix would follow the troupe all the way down to Marseille. He would have two or three weeks in which to take another shot at Maurice."

"Estelle, I'm certain the American minister can provide

you with papers of some kind so you can travel safely to port," said Maurice encouragingly. "After all, you're coming to America to live, and maybe he can stretch a point."

"We can ask that favor," Estelle agreed. "But what of Félix—why does he want to kill Maurice?"

Jules shrugged.

Maurice said thoughtfully, "Maybe he thinks my death will make Claude rush to the scene, exposing himself to his enemies."

"He went through Claude's letters," said Estelle. "He must know I'm to leave the country with Maurice. Perhaps he wishes to keep me in France, and thus double his chances of locating a Donard."

Jules nodded agreement. "Félix must think you are more likely to know where Claude is than would Maurice."

"Yet I'm Félix's sole link with the Donard family," objected Maurice. "Would he really want to kill me or just scare me into running for Claude's hiding place or Estelle's?"

A thoughtful look stole into Jules' eyes. *"Oui,* you're right! He need only frighten you away from the protection of the troupe, then follow."

"Perhaps," suggested Estelle, "perhaps we could even return, and let Sebastien take us down to Marseille."

"No!" Maurice stood up, checking the impulse to run. "Every time I went onstage, I'd risk a bullet. I could easily turn the wrong way, as Timothée did, and die. And if Félix saw he couldn't scare me out of the troupe, he might kidnap me."

"I agree with you, Maurice," said Jules. "Félix thinks you're dead. But if you showed up among the players again, he would surely hear of it through some cohort of his."

Estelle shrugged. "It was only a thought. *Mais oui,* then, we shall go to Paris."

Jules fetched loose cushions from a divan and flung them on the floor for him and Maurice. Estelle was gallantly allotted the huge four-poster bed, and Maurice helped her shake the dust out of the covers and draw the canopy curtains to make a secluded enclosure.

Just before Jules blew out the candle, Maurice asked about rats. His friend shook his head. "There's been nothing to attract them here for years."

Out went the candle and moonlight flooded the room. Tree shadows swaying across the window swept Maurice into memories of Sebastien's wagons lurching through the night.

More than the ease of travel and protection against Republican officiality, Maurice would miss the feeling of kinship with the troupe. With surprise, he discovered he had grown fond of them; Sebastien, vain, flamboyant and brilliant; Sebastien, vigilant of their welfare, exhorting them to as high a standard of performance as his rustic circuit allowed; Yvette, mother to the troupe, leaven to her husband's temperament; Guy, an older brother, quick-witted and light-hearted; old Timothée, a kind if perhaps faltering grandfather . . . whom death had seized with cold and violent hands.

And Maurice Fabry had run.

It would look to the troupe as if he had deserted them the moment serious trouble struck. Maurice yearned to explain how the bullet was really a threat to him. Somehow, he would send word to Sebastien Brillon when he and Estelle were ready to embark at Marseille.

Yet how would they get to Marseille?

How, indeed, to get to Paris?

City of Light

X "THERE'S OUR TRANSPORT," said Jules, pointing to a battered wooden shape at their feet.

After a breakfast of dried bread, he and Maurice had left Estelle making their quarters more comfortable while they explored the boathouse.

From the overflowing pond outside sunlight ricocheted inward through mossy stone arches, flinging dazzling circles amid the masonry-walled gloom. Higher up, daylight squared itself against windows where the glass had been smashed out. The brick floor and the ramps sloping into the water were littered with splintered trestles, stove boats, smashed oars and paddles, broken fishing rods, traps, and nets.

Among the hopelessly shattered small craft they had found a badly sprung punt and now this skiff with a hole in its side.

Maurice frowned. "It would be easier to fix the punt."

"But the skiff travels faster and more secretly," Jules argued. "We can even use paddles to get through narrow canals and irrigation ditches. This gives us a greater choice of routes."

Jules had explained to Maurice that France was webbed by an intricate network of waterways, many so small and subtle that they were virtually invisible. Jules had come to know many of these routes by reputation and some from having begged occasional rides on passing craft.

Together they shifted the broken boat into a direct shaft of daylight in which to work. The actual labor of repair was up to Maurice, trained in cabinetry and somewhat experienced with boats. He examined the skiff critically. "I'll need wood and tools to work it."

Jules began picking through the rubble. "Here's a rusted drawshave. And a length of planking. Nails are all over the place. Ah, a fishtrap! A minor repair and I can set this in the pond. *'Revoir, ami!*"

Whistling, Jules ducked under an arch and went along the pond bank. Water rushed over a dam at the far end, and Maurice saw Estelle filling a battered pail.

Maurice kicked through the litter and found a saw and a hammer with a broken handle. Now he could begin work.

For the next two days Maurice worked long and hard in the boathouse, feeling competent and useful for the first time since entering France. Jules kept them fed with fish from traps and nets. Estelle, rummaging in storerooms after having washed and repaired their clothing, discovered a cache of thickly waxed cheeses, aged to an incredible deliciousness.

At last the skiff was repaired, caulked, and pitched. Jules helped Maurice set it in the water to let the joints swell tight. Maurice put the paddles and mended oars inside.

Jules glanced at the sunset. "One more night, and then we'll be on our way to Paris."

"How long will it take to get there?"

Jules shrugged. "Perhaps a week. It's hard to say. We may have to hide often, and make stops in order to secure food."

Maurice studied the tiny trickles of water spreading in the bottom of the skiff. "I'm positive the American minister will lend us money. He might even shelter us for the ten days until Estelle and I take the coach to Marseille." He reckoned swiftly. "Yes, we'd arrive there in time to board the *All's Well*. But, Jules, what if something should hold us up on our way to Paris?"

"*Bien,* we could travel faster by going day and night," suggested his friend. "The less we linger, the less trouble can befall us. There'll be moonlight all this week. You and I, Maurice, we could take turns rowing, *n'est-ce-pas?*"

The next dawn while mist still hovered above the overflowing pool, they loaded their few possessions and a basket of cooked fish and cheese. Then Jules and Maurice shifted the skiff over the pond bank to the stream below the little dam. Jules cut a long pole out of a sapling to push the skiff through swamps until the water deepened to permit oars.

"Do you know which way to go, Jules?" asked Estelle, her voice soft against the hush of early morning. Once more her long dark hair was tucked up under a grimy red knit cap.

"The land lies flat, and the stream puddles into bogs," replied Jules. "Yet somewhere the water has cut a channel, for it flows onward instead of backing up. It is this current we will follow." Standing in the stern, he leaned on his pole, sending the skiff along the stream.

For the first hours they traveled slowly but steadily, Jules questing through the swampy land, nosing the skiff into one slough after another, sometimes tossing chaff into the water to detect the sluggish current. Gradually the mist thinned, and the air grew warmer until Maurice could smell the rich hot green of the forest alive with the buzz of insects and the flittings of invisible birds. "What if we come to a village?" he asked, suddenly thinking of it.

"Not in this region," answered Jules, pushing tirelessly on his pole. "The châteaux in this district were built as hunting lodges, away from farms and villages. These vast forests are still home to wild boars, wolves, stags, and even bears!"

Estelle said, "Maurice must be thinking of the château where we stayed. The mob that devastated it could have come from anywhere—from as far away as Orléans itself."

"Maurice, not all destruction throughout the country took place at one time, you understand," explained Jules. "It was, and is, a random violence. There's no way of knowing what sudden anger or fear inspired a mob to surge against any particular château. Rumors, old scores to settle, desire for loot—anything can whip up a ravaging crowd. I have seen it happen many times in my travels, and so far I've been lucky enough to keep out of the way." He cocked his head suddenly. "Listen! Hear that current? That river will surely carry us to the Loire well upstream from Orléans. Once across we can head directly north toward Paris."

That night they crossed the Loire, leaving the thick forest behind. They made a short stop in an alder thicket to cook fish over one of Jule's tiny smudgeless fires. Then, back in the boat, Estelle snuggled in one of the blankets they had taken from the ruined château, for a cool breeze traced the waterways. Maurice and Jules worked at the oars together in the moonlight, following a canal until it joined a river flowing north. Now it was time to take turns rowing and slumbering until moonset. "We'll be passing an occasional village," said Jules. "But anyone awake at this late hour must be up to some business he wouldn't want other people to know about, so we need fear no alarm. And there are no guards and watchmen outside the larger towns."

Night and day Maurice and Jules kept the skiff moving, stopping only to wait for the moon to rise, rowing in turns until it set, their exhausted slumber broken by the first gleam of dawn. During the day they trailed fishing lines, not so much for the needed food as a rebuttal to the inquiring eye of local citizens through whose district they rowed. Jules worked amazing calculations in his mind, tasting the wind, sighting the sun, lining up the stars, and racking his memories to guide them through a watery maze as intricate as the veins in a leaf. They paddled their way like a minnow through canals and irrigation channels, some so narrow that it seemed they were floating on the very grass of a meadow. Estelle, once again a grubby-faced gamin, kept a watch out for possible danger, perhaps a peasant who looked twice in their direction, or a troop of local National Guard at their weekly drilling. At those times they huddled far down in the skiff, close to the bank, pulling reeds over them, or inched along through some brush-grown ditch.

Once they clung beneath a low dark bridge, Maurice bracing his hands against the rough stone as spiders ran down his arms while above a vigilante group beat to death an army deserter they had found in a nearby hedgerow.

The next day they came to a village solemn with the steady rap of drums, and they hovered under some willows while cannon cut down a group of condemned people. Estelle turned very pale when the shrieking wounded were being finished off with hatchets, and when the bodies were thrown into the river Jules got out a paddle and worked the skiff backwards and then squeezed through a little canal cross-set with stone laundry slabs that had been ditched around the village.

It was near Fontainebleau that their river joined the Seine whose current would carry them to Paris. The great royal forest was cool and dark, teeming with game. But they dared not tarry, as roving bands of men inhabited the wood: fugitive conscripts, black marketers, political refugees, and vicious criminals. The three in the skiff went through the district as fast as they could on the river rushing north toward the distant city.

And then on their fifth afternoon in the boat it appeared before them—Paris, the City of Light!

Clear against the sky shone church spires, massive fortresses, and palace turrets. And in Maurice's mind, from home and school, from talk of travelers and those who yearned to travel, there crystallized all that Paris meant. For over a thousand years the Île de la Cité had been the heart and brain of European civilization . . . an ideal from which men might draw inspiration in art, science, and humanity.

Awed and thrilled, Maurice stood up in the skiff and stared at the distant skyline, low and lovely in the apricot afternoon. His heart thundered at attaining this matchless city, the hope and goal of past centuries—Paris, Paris, Paris!

"Sit down," said Jules sharply. "You're rocking the boat."

Traffic thickened as they drew nearer the city, both on waterway and road. Strangers themselves, the passersby paid scant heed to the three young newcomers who were as ragged as everyone else. Indeed, it seemed as if the most starving, most desperate from all over France were coming to fling themselves upon the charity or conscience of the National Convention. But they would find nothing for them in Paris, according to Jules. "Poverty has been abolished by decree, and no begging is allowed. If a man needs food or work he can always join the army. Nor must one believe the rumors about our soldiers dropping from hunger in the face of the enemy."

Grassy banks gave way to mud littered with rotting fish, rags, broken boards, pieces of metal with their identity long rusted away. Crumbling stucco cottages and wooden shacks teetered precariously near the water. A grain barge, burdened with armed soldiers, drove ruthlessly through the river traffic. A fishing boat landed and at once a yelling tattered mob hurled itself upon it while uniformed National Guardsmen beat them back with muskets so the catch could be safely unloaded. Homeless people tending fishnets screamed curses at the indifferent boats ripping through their lines. Using paddles, Maurice and Jules nimbly skipped out of the way. As they floated farther into the city, the noises, the odors, and the press of people grew more confusing. Estelle stared around her in wonder at the great city. Maurice bent to his paddle, afraid of being swept beneath some burly freighter. Jules trained his eyes along the bank, then pointed. "There, to the left, under that bridge. Some bushes are still growing there."

They pulled the skiff to the dark green growth beneath a narrow crumbling bridge which appeared seldom used. "*Hé,* it goes way back underneath!" called Maurice, tugging the skiff's bow well into the bushes.

"Someone must have once dug under the bridge's foundation," said Jules when they had the skiff inside the little brush-screened cave. "But this place has been unused for a long time. Now stay here while I find out how to reach the American minister."

But Maurice was tired of hiding and anxious to see the city. "I'll come with you, Jules. Estelle—"

"You won't leave me behind," she said determinedly. "I'll come as I am, though I wish I could clean up for the

American minister." She looked down at her torn soiled garments and sighed. "Yet they say Paris is the most dangerous place in all France. One must be more Republican here than anywhere."

"Never mind, Estelle," said Maurice, his heart light though the long furtive journey had wearied him. "When the coach leaves for Marseille, you can be dressed like a girl again. Our passports will protect us."

They scrambled up the muddy bank, hesitated briefly, then plunged into the first street running crookedly between houses. Jules directed them through narrow twisting streets. Maurice was at first bewildered, then disappointed at what he saw. This, the City of Light, was one dark cavern after another with uneven cobble meandering between close-set hovels, the streets threaded with the stinking slime of sewage. Dogs, idle children, a vast restless hungry mob pushed and shoved, even arrogantly. Then unexpectedly the three burst out into a huge sunlit concourse where wheeled and hoofed traffic mixed purposefully, leaving one broad avenue and taking another. Jules stopped. "Wait for me on the other side. I'll try my luck asking among the shops here."

Maurice and Estelle slowly went along the outer margin of the traffic circle. They had hardly reached the opposite point when Jules came carelessly bounding through the traffic straight across to them. "I learned that the minister's name is Gouverneur Morris, and he's the only foreign representative remaining. They say he's very sympathetic to people trying to emigrate to America."

"Where does he live?" asked Maurice.

"Across the river from the Louvre, on the left bank of the Seine where we are now," replied Jules. "We have only to make our way to the quay and go straight downstream to his address." He grinned at Maurice's distressed expression. "Don't worry, the houses improve as we get into the better districts."

Jules was right. As they wound riverward, the streets widened and straightened; refuse now ran in bricked ditches; but still paint peeled, woodwork sagged, and stucco crumbled amid grimy stony structures. More shops appeared, with windows full of toys, perfumes, and furniture. But of bread, shoes, soap, and meat there was little beyond dingy blank glass and drawn curtains. They passed a crew of men ripping out an iron railing to melt down for war cannon. A licorice-water vendor trotted by, his tank strapped on his back. An elderly chestnut-roaster trudged along under the burden of his charcoal stove. On ever broader sidewalks, restaurants spread their tables to escape indoor stuffiness during this intensely hot July.

The three arrived at the broad quay, where people idled along individually or in groups. A faint breeze circled over the river and languidly stirred the drooping tree foliage. Maurice felt the sweat drying on his forehead.

"Just down one more block," said Jules.

He led them to an imposing house well shaded by large trees. "Here we are. You'd best take Estelle in with you. I'll meet you near the statue by that bridge." He pointed to a shapeless mass of stone, and then went off down a side-street.

Maurice and Estelle went up to the large door. Their knock was answered by a tall man with a thin disapproving face. "No begging!" he said sharply in French, and began closing the door.

"Wait!" cried Maurice. "I'm an American. This is my cousin. I have to see the minister right away. It's urgent!"

"Monsieur Morris is very busy," said the thin face.

"Please, citizen!" pleaded Maurice. "We've come a long way. We must have passports. There's so much to be arranged."

The man frowned his uncertainty, but finally tugged the door wider. "*Bien.* Go down the hall and take the second door to your left. Give your name and wait until you are called."

Maurice and Estelle crept softly down the carpeted hallway. At Maurice's tapping, a voice within called, "*Entrez!*"

They entered a well-furnished and richly carpeted room crowded with men and women standing or sitting, murmuring among themselves or staring blankly into space. A young man glanced up from behind a polished desk near the door. His eyebrows rose as he looked at their tattered garments, but he said only, "Name, please?" as he dipped his pen in ink.

"Maurice Fabry."

The young secretary's hand jerked. "Fabry," he repeated as if he did not believe it. But he wrote it down and carried the paper through a closed door on the other side of the room.

Maurice and Estelle found an empty bench in a far corner. They sat there ignored by the others who were discussing their mutual anxieties in vibrant French and English. It was not long before Maurice, to his surprise, heard his name called. He and Estelle made their way through the inner door to the minister's office.

This room was large and airy, well lighted through generous windows, and furnished with such taste and beauty as to have cost the minister his head had he been French. Maurice's eyes roamed over familiar patterns, for some of these he had helped his father make in the Boston cabinetmaker's shop. This was the France of which his mother often spoke and which no longer existed except in the quarters of an American. There was much about the old regime that had been despicable, but Maurice wondered why the Revolution had had to destroy the good along with the evil. Possibly the general mass of people was unable to distinguish between the two.

Gouverneur Morris, American minister to France, sat writing at his splendid desk. Maurice was surprised to see a man younger than papa, though surely older than his cousin Claude. Through the kneehole of the desk he could see that the minister's left leg was of polished wood. Gouverneur Morris laid aside his pen, and the general good humor of his features sharpened a bit as he said, "Fabry."

Maurice approached the desk, aware that Estelle followed closely. "Monsieur, I'm an American. I need help—"

The minister gestured an interruption. "I quite understand your need for help. Dozens come every day, begging for money, for letters, for passports. A man came last week, and I was obliged to refuse aid. The moment he reached the street, police seized him. He was guillotined that afternoon." He sighed. "There is a limit to my powers of assistance."

"Monsieur, I had papers but I lost them on my journey," said Maurice. "I came to France to take my cousin here back to Boston to live with my family. But I must have a passport—and—and the fare to Marseille."

Gouverneur Morris frowned. "It's useless to deceive me, poor lad. You see, I know all about Maurice Fabry."

"You've heard of me!" It was these clothes, then, which made such a bad impression upon the minister. "Did my father write you?"

The minister pursed his lips. "Please desist from this ridiculous imposture! I have already issued a passport to

Maurice Fabry, and by now he has left France and is well on the way toward Boston."

Maurice heard Estelle gasp, and through the haze of his own shock he whispered, *"C'est une impossibilité!"*

Gouverneur Morris amplified. "Fabry came nearly two weeks ago and showed me letters written in Boston, one certifying his American citizenship, the other confirming his identity."

"Mine—those were my papers!" cried Maurice in outrage. "There was a letter from my cousin Claude and money—American money. This man must've found my valise in the road. Three horsemen stopped the night coach to Paris—"

"Enough of that!" said the minister firmly. "I have fully demonstrated your lie, and now you must leave."

"Wait!" pleaded Maurice. "I can prove my name. Here is my identification, made out before this impostor came to you, as the date must show." From an inner pocket he tugged out the worn wallet of papers Sebastien Brillon had given him.

The American minister took the dirty packet with reluctance, but he dutifully read through the contents, saying aloud, "Jacques Lebois, description follows. Employed as animal handler by Sebastien Brillon's Traveling Theater. Bread card: Jacques Lebois, no fixed residence. Citizenship certificate: Jacques Lebois, French. . . ." The minister handed back the wallet and shook his head. "I don't know why you showed me this except to arouse my sympathy for your situation."

Stunned, Maurice stared at the wallet in his hand. It seemed the same familiar worn canvas pouch he had carried for two weeks. But that strange name! "There must be some mistake."

Gouverneur Morris said reflectively, "I used to give a

few sous now and then to the needy at my door. And once in a while I stretched a point to give extraordinary aid. However, some high French official made known to me his disapproval, and I had to stop." Duty and charity warred in his features. Then he said decisively, "I am here on the sufferance of the French Republic, the only foreign representative left. As the United States is a neutral power, there are in France many Americans who need all the aid I can officially render them and their relatives. I also (informally, of course) look after the affairs of the other foreign ministers who have had to leave this country. All of this official duty and moral responsibility will be seriously jeopardized if I allow my natural sympathies to exceed the tolerance of the French officials. And should I be ordered out of the country, the United States may be obliged to declare war. This is why I must ask you lads to go away and not come back, for I can not interfere in the affairs of French citizens."

"Please, monsieur—" Anger and frustration choked off Maurice's words.

The American minister spoke with finality. "I will tell my secretary that if he sees your faces again he is to call for the police." He stood up nimbly, despite his wooden leg, and made a gesture of dismissal.

Maurice stumbled from the room, vaguely aware that Estelle followed. He pushed through the crowded anteroom, went down the corridor and came out of the house onto the quay, blinking in the sun.

They sat near the base of the statue Jules had indicated, their backs against the hot stone railing of the bridge, neither speaking as they waited for their friend. People passed them with scarcely a glance, intent on their own affairs. Smoke from a fire on the mudbank below wafted up to them, soon followed by the smell of browning fish. But

Maurice was too miserable to feel hungry. At last Estelle pointed out Jules Volant coming toward them with his bag swinging jauntily over his shoulder.

"Two bound for Marseille, is it?" said Jules cheerfully. "Then why such long faces?"

"Oh, Jules!" cried Estelle. "The American minister didn't believe us because someone else has already used Maurice's name!"

"Hein! What happened?"

The story came out haltingly and Jules asked questions until he knew every word that had passed during that futile interview. *"Bien,* it's plain what happened to your missing valise, Maurice. Félix took it with him and sent one of his men to use your papers in order to keep you in France, and helpless."

"So that they might force Maurice to seek out Claude," added Estelle.

Maurice nodded in gloomy agreement.

"Even so," said Jules, "didn't the American minister think it unusual that you could speak English to him?"

Maurice looked up. "English? I—I don't remember which language I used. One is like the other to me now."

Estelle exclaimed, "That's it, then! Maurice and Monsieur Morris both spoke in French. I understood every word they said. Perhaps if we went back and explained—"

"You'd never get to see him," Jules reminded her. "By now his secretary has orders to hand you over to the police as beggars or attempted impostors. If only Maurice hadn't showed him his wallet!" He shook his head. "What ever made you do such a foolish thing? Have you never examined the papers Sebastien gave you?"

"Why should I?" Maurice retorted. "I knew who I was. And when the troupe needed to buy food or pass a checkpoint, someone always collected everyone's papers, then handed them back." He flung a pebble over the railing into the river below. "It's Sebastien's fault! Why didn't he ever correct the mistake he made in filling out my papers?"

"Sebastien Brillon does not make mistakes," said Jules testily. "And he has a reason for everything that he does." He sighed in exasperation. *"Néanmoins,* the problem of getting to Marseille remains."

"It was a miracle we reached Paris without incident," said Estelle, tucking a stray lock under her red knit cap. "If only we could find my brother Claude!"

Jules Volant gazed into the distance, musing aloud, "Eastward one comes to a river and canal system flowing all the way down to Marseille."

Maurice regarded him stonily. "If you're thinking of the skiff, then you are out of your mind."

"We can neither work nor beg our way because of this girl," Jules argued. Then as Estelle flushed with growing indignation he added swiftly to her, "Your papers bear a boy's identity, 'André.' If you lose your cap, we all lose our heads."

"But going by skiff is out of the question," Maurice protested. "Marseille is hundreds and hundreds of miles away. And even if we managed to get there, the *All's Well* will surely have sailed by then. Without money or papers, how could we get another vessel?"

"Easy enough!" Jules grinned. "One merely boards the nearest foreign ship. The captain need not be bothered until you are well away from France. And then he would just put you off at the next port. There you could ask the nearest American minister for aid, remembering to speak English, of course!"

This wildly improbable plan had slim chance of success. Yet Maurice found himself considering it. "If we could only feed ourselves for the next three or four weeks . . ." A ray of hope and the thought of food touched off a raging hunger. Maurice winced as his stomach cramped painfully. "Got to eat!" he groaned.

Jules glanced at the late afternoon sky. *"Oui,* there is time. You and I, Maurice, can soon earn twenty sous each. That's enough to buy two pounds of bread."

"And what of me?" asked Estelle. "Can't I earn twenty sous also?"

Jules shook his head decisively. "No, not you. But first we must find a place where you can wait for us."

Twenty Sous for Bread

XI It was Estelle herself who thought of the National Convention. "I have often heard Claude speak of it, what late hours the deputies keep, and how the gallery is always open to the public."

Jules applauded the choice. "I've been there two or three times myself. You can gossip with friends, or sleep all day, or yell down at the deputies. People are coming and going all the time and nobody bothers about papers."

"Aren't the deputies ever afraid of the crowd's anger?" Maurice wondered.

"Certainement!" replied Jules. "I have heard many times how Robespierre has filled the gallery with his brutal, starving street ruffians or set a mob raging outside the building in order to make the other deputies agree to his proposals."

Maurice remembered the portrait in the Blois Jacobin Club. "He doesn't seem the sort of man who has friends among the street rabble."

"He hasn't," Jules said. "But he has friends who have."

They crossed the bridge to the right bank of the Seine, walked past the Louvre and the mob-battered Tuileries from which the Royal Family had once fled in fear of death, and turned the corner into a broad avenue. Here the pace quickened as people walked with purpose. Shop windows showed off rich goods and the houses seemed in better repair.

"Rue St. Honoré," said Jules. "All the important events happen on this street."

Estelle, amazed and delighted by the luxurious shops, had to be pulled along until they reached the huge rambling building that housed the ruling body of France. Maurice gestured at some shapeless statues. "What are those supposed to be?"

"Intellect, I think," said Jules. "That one must be Liberty. The Republic has a passion for putting up statues, after having taken down the ones of kings and victories and saints."

"The Republican statues melt in the rain," explained Estelle, "because they are made of cheap materials."

"Hush," warned Jules, for any criticism of the government was treason.

They pushed their way through knots of people idling before the building and entered.

Though white-belted blue-uniformed soldiers stood rigid with their muskets, and men hurried through the halls on important business, no one stopped or questioned them as Jules led the way to the entrance of the public gallery. Estelle promised to sit close to the door, and went inside.

Maurice hurried outside after Jules, who set a stiff-legged pace down the Rue St. Honoré. They pushed their way along the splendid boulevard, past the luxury shops well stocked with perfumes and silks and jewelry, the restaurants where plumed and daggered merchants and lawyers bought forbidden tidbits with furtive bundles of assignats, past gambling clubs and a dance hall just opening for the evening.

Officers on leave roamed the street in war-worn uniforms. Civilians idled along garbed in the dirty common style of sans-culotte patriotism. One shaggy-haired Republican who had forgotten to wear his tricolor rosette was being roughed up by a gang of noisy young men. Two children squatted near the gutter playing with a toy guillotine. Dogs scuttled between people's legs, horses forced their way among the pedestrians. A lemonade seller, her long hair hanging in dirty strings, tinkled her merry bell. Boys hawked pamphlets, and chestnut-roasters cried their ware.

"Hurry or we'll be late!" urged Jules as he turned down an angled street.

At the right bank of the Seine they hastened along the quay then crossed a bridge to the Île de la Cité in the middle of the river.

Jules nodded toward a grim towered fortress ahead of them. "The Conciergerie. It is the chief prison." They hurried along the side of the massive building until the wall gave way to great iron palings. Huge gates stood open, and they entered the prison's large courtyard.

A crowd of men and women loitered in this square, some sitting upon the big stone steps leading up to the Palais de Justice. Here and there guards in threadbare uniforms stood stiffly, ignoring the rabble. As the two strolled over to join a group of young men, Jules whispered urgently, "Now follow along with great enthusiasm."

"But what—?"

Jules' elbow stabbed him in the ribs. "Shut up." He raised his voice in greeting as they joined the group. Two of the young men squatted on the ground, gambling with dice against their evening's future earnings. "You're early," a bystander told Jules.

"No," said one of the gamblers, not looking up.

"There's been a mixup about the tumbrils. Sanson's in a rage— Seven! See, idiot, you owe me four sous," He swept up the dice and cast them again.

No one seemed inclined to conversation so Jules and Maurice strolled off to a huddle of women, some with hands busily knitting and tongues wagging. But it was only some foolish neighborhood gossip, so the youths moved away. A man jerked his chin toward the entrance at the top of the stairs. "There's a trial going on."

Jules nodded. "I know. Same time, every day, twice a day." But he glanced at Maurice. *"Bien,* it will pass a few moments." They mounted the stone steps, struggling between squatters who did not move aside.

Within the great entrance they moved through huge corridors to the courtroom of the Revolutionary Tribunal. Two soldiers stood guard. "Go ahead, young citizens," invited one, opening the door far enough for them to slip inside. They sat down on the nearest empty bench among those lining the walls, half filled with people who muttered or shouted their hatred for the traitors standing between the judge and jury.

A stubble-chinned man grinned at Maurice, showing rotten yellow teeth. "You missed the big one," he muttered, stabbing the air with a gnarled finger. "That one down there. Chemist, he was, one of them what tries to poison folks with mysterious stuffs."

"Is that his crime?" asked Maurice.

"Non, non, he was a tax collector under the tyrant king." The fellow spat and cursed all tax collectors. "We'll get every one of them if it takes ten years."

Down in the court arena a clerk called out a name. An old man shuffled forward from the waiting group of prisoners. The judge asked him, reading from a list on his bench, "Are you one Raoul Gillette, age 72, wigmaker?"

Hardly waiting for the aged man to mutter, *"Oui,"* the judge raised his voice to the jury. "Citizens, how do you find this criminal?"

One of the jurymen stood up, obviously the spokesman. "We find him guilty of treason for failing to support the Republic with sufficient vigor."

The judge said solemnly, "Traitor, you are condemned to die on the guillotine tomorrow morning."

Amid the catcalls of the audience, a guard directed the old man back to his place. The clerk read off another name in a bored tone, and a young girl stepped forward hesitantly. The identical ritual took place word for word; the watchers shouted their indignation, and another name was called.

Maurice listened to the farcical trial in growing rage, his fists clenched tightly. When Jules tugged on his sleeve, he was glad to follow his friend out of the courtroom. One of the guards said, "The tumbrils are here, if you want to pick up a few sous."

Jules nodded. "That's what we're here for."

As they went through the huge corridors, Maurice stuttered, "Those people—condemned—for nothing!"

"Yes, yes," said Jules impatiently. "I hope now you believe my warnings. It is very important to avoid arrest. Once a gendarme lays hands on you, all is lost!"

The stone steps outside were empty, the loafers having gathered around three carts that Maurice recognized as the one-horse, two-wheeled tilting wagons peasants used for dumping manure. Jules whispered in his ear, "Our job is to cheer the executions."

They stopped in front of a man cradling an open ledger in one arm. He glanced at them briefly. "Name?"

Jules gave the names on their bread cards. The clerk wrote them down without asking to see their papers.

"You'll be paid at the scaffold when the executions are over."

Jules looked across the courtyard. "They're opening the prisoners' gate. Quickly!" They jogged across the square to join the group around the tumbrils. Three muscular young men in sleeveless vests held the horses, bantering cheerfully among themselves and trading jokes with the crowd. An older man was giving crisp orders. Jules muttered, "That's Sanson. He is the chief executioner."

Sanson called out, "Two or three more for the lower court. How about you two there?" He stabbed a finger in their direction.

Jules replied, *"Oui,* citizen!" and at once began shouldering through the crowd. Maurice followed him down ten stone steps and through a narrow iron grill to a small, dark, lower court to join the lesser crowd waiting on either side of a single door.

Maurice looked at the huge rise of stone around him and felt suffocated. Along the foot of the nearest wall faces peered out of barred windows, arms thrust up scraps of torn papers, and voices lifted in a chorus of last messages and names soon to be forgotten. "Please, tell my little children. . . ." "I'm only a simple toymaker. . . ." "My father doesn't know where I am. . . ." "Take this note to my wife. . . ." "Water, water for the love of God. . . ."

One of the rabble spat in answer to this last. "God is dead, you worthless scum!"

The little door opened, and two armed guards came out to post themselves next to it. Sanson pushed his way forward, a paper in his brawny hand. The jailer appeared, a fat fellow in patched pants and greasy leather vest, jingling a ring of keys. He bawled into the black cavern behind him, "Corbette, Alphonse." Sanson carefully made a mark on the paper in his hand.

A young man stepped out, blinking in the dim light of the small court. His hands were tied behind him, his shirt was open wide at the neck, and in the back his hair had been shaved off to above his ears.

"Death to traitors!" yelled one of the crowd. Then all shouted together several times, *"Vive la Rèpublique!"* Jules dug his elbow fiercely into Maurice's stomach until he joined the chorus.

The jailer gave the young man a push, and he stumbled to the steps where one of Sanson's muscular assistants grasped his elbows to help him up and into one of the tumbrils that had been backed up with the tailgate down on the top step. The crowd in the upper court began screaming patriotic slogans. Beyond them Maurice saw a file of waiting cavalry.

The jailer cried out, "Dachelet, Thérèse!"

This time a middle-aged woman came out, arms bound, with hair cut short and shaven at the neck. Again that confused pause while the crowd yelled, "Death to tyrants!" The jailer pushed, Sanson checked the name on his list, and his assistant hurried the victim up into the tumbril while the crowd on the upper level shouted with enthusiasm.

"Denil, Richard!" An old man, this time. He fell twice and some of the crowd kicked at him, laughing, until Sanson's brawny helper actually took the frail man in his own arms and carried him up the steps, dumping him into the tumbril to the amusement of the upstairs audience.

One by one they came as their names were called; a young crippled woman, a tattered starveling staring through sunken eyes, a grandmother walking with immense dignity ("Dirty aristo!" yelled the crowd), two nuns, a secret priest dressed as a stone mason, a poet, a gunsmith, a baker, a printer, and a dozen more enemies of the state. The crowd cheered their coming death. Maurice joined in with feigned enthusiasm. Once he failed to shout, and a grimy tough jostled him, demanding, "What's the matter, you *sorry* for them?" Hasty cheering saved Maurice from a beating.

The tumbrils were filled. Sanson gave a receipt to the jailer, and the crowd followed the chief executioner up the steps where he swung into the driver's seat of the leading cart. A column was swiftly formed, cavalry with drawn sword riding on either side of the tumbrils, footsoldiers rattling drums as they marched in front and brought up the rear. In the wake of the column surged the rabble, occasionally shaking fists and crying out patriotic insults but mostly talking among themselves. Jules and Maurice walked along in the midst of the crowd.

The death march passed through the prison's great iron gates, turned left, and followed the street over the bridge to the right bank, the way Jules and Maurice had come. Then the column swung to the right. Jules exclaimed in surprise, "Aren't we going to the guillotine?"

A man plodding alongside him grunted. "You've been away from Paris, then. They moved the guillotine a few weeks ago to the poor people's quarter."

A young fellow walking beside Maurice added, "The shopkeepers along the Rue St. Honoré complained that the execution crowds spoiled their business. Truth is, the fine people didn't want to watch the daily parade anymore."

The man next to Jules spat in disgust. "As if we poor folk don't have any feelings! I tell you, there's days I can scarcely make myself come."

"Why do you, then?" blurted Maurice.

The man rubbed horny fingers together. "Twenty sous, *mon ami!* I've got three little ones to feed. Work? There's no work to be had. Factories are closing every day for want of materials and customers."

"Join the army," advised the young fellow with a laugh. "Or get a job making cannon."

"I'm a glass blower," replied the man. "How am I to apprentice myself for no pay to learn a new trade? At least I can yell for the Republic and earn a few sous for my children's bread."

"I come and cheer to make myself strong," said the young man seriously. Then he winked at Maurice. "You know, they won't put you in the army then, for they always need a good audience at the guillotine."

"There was a time when the crowds flocked thickly there," said the man with three children. "Now everyone is bored with the spectacle." He shrugged. *"Bien,* it makes a job for us."

"That one there—" said the young fellow pointing to the ruffian who had jostled Maurice at the prison. "That one goes because it makes him laugh. He cheers at the morning executions as well. Then he spends all his sous on wine and talks about how the blood ran off the knife."

The houses were becoming shabbier, the stucco scaling off in large patches, timbers bare of paint, broken windows stuffed with rags. The streets narrowed and grew more crooked while cobbles rocked loosely under their feet. The solemn rapping of the drums drew people to windows and from adjacent streets. Volunteer marchers swelled the ranks, and from time to time a ragged *"Vive la République!"* went up, hurriedly reinforced by the paid witnesses. But too many of the onlookers just stood and stared silently at the swaying tumbrils, the prancing cavalry and drumming footsoldiers with their tattered escort. Now and then a small child was snatched indoors, or a shutter creaked in place over a window. But relentlessly the death column wound through the filthy, stinking streets.

"It's a longer way than to the old place near the National Convention," grumbled a woman who had dropped back in the column from fatigue. "And not a sou extra!"

At last the marchers halted on the edge of the execution square. In the center on its high platform rose the bloody finger of the red-painted guillotine, its base hemmed in by a milling crowd.

"Look at those innocents, ready to cheer for no pay," sneered one of the professionals, watching the crowd give way before three or four cavalrymen clearing a space for the tumbrils. "Dupes! Simple ones!"

Maurice turned to him. "But isn't it known, then—about the twenty sous?"

The man who had three children to feed explained. "Many who hear of it do not wish to believe it. And those who do, think it's just a form of charity for the poor."

The column started up again, its components neatly deploying as the cavalry trotted up to guard position, the tumbrils wheeled into place, and the ragged escort split up to drift among the innocent volunteers and by their presence and voice urge them to cheer against traitors and for the Republic.

A woman, probably one of the regulars, opened a folding stool and sat down to pass the time knitting. Some boys darted among the watchers, hawking government-approved pamphlets or licensed newspapers. A man went by selling lists of names of those waiting in the tumbrils to be executed. Old crones forced their lemonade carts through the crowd, bells tinkling invitingly. Girls jostled their large trays of cakes for sale. Maurice saw a cunning thief slip a bundle of assignats out of a spectator's pocket and vanish before he could shout a warning.

Jules nudged him. "Get ready."

The scaffold towered over the square so that every detail of the executions would be clearly visible. On the platform, Sanson began cranking the polished slanting knife-blade high up between the twin red posts. At the foot of the uprights a wooden collar with a hole cut in it awaited the victim's neck. One of the executioner's assistants pushed up the top half of the collar, then placed a stained wicker basket just in front of the lower half.

Sanson signaled.

The watching crowd stilled.

Drums rattled. Death. Death. *Death.*

Two of the assistants pulled a man out of the first tumbril. He stumbled up the scaffold steps between them. Swiftly they strapped him to an upright plank, then swung it level with a thud, his neck falling neatly in the half-circle. The top of the collar slammed into place and only his head was visible to Maurice. Sanson tripped the release.

Down hurtled the great bright blade with a roar that ended in a reverberating blow. And before Maurice's horrified gaze, the head slipped away from the wooden collar, disappearing into the wicker basket while the fleshy stump sprayed great gouts of blood over the platform.

The yelling from hundreds of throats roared in Maurice's ears. *"Vive la République! A bas la tyrannie!"* A sharp punch in his ribs made him turn toward Jules who was cheering in a hideous mimicry of rejoicing. Between cries, Jules hissed, "Shout out, you fool!"

Sanson carefully wiped the edge of the knife so that nothing might interfere with the precision of the executions and then began cranking the blade upwards again while the crowd yelled for him to hurry. One of his assistants, clenching a rose between his teeth, swept the blood from the scaffold, laughing as it splashed those directly below. The other helpers unstrapped the body from the plank and casually flung it down on the cobblestones.

Drum taps sprang up, beating down the crowd noises.

The executioners dragged a woman to the top of the scaffold steps where one ripped her shawl from her neck. Quickly they strapped her to the board. Down slammed the plank, the wooden collar thudded into place. Sanson tripped the knife, and it rumbled downward to its final crash. Another head tumbled into the basket.

"*Vive la Révolution!*" screamed the crowd.

Jules kicked Maurice in the leg, and Maurice forced his lips to move, though his dry throat was voiceless.

The fellow with the rose in his mouth reached into the basket, pulling out the woman's head by the hair, the dead face frozen in a look of final terror. He shouted through clenched teeth, "She saw one egg in the basket waiting for her!"

Raucous laughter greeted his brutal, senseless humor.

"Hurry up there!" ordered Sanson crisply, all business. He started cranking up the knife as his assistants quickly cleared away the mutilated traces of a human life. Then with practiced efficiency the next victim was snatched from the patient tumbrils.

Thump! went the tilting plank.

Boom! echoed the wooden collar.

The slanting blade flashed down in the mellow afternoon sunlight with a thunder of sudden death.

Whack!

The cheers arose, and when they flagged, the paid professionals screamed all the more urgently, glaring threateningly at the slackers. Jules shouted lustily. Maurice yelled at full strength. "Death to traitors! Long live the guillotine! Long live France!"

Thump! Boom! Whack!

A bloody flower burst into brief bloom, and a stained

broom swept the fallen drops away.

"Liberté! Égalité! Fraternité!"

In the close-pressed heat of that afternoon the raw blood stung Maurice's nostrils with a stench of salt and iron. Ravening dogs fought through the dense stand of human legs to reach the foot of the scaffold. There from time to time a battle broke out among the animals, to be broken up by cavalrymen with swords.

Down slashed the mighty blade! Another head dropped free. Maurice yelled for peace and honor and justice. Rose-in-teeth took away the full basket and put down a new one. Other helpers pitched bodies into an empty tumbril. Sanson inspected his beloved blade, frowned, took out a file and rasped methodically along the edge. A man next to Maurice bought lemonade for his giggling girl friend. An old woman began nibbling on roasted chestnuts. Two soldiers on leave discussed what to do during the rest of the evening. Up, up clicked the great blade on its ratchets. Drums rattled, the crowd drew its breath, then let it out in one patriotic voice when the knife roared downward.

Behind Maurice someone muttered a complaint. "That makes eighteen. Hurry, Sanson, my stomach rumbles with hunger!"

Maurice's own stomach turned uneasily. How could anyone think of food when the air was fouled by the smell of death, the hysterical rejoicing, the appalling sight of tumbrils crammed full of headless corpses? He, Maurice Fabry, could never eat again. No, not even after escaping the heat, the press, and the noise of this insane crowd, the callous rabble with its obscene jokes.

The last ten executions went by in an unreal blur for Maurice. It was like watching a play, and the guillotine was only a theater property like the one Guy had invented for Sebastien's troupe. None of this could be real. No one, no matter what the pretext, could possibly gather up twenty-eight humans at random and methodically cut their heads off, one by one.

Drums rattled.

Thump! Boom! Whack!

Cheers rose for a fine performance.

When the last joyous cries echoed away, Jules pulled Maurice along to where the professionals were gathering. They began singing the *Marseillaise* while the crowd slowly broke up and drifted away. The burying gang took over the full, dripping tumbrils, the cavalrymen wheeled their horses, and this smaller column moved out toward the cemetery. The footsoldiers, dismissed, swung jauntily away from the square, practicing tattoos on their drums. Sanson directed the cleaning of his guillotine with sand and water. The dogs, unhindered, leaped snarling up the sides of the scaffold. Sanson dismounted the precious knife blade and loaded it into the last remaining cart. The professional cheerers were well into the third verse of *Ça ira* by the time square and scaffold were empty.

"There's the man with the ledger," said Maurice.

"That's who we were waiting for," remarked Jules.

The ragged witnesses lined up to receive their pay as the man carefully checked off each name in the ledger before handing out the twenty sous.

Maurice jingled the coins in his hand. It seemed to have taken hours to come by this small sum.

"Come on, Maurice," urged Jules. "Let's find a bakery!"

They ran through the crooked streets, now and then slipping on the loose cobble. They passed one baker's shop crammed with people fighting for their turn at the rationed bread. Then Jules spied a modest sign down a narrow dingy side street. When they reached the tiny shop, Jules ruthlessly elbowed his way through a group of old women and dropped their coins on the wooden counter. "Two pounds of bread, my good woman!" he commanded.

"Out of turn!" screamed a frail elder at Jules' elbow.

"Bread card!" rasped the pinch-eyed woman behind the counter. "Both of them. There's only a pound allowed for each citizen."

They let her have their cards briefly. She swept up their coins and then indifferently tossed down two long warm loaves before them. Jules snatched them up and fought his way out of the shop, Maurice receiving most of the kicks aimed at him. "Beast! Monster! Filthy aristo!" snarled the frail elder at their backs.

Farther down the tiny street, Jules stopped to drink from a little fountain set in a niche. "Got to wash the blood out of my throat."

But water did not help Maurice. He would strangle on this evening's blood for the rest of his life. Dully he watched Jules tear open one end of a loaf and thrust it into his hands. "Food, Maurice. Eat!"

"How can I? How can anyone . . ."

But Jules was already wolfing his down.

The crust was crisp in Maurice's fingers, and the soft white bread inside was still warm from the oven. The yeasty tang overwhelmed the lingering taste of salt and iron. The cheers for every death died away under the crackle of the rich crust in Maurice's teeth. And his stomach, awakened to its long hunger, embraced the food with painful eagerness.

"More!" demanded Maurice. "Quickly, quickly!"

The methodic thunder of the guillotine faded from Maurice's memory as his entire consciousness sank deeply into the sight and smell and taste of the bread he crammed into his mouth.

Shadows for Robespierre

XII In Paris one was never far from a bridge, it seemed to Maurice as, stopping at the gallery of the National Convention to fetch Estelle, the three soon crossed over to the left bank. Clutching her share of the bread, Estelle said, "I thought I recognized someone in the Convention, a deputy. . . ."

"Talk later," said Jules shortly. "We want to reach our skiff while it is light enough to make a camp for the night."

As they went along the bank in the violet dusk, small cooking fires sprang up before makeshift hovels or caves dug into the mud. Ragged figures huddled over roasting sticks or battered pots. A small boy scooped a pail of water from the river, and farther upstream someone emptied a bucket of slop. The river split, the buildings of the Île de la Cité rose on their left. Much farther along the island dropped behind them and they came to the low crumbling stone bridge where they had first landed in Paris.

"Home!" exclaimed Jules, joyfully springing down the muddy bank to the brush screening their skiff. A moment later he shouted, *"Hein!"* and began thrashing through the bushes.

Maurice ran over to him. "What's the matter? *Hé,*

where's the skiff?"

Jules tore through the bushes like a madman. He crawled deep beneath the foundation of the bridge and backed out again, muttering with fury. He thrust past Maurice and Estelle and stalked purposefully up the bank. Maurice hurried after him and grabbed his arm. "The skiff is missing? Perhaps it drifted off into the river!"

Jules shook his head violently. "No, no! The skiff was high up out of the water. Someone has made off with it!" He twisted his arm free and strode downriver.

"I'll search upstream," said Maurice. Leaving Estelle to eat her bread beneath the bridge, he stumbled and slid along the muddy bank in the deepening gloom. Twice he blundered over figures camping without a fire, was sent on his way with a curse the first time and a blow the next.

Maurice could see almost nothing in the growing darkness. And the thief would not have lingered in the area. By now the skiff could have changed hands many times. It could even be aboard one of the many freighters, miles away from Paris. He returned to the bridge.

Jules was a long time in coming. It was pitch dark by the time Maurice and Estelle, sitting under the bridge, heard the bushes stir. "It's me, Jules." He sat down next to them with an exhausted sigh. "Eh, Maurice, now we are truly Paris-bound!"

Maurice felt his heart give a sickening lurch. Up to now it seemed that Jules had always been able to find a way out of their difficulties. But if he gave up . . . "We've got to get out!" Maurice said. "Tomorrow I'll go back to the American minister."

"Don't!" warned Estelle. "He'll have you arested."

"I don't care. He'll listen to me. He's got to!"

"You saw the National Butcher at work today," Jules reminded him. "You are not afraid of it?"

"I have no choice. . . ." Maurice's voice trailed away. He had never feared death. Indeed, he had often envied the heroic martyrs of the American Revolution. But it was one thing to offer your life for a purpose. And quite another to be capriciously seized, trussed up, and dumbly slaughtered for no reason whatever save that of terrifying those who watched you die.

The impersonal rattle and thump of the guillotine blade echoed in his ears. And in his mind's eye death blossomed in dripping red over the scaffold.

Fear sank deep into his bones. He began to tremble.

Maurice Fabry now understood the meaning of Terror.

The smell of cooking fish woke Maurice up early the next morning. Hearing Estelle and Jules talking on the bank, he scrambled out of their rough shelter beneath the bridge to find breakfast nearly ready. Jules used a stick to turn a filet sizzling in a battered, salvaged frying pan, while Estelle, still grubby in her role of street boy, carefully prodded a roasted potato. Maurice exclaimed, "Where did you get those, Estelle?"

Jules grunted. "Went begging in the marketplace across the river while I was downstream fishing."

"I worked for them," retorted Estelle. "I fetched and carried for some of the farm women bringing produce in for sale at dawn."

Breakfast was served on pieces of sand-scoured driftwood planks. No one spoke until the last crumb had been licked from plates and fingers.

"That's one meal less to worry about," said Jules, recovering some of his usual cheerfulness. "Maurice and I will look for work today."

"We'd do better to look for Claude," said Estelle, tucking a stray lock under her dirty red cap. "He is somewhere in Paris, I am certain."

"You told me you didn't know where he was," Maurice reminded her.

She nodded. "But I have been thinking very hard about it. Claude said—" She glanced around, then lowered her voice. "He said he was going to tumble Robespierre from his mountain of power. From the talk of the people in the gallery yesterday I learned that Robespierre never leaves Paris. I also learned that the major group of deputies in the Convention who votes for everything he wishes is called the Mountain. They made him President of the Convention. That is the source of his power."

"Plus the fact that he is Chairman of the Committee of Public Safety," added Jules. "This is the police authority of the country, Maurice. Robespierre also heads the Jacobin Club, the only political party permitted. The other clubs have been disbanded, their leaders guillotined under the pretext of being traitors to France."

"With no proof, no trial?" And then Maurice remembered the sham trials of yesterday. "Why do the people let this happen? Don't they know that if this isn't stopped they have only to await their turn to put their heads under the knife? Why don't they protest, if only to save themselves?"

"The first few protesters would be certain to die," said Estelle.

"They've already died," declared Maurice. "And the ones after, and the next, just as if the Republic were going through the tax rolls. There are no more protesters, only mute victims."

Jules nodded. "But perhaps one may make himself safe by screaming his patriotism loud and long. Best of all, you can always accuse someone else of treason. For myself, I find country roads the safest place."

"Claude would keep us safe, if we could only find him," said Estelle.

Maurice agreed readily. "He could solve most of our problems. Claude could swear to the American minister that I am a citizen, and I'd get my passport. And Monsieur Morris—" Maurice frowned. He must remember to speak English the next time he saw the minister. "*Mister* Morris would get up some kind of paper to keep Estelle safe until we boarded a ship."

"The problem," said Jules, "is how to begin looking for Claude."

Estelle folded her hands in her lap and said calmly, "We will start with Maximilien Robespierre himself."

Maurice began sputtering, but Jules held up a hand. "One moment, *mon ami!* Perhaps she's remembered some clue."

Estelle bit her lower lip. "Not exactly. But I know Claude would understand that I would be watching Robespierre, because he is our only link to my brother. Claude must have ways of doing things. Look how he arranged for Sebastien to take me and Maurice with him down to Marseille!"

"Sebastien's instructions might have been sent to him in some roundabout way," Jules pointed out. "Perhaps even he could not get in touch with Claude."

"But even so," said Estelle, "there must be some signal by which Claude would know whether or not Maurice and I were safely delivered to our vessel."

"And when Claude learned we were not," added Maurice, "you think he would be alert to all possibilities, is that right? You might even have gone back to the family which had been sheltering you."

"Or, in hopes of finding my brother, I might have gone on to Paris, which is much closer," said Estelle. "Either way, Claude would try to find me."

"And there are only half a million souls in Paris," mused Jules.

"That is why," said Estelle in patient tones, "we must become Robespierre's shadows. Sooner or later I will recognize a face or hear a name—"

"No, you won't!" interrupted Jules. "We can't let you roam the streets, Estelle, for your safety and ours! One mischievous or thieving brat snatching off your cap, and we're all going to see the guillotine from very close up."

"If I could somehow contrive a real dress—"

But Jules still shook his head. "You don't know Paris the way I do. A girl in the streets is at the mercy of the populace. There was a time when law kept things in order. But now . . ." He shrugged. "Maurice and I will be Robespierre's guardian angels. As for names and faces, we must count on your brother's cleverness in figuring all this out for himself."

"We might run into someone else searching for Claude," said Maurice. "Our friend, Félix Missing-finger."

"Never fear!" said Jules. "If he thought Claude was in Paris he would never have bothered with you at all, Maurice. Even so, Félix believes he's killed you and his supposed lead to Claude is gone. And if he discovered he has shot old Timothée by mistake, then he must still be trailing Sebastien Brillon's troupe all the way down the Rhône valley toward Marseille. We may safely dog Robespierre's tracks. We must also watch out for occasional jobs in order to pick up a sou here and there. Of course, every morning and afternoon there's always—"

"No, no!" Maurice burst out. "Not that, never that, Jules!"

Jules kicked dirt over the hot ashes of their breakfast fire. "Then let's go to the National Convention and listen to President Robespierre."

Estelle insisted on coming along this first day of their search, and Jules agreed, for who knew if chance would favor them at the outset?

Early as it was the gallery was already filling up with the homeless, the unemployed, the bored, and the fervently patriotic. The three found places in the front overlooking the Convention floor. Stretched out on a bench beside them a ragged sans-culotte slumbered away his wine. Behind, a knot of women whispered viciously among themselves as their hands knitted ceaselessly. And all around them, spectators talked and ate, spat on the floor, occasionally calling down in derision or approval to a deputy below.

The deputies themselves came and went on business, though the Convention had begun its daily session. Someone was speaking with impassioned gestures, and many of the representatives below nodded as they listened while their fellows roamed around the vast chamber, whispering with one another, going over notes, or hurrying to and from the various committee rooms and offices down the halls.

The speaker finished; the deputies applauded; the gallery sitters yelled with enthusiasm. The presiding officer rang his bell for order, and the next deputy rose to speak. Maurice listened intently. The speeches were full of Liberty and Justice and the Fatherland, but gradually he understood that the deputies were struggling with the complaints of the Paris poor over the scarcity of bread.

Estelle nudged him, whispering, "There he is!" Then as Maurice searched about she added, "That deputy walking down the aisle, thick-set man, heavy face, dark curly hair. No, silly, it's not Robespierre. It's the man I saw in Orléans, I'm certain! He came to see Claude. Wait here."

Estelle slipped away, a dirty little gamin wriggling among the close-packed spectators in the gallery. When she came back she whispered her harvest of information. "His name is Wautier. He's from a central district, so he must have traveled to Orléans in order to see my brother." She spoke so quietly, lips next to Maurice's ear, that he could scarcely make out her words. But he studied Deputy Wautier carefully as that representative of the people consulted with some colleagues, and finally took his own seat on the Convention floor.

The three stayed about an hour in the gallery. At last Jules left his place and when he came back he said, "They say in the hallways that Robespierre has not come to the Convention for over a month. We might as well leave."

Outside on the streets they watched a column of soldiers with drawn swords escorting a train of grain carts while a gang of gaunt sans-culottes trailed along, some cradling broken cobblestones. "Waiting for some grain to spill," said Jules. "You'll see a fine fight then. Come on, Robespierre often strolls in the Bois de Boulogne. The forest is on the western edge of the city."

They went along the right bank, pausing to watch the big freight boats docking beside the quay. Many of the poor were out with their fishlines and their nets, and some were cooking their catch. Barges carrying foodstuffs were protected by soldiers against looters.

A small fishing boat wallowed toward the bank. The man aboard shouted to the three and threw them a line. After they had helped him moor near a shed he owned, he offered them the job of unloading. For three sous each, they lugged boxes and barrels from boat to shed.

The rest of the morning was spent tramping through the lovely forest bordering the city with no results except the catching of five fish in one of the ponds. Estelle met with a peasant woman going home with her unsold produce and bargained fiercely for three potatoes. In a small clearing by a stream they made a fire and cooked their meal.

They briefly visited the Convention once more, and then a café owner singled Jules out to run an errand for a sou. While waiting for him to come back, Estelle went off and returned with a mysterious package wrapped in yesterday's list of the guillotined. Maurice meanwhile fell to talking with a journeyman printer and learned of a job posting newspapers on walls. When Jules returned he told him about it, and together the three went to the printer's shop.

"Only pay for one boy," grunted the printer, filthy from ink.

Jules argued with him and finally got pay for one and a half boys if all three of them did the work. Estelle carried the paste bucket and brushes, and they spent the rest of the afternoon posting newspapers so the poor could read them free. Sometimes they scarcely had pasted one up before a crowd gathered and someone began slowly spelling the news and editorials aloud. The printer gave them their few coins and told them to come back the next afternoon. "But," muttered Jules as they left, "without our 'André,' eh, Estelle?"

She smiled mysteriously. "I have something of my own to do."

They did not have enough money for a loaf, so Jules bought three hard day-old rolls and as many duck eggs. The other coins were saved for tomorrow. That night, back at their crumbling bridge, Jules' fishing failed them. They went to sleep on a slender dinner, their stomachs still clamoring for food.

Maurice woke up with a headache that he realized was

connected with the hollowness of his middle. He crawled out from under the bridge into a bright sunlit morning. Just then Jules came running down the bank. "Look, Maurice! I caught him in a snare just two miles out of the city!" He produced a large rabbit, fumbled for his knife and began working on it. Maurice went off to collect wood for a fire. The rabbit was nearly roasted to a turn when Estelle woke up to greet the meal with glad cries.

When they finished eating, Jules slung his bag over his shoulder, and they left Estelle under the bridge opening her mysterious package.

Once more Robespierre was absent from the National Convention. Just a block away, across the Rue St. Honoré, was the Duplay house, where the Incorruptible boarded in Spartan simplicity, so went the talk in the wine shops. Maurice and Jules made a point of passing before it three or four times on their various errands and wanderings that day, in hopes of catching a glimpse of Robespierre and so beginning their covert study that might by chance lead them ultimately to Claude Donard.

They spent two hours in the streets hawking the merits of a painter of the popular miniature portraits. Maurice helped a café owner shift some wine casks, hot and heavy work. Jules struck up a friendship with a sick old man, borrowed his portable stove, and spent the afternoon roasting chestnuts for sale, giving the old one half his earnings. Maurice posted newspapers for the printer, who tried to cheat him of his wages, but luckily Jules came along from his chestnut roasting and berated the man so loudly that he paid what he owed and threw them out of his shop.

Jules counted their sous. "Not enough to live on, Maurice, this scraping up of coins here and there."

It was early evening and neither of them had eaten since morning. Gloomily they walked toward their distant bridge, directing their steps to take them through the Rue St. Honoré. Just beyond the National Convention Jules stopped and gestured across the street toward what had once been a monastery. "That's the Jacobin Club, right next door to the Duplay house. I wonder if he would be in there. Why isn't he in public? There are all kinds of rumors."

Maurice nodded. He had heard the same rumors and counterrumors all day, Robespierrists muttering worriedly in the restaurants while others, risking their heads, murmured oblique deprecatory remarks.

They took a few steps and then lingered across from the Duplay house with its carved wooden eagle over the door. People passed in front of them in the street, dogs slunk by, an occasional rat darted from one building to another, and once in a while a coach rattled over the cobble. In spite of this traffic Maurice's ears detected a familiar sound. "There's hammering and sawing going on. Are they building something over there?"

"This Duplay is said to be a carpenter," replied Jules. "Look, someone's coming out of the house! Let's cross over."

They darted through the traffic, gaining the other side as two men stepped away from the door. Suddenly there was a shout from behind and an officer of the National Guard ran up to seize Maurice and Jules by the collar. The men leaving the house turned and stared in surprise.

The officer addressed one of the men. "Citizen Robespierre, these boys were lingering before your residence. And several times today I saw them passing by slowly, watching the house closely."

The eyes of Robespierre widened in alarm. "Who sent you?" he demanded of them. "What do you want?"

Maurice sensed that Jules was trembling. But he himself

merely felt astonishment that the Terror of all France was embodied in a man of such indecisive appearance.

Not quite as tall as Maurice, Maximilien Robespierre held himself stiffly poised in his old-style frock coat, knee breeches, and ruffled shirt. A tricornered hat sat on his powdered hair, neatly combed back from a broad forehead that tapered sharply past a stubby nose to a pointed chin. Green eyes flickered nervously in a pale, pockmarked face. "What do you want?" he demanded again, lips pressing tightly over his words, uttered in a surprisingly mild voice.

Maurice spoke up without thinking. "We've only been going from one job to another all day."

"Job? What sort of job?" Robespierre's eyelid began twitching, and as Jules found his voice and told of their day's labors, the Incorruptible ruler of France fumbled for a pair of green tinted spectacles.

The grip on their collars relaxed and the officer's voice was suddenly friendly. "*Bien,* citizens, so you are only looking for work. You needn't be afraid to approach our Citizen Robespierre for help. Many come every day, and none is turned away."

Robespierre said to his companion, a rough-looking fellow in sans-culotte dress, "Come, Duplay, we'll be late for the meeting."

The officer nudged Maurice and Jules ahead. "Here's your chance to ask what you will. So, speak!"

Maurice's heart shrank as Robespierre's features altered into an expression of cold arrogance. But the friendly officer seemed not to notice. He said, "Citizen Robespierre can find work for you lads; can't you, citizen? No one starves in France these days!" He spoke on in friendly insistence, and Maurice could see that Robespierre felt unpleasantly trapped.

At last the Incorruptible gestured for silence. "Duplay,

can you find something for these urchins?"

And Duplay was a carpenter! Maurice blurted, "I can work with wood, citizen!"

Citizen Duplay grudgingly agreed he could give Maurice a few hours' work the next morning. Robespierre sounded relieved as he added to the officer, "Ask Madame Duplay to give them a little food for the night." Without another word he and his companion turned and walked down the street.

Broken Type

XIII

CHEESE! BREAD! How did you come by this?" cried Estelle in delight when the youths returned to the shelter beneath the bridge.

"It was because of the adjutant to the Commandant of the National Guard," explained Maurice.

"The adjutant forced Robespierre into playing the hero he thought him to be." Jules laughed scornfully as he divided the food, but Maurice knew he had been badly frightened.

As they ate in the growing dusk, Maurice recounted the incident in front of the Duplay residence where Robespierre dwelled. "And so tomorrow I am to work right inside that house."

"You must make the most of those few hours near Robespierre," said Estelle. "Try to get close enough to overhear what his visitors say."

Maurice shook his head. "Half a day near Robespierre wouldn't be any use. My idea is to work long and hard for low wages so that Citizen Duplay cannot resist having me come in regularly. If I am to learn anything about conspiracies, and especially about Claude Donard, it will be from the ordinary talk of the household day after day." Then he shook his head. "But such scant pay will not support the three of us."

"Jules and I can do that." Estelle smiled. She brought out a bundle and unwrapped it to display dozens of red-white-and-blue ribbons and rosettes. She had spent the day beneath the bridge sewing these from ribbon she had bought yesterday. "That's what was in my mystery package," she laughed.

Jules quickly agreed to sell these patriotic decorations in the streets, buying more ribbon to keep Estelle busy during the day.

Early the next morning, with only a left-over crust in his stomach, Maurice boldly knocked on the door of the Duplay residence. Madame Duplay herself let him in, a forbidding woman who stood guard over the entrance. She led him through a long porch to the courtyard where her husband and his helpers were already sawing and planing under the bright sun.

Citizen Duplay looked Maurice over with distrust, but set him to work squaring up some boards. When Maurice finished the task, he looked around to find himself ignored in the general activity of the courtyard. Duplay and his helpers worked on amid cheerful banter. A young woman hung up laundry while her sister watered the garden. Madame Duplay peeled vegetables on the porch as a neighboring woman visited with her. Through the open entrance, Maurice saw an old man pass by on a tired donkey. Upstairs a door opened, and Robespierre came down the outside stairway, pausing to speak with Duplay and then Madame Duplay before going to his study on the ground floor of the house.

Maurice poked through the sheds against the brick courtyard wall. Finding some dull drawshaves, he began sharpening them. As the July sun climbed higher and hotter, he managed to find one task after another for himself.

Finally, at noon, Duplay became aware that tools were suddenly in excellent shape, that nails were kept picked up and sorted, that boards were neatly stacked, and mounds of shavings were swept out from underfoot. "*Bien,* young citizen, you are no stranger to work," he said, counting six sous into Maurice's hand. "You may come again tomorrow."

Maurice fingered the coins, enough to buy a few stale buns. "Tomorrow, Citizen Duplay, I must have ten sous."

Duplay growled in feigned outrage, and then settled down to a sharp bargaining session. Maurice went away with an agreement of eight sous for half a day's work, far less than he was worth, and a sum any true Frenchman would despise even in times as harsh as these.

Maurice hurried back to their shelter on the left bank to find Estelle busily sewing more patriotic decorations. Jules soon joined them, empty-handed of ribbons, jingling sous in his pocket, and asking what they wanted to buy for the noon meal. Then off he went to the market, to return with some dry sausage and a whole loaf of day-old bread, remarking casually that for an instant he thought he had glimpsed Félix down a dingy side-street. "But it could only have been someone who resembled him."

The next morning Maurice was pleased to find himself received as part of the Duplay household. Even the guardian Madame allowed him a stingy smile of welcome. Again he worked hard, not enjoying a single moment of idleness, feeling Duplay's approving eye upon him.

Shortly before noon Madame turned away from someone at the open door and beckoned to Maurice, who was nearest. "Go to Citizen Robespierre in his study," she commanded. "Someone has sent to ask if he will be at today's meeting of the Committee of Public Safety. Bring me his answer." And she turned back to guard the entrance.

Maurice entered the house, dark and cool, sounds muted by carpeting and drapery. His eyes grew used to the dimness, and he saw he was in a hallway. He walked its length and found himself in a large sitting room. Voices sounded through a partly-open door in the farther wall; Robespierre and a visitor. Maurice hesitated, then knocked.

Robespierre's mild voice rose. *"Entrez-vous."*

Maurice pushed the door all the way open and stepped in, blinking in amazement.

A dozen portraits of Maximilien Robespierre lined the walls of that cramped study. Along the mantlepiece, on dainty tables, atop shelves in corners stood busts and full figures of the Incorruptible in metal and marble. Several highly polished mirrors reflected the paintings, the statues, and the man himself, so that wherever one glanced in that room, there looked back Robespierre, Robespierre, Robespierre. . . .

The living Robespierre spoke from behind a gleaming desk. "What is it?"

"Monsieur—" Maurice stood transfixed with horror at his self-betrayal. Yet the old style clothing, the ruffles, and the powdered hair of France's master had conjured up this formal term of respect.

But Robespierre merely nodded. "Go on."

Maurice cleared his throat, not knowing whether it was conceit that accepted or wisdom that ignored his slip. "They have sent to know if you will attend the meeting of the Committee of Public Safety."

Now Robespierre's visitor rose from his chair, and Maurice was startled anew.

For even as the man said to his host, "I must not keep you from your duties," Maurice recognized him as Deputy Wautier. Estelle had pointed him out in the National Convention as a one-time visitor to Claude Donard's shop in Orléans.

Wautier added, "We can finish this business another time."

Maurice stood with his tongue stuck to the roof of his mouth, desperately wishing for some excuse to speak with the deputy, to somehow halt the man's departure, to make a subtle inquiry that might ultimately lead him to his cousin Claude.

Robespierre, flipping through an appointment calendar, caught Maurice's eye. "Tell them this time I will attend the meeting." He nodded an unmistakable dismissal.

Reluctantly, Maurice left the Incorruptible-imaged study as Robespierre said to his visitor, "Come again three days from now."

Maurice lingered in the cool dim hall just beyond the house entrance. Soon Deputy Wautier came striding through, a middle-aged, heavy-set man in threadbare garments and grimy shirt, the costume of the street patriot.

Still Maurice could think of nothing to say to him.

The deputy paused just inside the door, pulled out a handkerchief, blew noisily (a true compatriot would use his fingers), and stepped outside. A paper from his pocket fluttered along the carpet. Maurice pounced.

Outside he hurried along the porch after Deputy Wautier. Madame Duplay inserted herself in front of him. "The answer?"

"What?" Maurice, shifting his attention with difficulty, remembered his original errand. Fortunately, Madame appeared to take his hesitation for stupidity. He said, "Citizen Robespierre will attend the meeting."

The deputy left the porch, pushing past the messenger hovering at the entrance. Maurice, in sudden inspiration, said, "I'll tell him myself, citizeness."

He hurried through the entrance.

The threadbare coat of Deputy Wautier vanished around a corner.

The patient face of the messenger thrust forward inquiringly. Maurice told him shortly, "He'll attend the meeting," and stepped past him into the street.

"Come back here, boy!" shouted Duplay from behind.

Maurice swayed to a halt, longing to race after his tenuous link with Orléans, with, possibly, his cousin Claude Donard.

Duplay poked his head out of the doorway. "In a rush for your dinner, eh? *Bien,* here's your seven sous. You'll be back tomorrow?"

Maurice said, "That's eight sous, citizen. And I'll return in the morning."

A few moments later he jogged along the street down which he had seen Deputy Wautier turn, but he did not catch sight of the man.

Back at the bridge abutment that had become home, he found Jules screening off part of the bank beneath with a rough balk of scorched boards. "A bakeshop burned last night," he told Maurice. "A mob attacked it because the fellow was giving them moldy bread for their rations. I helped clean up the area and got some boards for pay."

Estelle's quicker eye read the agitation on Maurice's face. "What has happened—did you lose your job?"

"I saw Deputy Wautier," Maurice said. "He came to visit Robespierre!" He described his errand to the Incorruptible's study and his futile attempt to accost the deputy outside the house.

"But what would you have said to him?" asked Jules. "You don't dare give away Estelle's presence in Paris until you know if you can trust him. And would he tell you of Claude, if he himself knew?"

"I wouldn't have blurted everything out," Maurice said.

"But something would have occurred to me as I returned his lost paper." He smoothed the small square sheet on his knee. It was a blank form, a certificate of identity.

With a startled exclamation Estelle pulled the form out of his fingers. She examined it closely. "I know this type! It was in the box Claude took with him from the shop, the only complete set remaining."

Maurice's heart pounded in his throat. "Are you certain?"

She nodded so eagerly a black curl slipped from beneath the knitted boy's cap. "Claude put the set in the cellar because it was worn and parts of it were broken. That's why it escaped destruction. Here's the chipped *f*, the crooked *j*, and see! the *i* has almost lost its dot." She pointed out several other marks. "I know this type face well from having often proofread for Claude."

"Then this Wautier must be in contact with your brother," said Jules, excitement rising in his voice. "If Claude is working with a secret organization against Robespierre, how better to get ration cards and other needed forms than by printing them yourself!"

"Unless," said Maurice doubtfully, "the men who attacked the shop took some of these forms away with them."

"C'est impossible!" exclaimed Estelle. "That type had not been used for two years when Claude and I parted. Citizen Wautier knows Claude is here in Paris. Oh, Maurice—Jules! Soon we can stop living like wild animals in this—this wretched cave!"

Jules looked offended. "We've made a good camp here, far better quarters than many people have."

Maurice said, "The deputy returns to Robespierre in three days."

Estelle seized his arm. "You must speak to him as soon as he arrives!"

"It is best to wait until he leaves, so we are not overheard," Maurice corrected. "But what shall I say?"

"Something will doubtless occur to you," said Jules with a grin.

During the next three days Maurice rehearsed many speeches in his mind while spending his mornings working for Duplay. The courtyard was lively with the labor of both trade and house, as well as a fairly steady stream of people on official business or friendly visit. There was usually a uniform or two present, sometimes a professional officer bringing word from the front, most often a neighborhood citizen on National Guard duty. Once the adjutant to the National Guard commander came, and finishing his errand he paused beside Maurice busy with his plane. "Eh, young citizen, did I not say our Robespierre takes care of all his children?"

Maurice nodded at the guileless face. "I have a job now, thanks to you, citizen."

In this sunny courtyard it was possible to forget the horrors of the teeming alleys, the quays crowded with starving homeless, the riots against bakeries and meat shops. Once Duplay sent Maurice across the city with a message for a fellow craftsman in the suburbs. As he threaded through the narrow streets in this squalid corner of the city he heard the angry snarl of drums, then a ragged cheering. Around him shutters began closing and people either stepped into houses or pressed forward to the sound. He followed, turned a corner, and then saw the tumbrils, the soldiers, the paid patriots following dutifully. He recognized among the escort some of the people with whom he himself had marched.

Maurice shouldered his way back through the crowd to take a roundabout way to deliver his message. Back in the Duplay court a bird twittered briefly in the tree of the Jacobin Club yard next door. Over this pleasant scene of garden, trees, and birds looked Robespierre's private rooms.

On the third day of waiting Maurice was suddenly apprehensive that Deputy Wautier would come after he left at noon. But as the morning coolness was burned away by the July sun, the deputy came walking along the covered porch. Passed by Madame Duplay, he entered the cool dark house.

Maurice left his plane and began picking up nails so he could keep an eye on the door. Wautier's visit seemed to last forever, and Maurice had worked himself to quite near the door when suddenly it opened and the deputy strode along to the street entrance.

Maurice waited until the man left and then pulled the lost form out of his pocket. Hurrying up to Madame Duplay he said, "That man has lost this out of his coat. I'll run after him!" Without waiting for her reply, Maurice rushed into the street. He caught up with the deputy just as he turned a corner and called out to him.

Deputy Wautier stopped, studying Maurice uncertainly. "What is it?"

"This came out of your pocket, citizen." Maurice thrust out the blank form. And for all his careful rehearsing, he knew now he had but a few seconds to cut through this man's suspicion to his confidence. He lowered his voice and spoke rapidly. "Your name is Wautier, and you came to see Claude Donard at his printing shop in Orléans."

The deputy turned pale and glanced around quickly. Then he grasped Maurice's arm and pulled him farther down the narrow street where foot traffic was not so thick. "Who are you? What do you want of me?"

His fear was so real Maurice could almost touch it. This was surely proof enough that he was working with Claude Donard's secret group! With a feeling of relief, Maurice spoke swiftly. "Claude Donard's sister Estelle is here in Paris. I am her cousin, Maurice Fabry. We two, and a friend, have been searching for Claude. We need food and shelter, and help to get out of France. Where's Claude, citizen? Tell me, *s'il vous plaît!*"

Deputy Wautier licked his lips. "Cousin? Sister? I know nothing! Why do you come to me?"

"It's because of the printing on that paper I just gave you." Precious seconds raced by while Maurice explained how Estelle recognized the type. "Citizen, Claude will realize the truth of what I say. Only give him a message from me, from his sister Estelle, I beg you!"

Comprehension at last flickered in the deputy's eyes. "Perhaps I can do better than that, young Citizen . . . Fabry, is it? Where are you living in Paris?"

Maurice paused. Jules had made as good a camp as any, but Claude would probably be displeased to find his sister living like a begger on the river bank.

Wautier misread Maurice's hesitation. "Quite right, young citizen. One cannot be too careful in these times. I can arrange a meeting. . . ." He thought a moment. "*Oui,* there is a little café, Le Matelot, not far from the right bank." He described its location, adding, "Not a good district, but safe from inquisitive eyes. It will take time to arrange a meeting with Claude, so let's say, tomorrow night at eight o'clock. You will be there, *n'est-ce-pas,* you and your cousin Estelle Donard?"

Maurice nodded. "*Oui,* citizen, but—"

Wautier chuckled. "A matter of money, is it? I will make an arrangement with the proprietor. Order a good supper, with wine, and put it on my bill."

"*Merci,* citizen. Now I must hurry back to my work."

That noon hour as Jules raked baked potatoes out of the fire and Estelle carefully pared the mold from a lump of cheese, Maurice told of the appointment he had made with Deputy Wautier.

"Will Claude himself be at the café, Maurice?" Estelle's grimy face shone with anticipation. "Oh, how can I go looking like this? I must wash. And what of clothes? I have nothing to wear!"

"You will still have to go as a boy," Jules said sternly. "I know that district. It's a tough one, not fit for a girl."

"You have done well to shelter us, Jules," Estelle said gratefully. "But how glad I will be to wear dresses and live once more in a real house!"

"And I," added Maurice, burning his fingers on his potato, "how glad I will be to set out at last for Marseille." If events moved promptly, it might yet be possible to board Captain Hawthorn's bark, due within the week in that southern port.

In the Duplay courtyard the next morning, both time and work seemed to move slowly. The carpenter had gone to the National Convention, accompanying Maximilien Robespierre who was appearing there for the first time in forty days. The Incorruptible had secluded himself during that period, laboring over an important speech. He would deliver that mighty speech to the people's representatives today, setting the course for France's future.

Madame still guarded the entrance, but as she paced along the porch her mind was clearly with the National Convention. Once she paused beside one of the regular workers. "Mark this day, Leon, the Eighth Thermidor. It is the beginning of great times for our country."

Maurice, overhearing, wondered what new repressive law Robespierre would decree. He too marked the date, Eighth Thermidor Year 2, in the peculiar invented calendar of the Revolution, and Saturday, July 26, 1794, in the ordinary notation of the normal world.

When Maurice finished his morning's work, Madame handed him his coins. But Jules was not at the bridge when he returned to their camp. "Perhaps he hasn't sold all the ribbons I sewed," suggested Estelle. She poked something out of the fire, blew off ashes, and handed Maurice a hot roll. "Flour is cheaper than bread, so I bought some, and I begged a pinch of yeast from an old woman who lives farther downriver in a sewer. Jules had salt in his bag under the bridge. It's good, isn't it?"

Maurice chewed thoughtfully. It certainly filled his aching stomach, but it was doughy on one side and burnt on the other.

Estelle did not await his evaluation. "It's terrible!" she cried, tears starting down her dirty cheeks. "*Bien,* what do you expect me to do without an oven, no milk, not even a spoonful of sugar? I hate you, I hate this place, I want to go home!" She threw herself far under the bridge and sobbed into her ragged sleeve.

"Oh, shut up!" Maurice growled. Estelle was probably suffering the tension of waiting for tonight's meeting. But so was Maurice.

Jules came leaping down the bank, red-white-and-blue ribbons fluttering over the front of his shirt. "Maurice! Estelle—is that you crying? Come and listen to me!" He began taking off the unsold patriotic decorations. "I think we should leave Paris immediately."

"*Non, non!*" exclaimed Estelle, poking her head into the sunshine. "Jules Volant, you are quite mad."

"What's happened?" Maurice demanded. "Did you think you saw Félix again?"

Jules waved away the suggestion. "Not that. But I spent the morning in the gallery of the National Convention. Robespierre was there, just as the streets had rumored. He read out a speech, two full hours of it! It was filled with threats and accusations over some vast plot against him, against France. He swore revenge, he would root out all evil!"

Estelle gasped. "Claude's in danger!"

Jules strode up and down in agitation. "Who can say? Robespierre did not reveal his enemies though he says he has a list of names. Nor did he say what he would do. But I tell you, Maurice, it is the same as before the September Massacres! A great danger is declared, followed quickly by the purge, the indiscriminate slaughter. We must leave Paris instantly!"

"What happened then?" asked Maurice, remembering Madame Duplay's promise of great things to come. "Has the Convention passed another law?"

"All was silent when he finished this two hour speech. Then suddenly everything was in an uproar," said Jules. "The presiding officer rang his bell for order, but still deputies jumped up and shouted, wrangling, contradicting. Do you know—" Jules paused, a look of wonder on his face—"do you know, one of the deputies stood up and actually denounced Robespierre as a dictator!"

Estelle gasped. "The fool—he will be dead tonight!"

"But," Jules added, "others raised their voices also, and another deputy called Robespierre a murderer. All this time Robespierre sat as if stunned. At first he tried to speak, but his thin voice was overwhelmed by the confusion. At last the noon break was declared and I left."

Jules flung himself down and accepted the slightly charred roll Estelle nervously handed him for lunch. He ate hurriedly, then asked for another. Between bites he spoke aloud, considering where to go and how.

"But perhaps Claude will have plans for us when we see him," suggested Maurice.

"We must stay for tonight's meeting at the café!" insisted Estelle.

"Never mind that now!" cried Jules. "We must leave the city before these madmen think of closing the gates!"

"You said the Convention itself is against Robespierre," Maurice reminded him.

"Bah, they sputter out their frustration and do nothing," sneered Jules. "Other deputies, whole political clubs of them, spoke out long ago and then walked the steps to the national blade. And not a citizen in Paris protested. There will be a bloodbath before tomorrow, I swear, and we must leave or die!"

Arrest!

XIV

THE HEAT WAS LIKE a thick blanket at eight o'clock that evening as three dirty ragged figures wound through the twisting streets and hovels near the right bank, following Deputy Wautier's directions toward the Café le Matelot. Jules, his bag over his shoulder, grumbled that dusk had brought no coolness. Estelle, as if to make up for that inconvenience, murmured gently, "I'm glad you came back to us, Jules."

"*Bien,* someone must watch out for you heedless ones," he muttered ungraciously.

During their bitter disagreement that noon, Maurice had suggested that Jules Volant might go his way alone since he was afraid to remain in the city. He and Estelle would keep their appointment. And Jules, his arguments failing to move them, at last shouldered his bag and stalked off in angry farewell.

As Jules told them later, he had made at once for the city walls, but arriving there to find the gates still open he had hung about, listening to the talk of people in the streets. He had then roamed around, actively seeking rumors of what might happen that day in Paris. Finding himself before the National Convention, he had gone inside, fought for a seat in the unusually crowded gallery, and had spent the afternoon observing the deputies raging fiercely over whether Robespierre's morning speech, two hours of threats and accusations, should be printed for distribution throughout France. "This speech would have spurred every Jacobin in the country into another orgy of slaughter," Jules had explained. By the end of the session, Robespierre had lost the vote. Jules had described how the Incorruptible had slumped into his chair, muttering, according to report, "I am lost!" The gallery itself had been evenly divided in its sentiments over the master of France, many of the people still cursing the law of maximum wages passed only that week which limited the amount anyone could earn.

Jules had picked up a few sous by hiring out to run through one section of Paris, announcing the names of those guillotined that day. Then after having made certain the city gates remained open, he had returned to the makeshift home under the bridge in time to join Maurice and Estelle setting out for their appointment.

Le Matelot was a squalid little coffeehouse bordering a square that was but a widening of the crooked ill-smelling street. Like other places in this intense heat, Le Matelot had set tiny round tables and chairs outside where customers could be jostled by passersby and have their pockets picked by adroit *filous*.

The proprietor, a short man with a large, flabby stomach despite severe national rationing, examined the dirty three with distrust in his porcine eyes. "Wautier," he repeated. *"Oui,* he made an arrangement. Charity to three orphans of dead soldiers, eh? A large supper, he said, and me with nothing but a sliver of fish in the house. *Bien,"* he sighed. "You shall have it, but my customers must not suspect favoritism." He cast an appraising eye over his ragged clientele, men hunched over their thin soup, tired women picking up every crumb of stale bread, a soldier with an overdressed girl friend counting his money a sou at a time. The restauranteur pointed to a cramped corner. "Seat yourselves over there."

A rickety table had been jammed between the very edge of Le Matelot's allotment of sidewalk and a huge stone vase planted with wilting geraniums. The three squeezed into flimsy chairs, hidden from the other customers but exposed to the street traffic. A lemonade seller trundled her cart close enough to scrape the back of Jules' chair. The old woman stopped and began whining an apology when Jules, knowing she only wanted to dispense her sweet drink, impatiently ordered her away.

The proprietor brought them each a sliver of badly cooked fish, a boiled potato with a slice of onion, and a mug of sour wine. Jules got up and went into the café to fetch some spicy sauce for the fish, and on his return he had to push his way between the lemonade seller and an old man on a donkey who had stopped to speak with her. The tiny square's few lamps flickering in the deepening gloom shed scant light by which to eat.

Estelle picked at her food. "Where is Deputy Wautier?"

"He'll probably come after our supper," Jules replied.

"The proprietor may make us leave as soon as we finish," worried Maurice aloud.

Jules shook his head. "No fear, we can keep on sipping wine. Slowly."

A bearded crippled man with a charcoal brazier limped into the little square and, setting up his stove across the street from Le Matelot, began roasting chestnuts for sale. The old man kicked up his donkey but had just drawn near the three youths when he stopped and dismounted to remove a stone from one of the hoofs. A very fat woman with a tray of flowers hung around her neck came out of a dark side street and bought some chestnuts, chatting with the cripple while she ate them.

Jules pushed his empty plate aside and reached for the wine bottle. Suddenly Deputy Wautier appeared out of the night. He seemed somewhat breathless, and his eyes darted all around the lamplit square while he spoke. "You've had your supper, eh? *Bien,* and where is the sister, Estelle Donard? What, this dirty gamin? Hah, a disguise, *oui.*" Playfully, he broke off a tired geranium blossom and with a flourish tucked it into a buttonhole of Estelle's ragged jacket. "Listen, *mes amis!* I must run an important errand, but stay and drink wine, and I will return in but a moment. *'Revoir!*" And off he rushed down one of the numerous unlit alleys.

Jules frowned as he splashed wine into their mugs. "I don't like this delay. Why couldn't he arrange his business more conveniently?"

"Something urgent came up, then," Maurice pointed out. "You said yourself, Jules, that the Convention is in an uproar."

"But don't you two understand?" Estelle's eyes shone as she whispered excitedly. "He only wanted to make certain of me. Now he's gone to fetch—"

Horse hoofs drummed a tattoo on the cobble. Estelle stood up and looked down the poorly lighted street leading out of the square. "That must be him now!"

Maurice struggled out of his cramped chair. "So soon?"

Jules gestured fiercely. "Sit down, Estelle! That madman cannot be— Listen! He's kicked his horse into a canter!"

The hoofs suddenly rattled faster and louder. Estelle shrank from the street, her back against the wall of the restaurant. Jules jumped up and forced his way around the stone vase to safety.

The cantering horse exploded into the square and his black-cloaked rider pulled him up, rearing and clawing the air with his sharp hoofs directly in front of Estelle. An arm shot out and seized Estelle.

Maurice yelled, "Félix!" and tumbled chairs out of his way.

Clutching Estelle tightly, Félix spurred his mount. A sudden lunge made the hoofs slip on the cobble. The horse staggered to regain his footing for several seconds while Estelle screamed and struggled in Félix's iron grip.

Jules shouted, "Stop him! Stop him!" He flung his flimsy chair, striking the horse on the flank and unfortunately spurring him on.

Maurice sprang toward the old man's donkey. "Out of the way!"

But the old fellow brushed him aside with a powerful sweep of the arm, leaped on his donkey and drummed his heels to pursue Félix who had reached the mouth of a dark alley, clutching his prey before him on the saddle.

Suddenly the old crone sent her lemonade cart spinning in front of the horse who shied with a frightened whinny. The crippled chestnut roaster ran up to seize the reins while the fat flower seller whistled shrilly. The old man forced his donkey between the frightened horse and the entrance of the alley, blocking it.

Maurice gaped. Jules struck his arm. "Come on!"

They ran toward the jostling, wrestling figures. The flower woman was biting the arm with which Félix clutched Estelle. Maurice pushed her aside, seized Félix's thumb, and bent it backwards until the man cried out and his arm sprang open. The flower seller caught Estelle as she slipped from the saddle. Someone—Jules perhaps—pulled Félix down the other side of his mount.

The chestnut roaster grasped Maurice's arm, muttering

in the unmistakable accents of Sebastien Brillon, "This way, quickly!" and pushed him down a tiny passage between two houses. A backward glimpse showed Jules pulled along by the old lemonade crone whose disarranged headcovering revealed Tante's wrinkled features. The fat flower woman whispered soothingly to Estelle in Yvette's voice. Beyond, still in the square, other figures converged on Félix, and the entire struggling crowd seemed to melt silently into darkness.

"Hurry!" urged Sebastien in his familiar agonized whisper. Only this time the play and the danger were very real.

Maurice followed blindly, guided by whispers and an occasional touch of hand to hand or a push from behind as the escaping group expertly threaded numerous dark passages and alleys, sometimes scrambling through a cellar or perhaps a dimly lit tunnel. Once when they passed a flickering lamp in some underground shaft, Maurice saw Jules behind him. "What happened to Félix?"

"The others who came when Yvette whistled were also of the troupe. Guy says Félix pulled out a pair of loaded pistols. They had to kill him in self-defense."

"That old man with the donkey—"

"Yes, that was Guy." Jules grinned. "Eh, I never knew he was that fine an actor!"

"Sebastien also," added Maurice. "Though I should have recognized that arrogant beard of his."

At last the group crammed into a tiny room smelling of its earthen walls. A door behind shut them up in darkness. The man in front, Sebastien, Maurice thought, seemed to be feeling along the wall. . . .

A doorway opened and the group stepped through into a stone-walled cellar filled with stored items, broken furniture, barrels, and a small printing press. And there in the flickering lantern light was a man with the same broad brow and dark hair as Estelle.

Estelle broke free and flung her arms around him. "Claude, Claude! I *knew* you were in Paris! Now you have arranged everything for us."

Claude greeted his sister warmly, eagerly asking after her well-being. Then he clasped Maurice's arms. *"Voila,* cousin! You do bear the stamp of the Donard family in your face. And this must be Jules Volant, *n'est-ce-pas?* Sebastien guessed you three had left Orléans together."

"He knew how to reach you then!" exclaimed Maurice.

Sebastien was already wiping off makeup. "But only in a time-consuming, roundabout way. When you three slipped away from the troupe in Orléans—*coup de tonerre,* all our careful plans utterly annihilated!" He struck his forehead in remembered suffering.

"It was Timothée—" But Maurice was interrupted by an impatient wave of Claude Donard's hand.

"We all have questions to ask of one another," said Claude. "But these must wait. Today Robespierre made a menacing speech which forces our secret group to strike swiftly."

Jules spoke up. "I heard that speech. Everyone in the streets has been debating it. I think it heralds another purge."

Guy removed the last traces of his old man's disguise. "At this very moment, Robespierre is repeating his two hour raving before his faithful Jacobin Club. We have a man there to give us a report on the club's reaction. The Convention was afraid, but the Jacobins are certain to approve of it."

Claude nodded grimly. "We must act tonight, instead of two weeks from now as we planned."

In a few terse sentences Claude Donard explained to Maurice and Jules that as a printer in Orléans he was often ordered by local authorities to suppress certain news. Some of the crimes committed in the name of Robespierre were so outrageous that Claude went to Paris to speak to a few of the deputies. The people's representatives listened politely, then said they needed facts, names, dates, before they could unite to act against Robespierre. "But every man signing his name would expose himself to certain death," said Claude. "The reports would have to be kept absolutely secret." Realizing that other pressmen also labored under censorship, Claude organized an information gathering network among his colleagues. At first he himself rode out to collect the reports, but having met with Sebastien Brillon's troupe one stormy day and taken shelter in his wagon, he found the actor sympathetic with his underground cause.

Sebastien stroked his daggerlike beard and smiled slyly. "Who alone travels without suspicion, eh? An actor's troupe! We became the artery of Donard's secret organization. That is not to say—" he shook a finger under Maurice's nose, "that the whole troupe was in on it. *Non, non!* We in this room, and one or two others. The rest—my little stray puppies! Sebastien puts bread in their mouths, and they turn eyes blind and ears deaf."

Supplied with bread cards and identity forms printed by Claude, the troupe carried messages, collected reports, transported people in flight, and contacted deputies hiding in fear of arrest. Slowly but incontestably the evidence against Robespierre and his cohorts mounted until even the most sluggish deputy would be convinced of the vast extent of the Terror and so act against the Incorruptible.

"Why do they call him Incorruptible?" Maurice asked.

Claude smiled wryly. "Because he is so devoted to the principles he set forth for governing the nation that he even sends his closest friends to the guillotine."

Guy added soberly, "Robespierre cannot open his heart to friendship, to love. He is dead inside."

"*Oui,* these reports show that," said Claude, tapping a thick folder on the table. "But how I wish I had the Rhône documents here! Those terrible crimes committed in Lyons—"

"Hugo is bringing them as fast as he can gallop," Sebastien said. "He will likely arrive late tomorrow."

"Before Robespierre's speech causes the Jacobins to loose a new patriotic massacre, we must notify those deputies hiding in Paris to be at the Convention tomorrow, ready to act," said Claude.

Guy laughed. "If they are afraid to be seen, we will take them through the streets made up as clowns. You, Maurice, you did not recognize me even when you tried to take my donkey."

When Claude, Guy, and Sebastien left the cellar through the concealed door, Tante and Yvette took the three young people up several flights of rickety stairs to cramped but very clean quarters. The rest of the troupe lived in various dwellings scattered nearby. Yvette shed her disguise and heated soup while Tante fetched blankets and allotted beds. Estelle, to her delight, was presented with dresses and linens and led away to a secluded washbowl.

Later, with stomachs full of soup, the three explained Félix's role in their flight from the troupe.

Yvette and Tante told how Sebastien had sent Hugo galloping down the Rhône valley in search of them and also to collect certain papers, while the troupe hastened to Paris to contact Claude through a coded ad placed in one of the state-licensed newspapers. When they met, Claude was certain Estelle would make for Paris, and the troupe began searching the city, in various disguises because Sebastien was convinced Maurice and Estelle had become suspicious of the actors' motives. Tante, finding the three at Le Matelot, sent a hasty message, and the rest gathered around to scoop them up. "Instead, we found ourselves as rescuers," said Yvette.

Weeks ago when Claude had had to go into hiding, he had sent Sebastien to meet Maurice in Nazaire. Hugo, riding ahead to the port, had just missed Maurice as he boarded the night coach to Paris. Later they learned Maurice had gotten off the coach when it had been stopped en route. Hugo, having glimpsed Maurice's face up against the coach window in Nazaire, searched along the sideroads until he saw young Fabry and Jules Volant, and the troupers at last caught up with their mission.

Maurice awoke very late the next morning. He hardly recognized Estelle in her dress. Tante was busy cutting down another skirt for her. Yvette served Maurice a delayed breakfast.

"Where's Jules?" he asked. "Did Sebastien and Claude come back last night?"

"Oui, and they've gone out again, Jules with them," said Yvette. "They're at the National Convention with the documents Claude has collected."

"Claude said you are to meet him there as soon as you are awake, Maurice," said Estelle. "He will go with you to the American minister to arrange for a new passport."

"Are you still coming to Boston with me, Estelle?"

She nodded gravely. "Claude said I must. Even if things change for the better, war still rages all around France, and if we lose . . ." She shrugged. *"Bien,* I want to meet my aunt and uncle. Perhaps I will even learn the English tongue, *n'est-ce-pas?"*

"Of course you will! Maman has already arranged lessons."

Yvette took his plate. "Now be off, Maurice! If all goes

well, you and Estelle will be on the coach for Marseille next Wednesday."

Maurice left the house in shirtsleeves, picking his way down narrow dark stairs to the dingy street below where the day's heat was like the blast from the blacksmith's forge. Sunlight reflecting from age-polished cobble nearly blinded him as he followed Yvette's directions out of the quarter. Sweat streamed down people's faces and dogs slunk in the shadows. The idle sat on the curbs of fountains with their meager trickles of water or gathered along the quays to get what cool air moved sluggishly over the Seine.

People moved more quickly past the smart shops of the Rue St. Honoré, and there was talk of some excitement inside the Convention. Maurice passed the Duplay residence on the other side of the street, then began working his way through the crowd before the National Convention. A tanner's apprentice told Maurice the gallery was so crowded to hear the grand fight inside that no one else was allowed. But Maurice pushed forward, shoving past a distracted armed soldier. Inside he went through cool, dim hallways up to the gallery.

He squeezed inside the crowded balcony, pushing and shoving until he found Claude Donard in the front row.

Claude nodded a terse greeting and gestured to the confusion on the Convention floor below. "So far they have succeeded in keeping Robespierre and his cohorts from speaking." As Maurice looked down, Claude pointed out and identified some of the men.

Robespierre stood by the speaker's dais, one foot on the bottom step. He was as elegantly groomed as ever, neatly powdered hair well set off by a blue frock coat and yellow silk knee breeches, his white ruffles stiffly starched. On a higher step stood a slim young man with golden hair,

Saint-Just his name, a partner in terror who particularly enjoyed sending people to the guillotine. He held the papers of a speech in his hand. Two men occupied the speaker's desk, men making Claude Donard's cause their own.

Surging around the speaker's dais were shouting, gesturing deputies, shaking fists, yelling accusations. Over all this the presiding officer of the Convention rang his bell furiously for order. One of the men at the speaker's desk signaled for recognition, and the bell ceased abruptly. As the uproar subsided, the speaker pointed to Robespierre and cried out, "Why did you create your own secret police, if you didn't mean to tyrannize all of us?"

Robespierre raised his thin voice. "Murderers—all of you, murderers!"

At once the furious pounding of the presiding bell drowned his words. A deputy secured the floor and waved a hand to the packed gallery above. "You good citizens up there, did you hear this man proclaim us to be murderers?"

And around Maurice and Claude, the intently watching citizens, reeking of sweat and sour wine, began yelling indignantly.

During a lull in the tumult, Robespierre raised clenched fists and began to shout. Suddenly his voice broke, and he mouthed wordlessly.

A deputy jumped up. "The blood of your victims chokes you!"

"Cowards!" Robespierre's voice came back, desperate, fear-strained. "Why did you not defend them?"

"Tyrant! Tyrant!" roared the representatives, and the gallery rang the cry back like a chorus. The bell clapper beat like a call to arms.

Robespierre paced up and down the aisles of the Convention, attempting to speak with one deputy or another under the continual noise and confusion. Representatives shrank away from him. Someone at the speaker's desk began a long harangue. The Convention members broke into conferring groups, or hurled their individual accusations into the growing turmoil.

Maurice realized this must be the same kind of indecisive milling around that Jules had described after Robespierre's scathing speech of yesterday.

Claude pounded the gallery railing in frustration. "Now!" he hissed to himself. "*Now* is the time to overthrow the Incorruptible!"

Maurice saw Robespierre wring his hands, his lips shaping the same word over and over as he prowled up and down the chamber: "Death! Death! Death!"

Claude was right. If this moment were not seized, Robespierre would never be stopped.

Suddenly a deputy leaped up and asked to speak. As the din ebbed, his words rang out: "I propose a decree of arrest against Robespierre!"

Shocked silence fell like a hammer blow.

Suddenly the representatives sprang out of their seats. "Vote! Vote!" And in a thunder of unanimity, the deputies passed the motion for Robespierre's arrest.

The gallery broke into cheers of relief and enthusiasm. Below, the representatives threw their hats in the air. Joy shook the windows of the Convention.

"Vive la République! Vive la Liberté!"

Maurice seized his cousin's arm. "Claude, you've won, you've won!"

"It's not over, Maurice." Claude shook his head. "Not yet."

Call to Arms

XV MAURICE AND CLAUDE hurried through the baking hot streets of Paris, crossed the river whose crowded banks were already buzzing with rumors, and went along the quay to the tree-shaded house of the American minister. They were taking advantage of a brief recess of the Convention to get a new passport for Maurice.

"I won't really need it now, will I?" asked Maurice. "Now that Robespierre no longer rules—"

Claude smiled grimly as he rang the doorbell. "Robespierre has so many supporters of his tyranny throughout the nation, Maurice, that a revolt could easily break out. If you and Estelle are to leave within the week, you will need the protection of an American passport."

From across the river and just a few blocks upstream sounded the urgent brassy clanging of a bell. "They're ringing the tocsin!" exclaimed Claude. "The Sections of Paris are being called to arms!"

Maurice's heart skipped a beat. "Has some trouble broken out at the Convention?"

Claude shook his head. "The Convention would rely upon its own troops first. It must be some Robespierrist who is summoning the Sections."

"The people of Paris—will they revolt?" Maurice looked

over the crowds along the quay. Heads were turning in the direction of the Hôtel de Ville, the seat of city government. But despite a restless stirring and some desultory debate, the citizens did not seem anxious to spring into action.

The door of the American minister's house opened, and the manservant directed them to the office. The anteroom to Gouverneur Morris's study was as crowded as Maurice had seen it his first day in Paris, but more agitated because of the alarm bell's clamor. Claude spoke to the young secretary at some length, then the man actually led them through the crowded room and into the study. The chair behind the elegant polished desk was empty.

"Please be seated," said the secretary, setting out chairs for them. "Monsieur Morris is out on an errand of mercy for the relative of a countryman. But he will be glad to meet you, Monsieur Donard. We have both heard much of your work from our French friends."

When they were left alone, Claude explained that remark to Maurice. "Monsieur Morris has always been sympathetic to the victims of Robespierre's Terror. I know from my own undercover contacts that more than once he has hidden inside this ministry certain fugitives from the frequent house-to-house searches."

Through an open window they could still hear the reverberating ringing of the alarm.

But what could anyone do now that Robespierre was under arrest? Leaderless, the Terror must surely crumble before lawful authority.

By the end of that turbulent, triumphant morning session, the Convention had voted the arrests of Robespierre, his young brother Augustin, Saint-Just with the golden hair, Le Bas who was Duplay's son-in-law, and the cripple Couthon who had authored the horrors at Lyons. These men were members of the dread Committee of Public Safety or had held other offices during the Terror. Arrest warrants had also been decreed for Commandant Hanriot of the National Guard, and for the presiding judge of the Revolutionary Tribunal, the court whose only sentence was death.

Then who was ringing the tocsin? Why didn't someone tell the *sot* that the Terror was ending?

As time passed, Maurice thought that the Convention had surely begun its afternoon session. He could see from Claude's restless pacing that he longed to be there. But Sebastien and Guy would see to things. Maurice had caught a distant glimpse of them as he and Claude had been working their way through the densely packed halls, and, upon meeting Jules, he had told him where they were going.

A delicate clock daintily chimed the hour. Maurice looked out of the window. The crowds along the quay had broken up into argumentative knots of people. Some men hurried along, buttoning the jackets of their National Guard uniforms. A few women pulled unwilling children into doorways. Across the river three or four artillerymen dragged a cannon toward the Hôtel de Ville.

At last the door to the study opened and Gouverneur Morris entered. He and Claude introduced themselves and spoke about the covert work to save the Revolution from Robespierre. Then Claude let Maurice explain in detail how he had lost his papers.

The American minister nodded. "Yes, I remember you from some days ago. I'm glad your story is true and that you can now prove your citizenship. In your new passport I'm going to write a full description of you so no thief can use it."

Claude spoke up. "There is the matter of my young

sister. . . ."

He and Monsieur Morris discussed this problem, for Estelle was not an American, and even an immigrant could not be granted citizen's papers. The average French citizen had not been authorized to travel outside his country for a long time. Even if Estelle secured a French passport of her own, it would probably not be honored by any French official between Paris and the docks of Marseille. At last the American minister devised a solution. He at once sat down and wrote out the passport for Maurice, signed it and stamped it with the official seal.

Maurice grinned as he read it. The pass was made out to Maurice Fabry, American citizen, traveling with his cousin Estelle Donard. It was written in English and French, and contained descriptions of them both. "Someone reading this hastily would think Estelle has American citizenship."

Gouverneur Morris carefully placed the tips of his fingers together and looked at the ceiling. "I didn't really state that, did I? The passport is entirely legal. I can't help it if people draw mistaken conclusions."

The dainty little clock struck three when Claude and Maurice took their leave to plunge into the thick heat of the streets. Sweating sans-culottes asked one another for news and exchanged contradictory rumors. Farther down the quay a group of dispirited National Guardsmen was disbanded by their officer and began trudging home. But not far away a corporal briskly marched his squad over a bridge toward the Hôtel de Ville on the right bank. The tocsin, silent for nearly half an hour, resumed its insistent clamor. A woman with a lemonade cart cursed the noise for overwhelming her tinkling little bell. A horseman galloped along the quay toward them.

"Look, Claude, it's Jules!"

Jules reined his mount to a prancing halt. "Claude, Sebastien sent me for you! Hanriot, the National Guard Commandant, is galloping around Paris, gathering soldiers, arresting any deputy he finds on the streets, and swearing he'll rescue Robespierre!"

"What! Aren't Robespierre and his friends in prison?"

Jules shook his head. "When the afternoon session began, they all sat calmly in the Convention with their arrest warrants in their laps, talking to one another as if nothing had happened. The deputies are beginning to lose their nerve."

"What is the Convention doing?"

Jules laughed scornfully. "They debate the pay of front line soldiers, but they falter nervously when they see the Terrorists staring insolently at them. And Hanriot—"

"Give me your horse!" Claude seized the reins and vaulted into the saddle. "I'll stiffen their backs until the Rhône documents arrive. Reading of those horrors will thoroughly convince any wavering deputies."

"The papers are due today, aren't they?" asked Maurice.

Claude nodded. "Hugo is bringing them directly to one of our men, Deputy Wautier, who'll take them before the Convention." Claude kicked up his horse and vanished down the street amid a clatter of hoofs.

"Wautier!" exclaimed Jules. "Maurice, I never thought of it until this very moment—"

"You don't think he had anything to do with what happened to us last night, do you?"

"Of course! Guy told me today that Félix was a member of Robespierre's secret police. They found papers on him last night which proved it. Wautier must have been selling him information from time to time. Remember how Wautier delayed coming until we had of a certainty arrived at Le Matelot? Then he was coy with Estelle, putting a flower in her boy's jacket."

"To mark her for Félix?"

Jules nodded. "Then off our deputy rushed with some story of a vital errand!"

"But really to alert Félix to capture Estelle, the 'boy' with the flower!" It seemed to fit. Maurice clenched his hands. Wautier would have endangered himself by revealing Claude's whereabouts in Paris, thereby exposing his own association with the conspiracy. But he could safely betray Estelle to Félix, who would then use her to force Claude Donard into the open.

"Our friends in disguise must have been around us by then," said Jules. "But this Wautier's visit was so hasty and sly, hovering as he was in the shadows, that he must have slipped past their notice. Let's go and warn Claude at once that this man is a traitor!"

"Claude's hands are full now," objected Maurice. "But we must prevent Hugo from handing those vital Rhône documents to Wautier. Where can we find the deputy?"

"Hugo wouldn't know of Claude's change of plans, so Wautier would still have to keep to the original rendezvous," reckoned Jules. "I'll wager he's waiting for Hugo in his own quarters, wherever they are."

"Then we'll have to stop Hugo outside the city."

Jules nodded. "The Lyons road. He can take no other. Let's go."

Despite the clinging heat, they hurried along the left bank. Others rushed too, small curious boys dodging among the loitering clumps of people, men responding to the insistent bell, a few furtive folk scurrying from one hiding place to another in fear of a blood bath to come. But some National Guardsmen lounged in the skimpy shade along the bank whose mud was cracking into baked earth under the brutal sun. And occasionally tradesmen standing in the open doors of their poorly stocked shops shouted derision at those citizens running in answer to the call to arms.

Sweat poured down Maurice's face, but he shivered as he and Jules drew abreast the bridge that crossed to the Conciergerie prison. Glancing at those grim spires on the Île de la Cité, he was startled to see people leaning out of adjacent buildings, waving rags, and making signals with their arms. Were they trying to tell the condemned that the Terror was over, that they might dare hope for life? Then a building cut off the view and Maurice hurried to catch up with Jules.

Farther up the Seine, past their camping place on the bank, they crossed the river on the last bridge within the city. Making their way among the hovels on the other side they finally walked through the city gate on the Lyons road.

They waited in the slender shade of a line of poplar trees. The heat weighed them down like chains. The very air seemed to have congealed so that the dust coating everything did not stir, and the only movement of shadows came from the slow reeling of the sun. From time to time during their long hot vigil the distant tocsin reverberated from within the city, but no life stirred in the parched fields, nor in the few scattered heat-blasted huts, nor along the sun-cracked road.

A long time later a finger of dust dragged along the south. "A horseman," said Maurice, shading his eyes.

The dusty plume grew larger and closer until they could hear the hoofs, then see the foam-flecked horse driven onward by its rider.

"Hugo!" Maurice yelled, and Jules joined him in shouting and waving.

The horseman swerved, wavered, then slowed. "Maurice! Jules!" Hugo pulled his mount down to a prancing halt. "Sebastien's looking for you! Where's André?"

They ran up to him and in a tumble of jerky sentences gave a rough account of recent events and warned him against Deputy Wautier.

Hugo did not waste time in questions, but nodded tersely. "Then I'll take these papers directly to Claude at the National Convention." He patted the leather pouch at his side, mounted his horse, and rode through the city gate.

Maurice and Jules followed on foot, coughing in the dust stirred up by Hugo's mount. Inside the city wall, as houses pressed against one another and leaned over the narrow streets it seemed hotter than a brick oven. People sat on their stoops or leaned against a shadowed wall, eating supper out of their hands—bread, boiled potato, the lucky ones a bit of hard cheese.

Hunger stirred in Maurice's stomach. "Can we find our way to Sebastien's and Yvette's quarters? We could get something to eat."

Jules nodded. "I noted well where they lived when we left for the Convention this morning." He led the way through the twisting streets of broken cobble.

Suddenly their way was blocked by a large hushed crowd of people all staring down the street. Others leaned from upper windows, grim-lipped, hostile. Even the dogs cowered in silence.

Then sounded the rhythmic clopping of trained horses, the squealing of cartwheels. And around a bend came the cavalry, the tumbrils, and a ragged band of paid witnesses. The death cortège drew nearer amid the unnatural silence of the assembled sans-culottes. The sergeant in charge glanced around in continual alert while his mount danced nervously on the cobble.

Then a woman in the carts began sobbing.

Never before had the weeping in the tumbrils been heard in these streets, for the rattle of drums and the roar of the crowds had habitually overwhelmed both sorrow and conscience.

"Drums!" ordered the sergeant sharply.

But only a few taps sounded before a burly soap boiler shook his fist and shouted, "Robespierre is under arrest! Commandant Hanriot has been seized! Let these people go!"

The crowd surged forward, surrounding the carts. "Let them go! Let them live!" The hefty soap boiler and some comrades seized the reins of the cavalry and put hands on the tumbrils.

Blades whipped out of scabbards and under sword blows the crowd fell back a few paces.

Sanson, the chief executioner, sat placidly in the driver's seat of the leading cart, but the sergeant of cavalry was furious. "Clear the streets!" he shouted.

A threatening murmur rumbled like distant thunder.

The sergeant's face glowed red with anger. "I have my orders, you fools, and I must carry them out!"

"Let them live one more day!" cried out a woman. "Perhaps tomorrow there'll be no more executions!"

One of the bound young men in the tumbrils raised his head. "Just give us a few more hours, citizens! Until tomorrow—" A sob choked him.

"Out of the way!" yelled the sergeant. "We're coming through!" He reared his horse and struck out with his sword. There was a scream, and the crowd dragged an injured youth from the cobble.

The cavalrymen wheeled their horses and laid about with their swords. The reluctant crowd was forced back against the mean houses lining the narrow street. Maurice and

Jules were squeezed tightly against a doorframe. "Drums!" ordered the sergeant once more.

The death march resumed with the orderly tattoo muffling any heart-piercing cries from the miserable victims. The cavalry rode with naked swords in hand.

As the paid witnesses at the tail end straggled by, one of them raised his voice. "*Vive la*—"

The soap boiler snatched the man out of line and shook a menacing fist under his nose. The fellow twisted in the hefty grip, pleading, "Please, citizen, I've got to earn my twenty sous—"

"Paagh!" growled the soap boiler in disgust, and he shoved the fellow down on the cobbles. The witness scrambled up and scurried after the procession.

Slowly the crowd broke up, talking, gesticulating, arguing. From a distance came the renewed clangor of the tocsin. One man gazed in the direction of the bell, then spat in the dust. Yet across the street another man hurriedly left his house, buttoning the jacket of his uniform with one hand while the other clutched his musket as he went to answer the summons. No one stopped him.

Maurice turned to Jules. "I wonder if it's true that the Incorruptible is at last in prison."

A woman paused beside them. "Eh, of course, it's true! I was there in the gallery myself when the Convention called the guards and had the entire lot of hypocrites hauled off to a distant room of the building. Later, that drunken fool Hanriot rode to the rescue with a handful of troops but was himself seized. Then the Convention ordered Robespierre and his fellow traitors off to prison and adjourned for their supper." She walked off, muttering, "Never did trust them, never!"

"It sounds as though Hugo arrived too late with the papers," said Maurice.

"Never mind. At least Claude stiffened the deputies' backs as he said he would," replied Jules. "They can see the documents during the evening session."

They wound their way through the dreary quarter, hearing the alarm bell and watching men answering or not answering it, and they listened to the good citizens cursing the National Convention or the Paris Commune, which opposed it.

An officer in a well-fitting fairly clean uniform came toward them, stopped and exclaimed, "You're the lad working with Duplay, aren't you?"

Maurice recognized the adjutant to Commandant Hanriot. "*Oui,* citizen, thanks to you." He wondered why the man was not on horseback while the tocsin was still ringing madly.

"What's going on, then?" the adjutant demanded. "The Duplay house is dark and shuttered, and no one answers my knock. Have you heard anything? I can't even find Commandant Hanriot!"

"He is under arrest," said Maurice, and Jules added, "Robespierre has been taken to prison."

The adjutant's eyes widened. "Is that really true? I have learned just now that the Committee of Public Safety has issued a warrant for the mayor, but Mayor Fleuriot-Lescot is still at liberty. They say he is organizing a defense at the Hôtel de Ville." He licked his lips and glanced around as if to deduce the mood of the city from the loafers in the street. "Tell me, has the Incorruptible actually been taken to prison?"

Maurice and Jules told the adjutant all the news they had, including a description of the last dismal march to the guillotine.

The adjutant glanced down at his impressive uniform. "It is over, then. I have served the Commune faithfully, and now . . . *Bien,* one must save oneself, *n'est-ce-pas?* It wouldn't be good for you to have it known that you worked for Duplay."

"I'm not afraid," said Maurice. "Besides, citizen, we are well known to those who have secretly worked to bring this very moment about."

The adjutant's eyebrows climbed. "Ah, you were spies, then?"

"Non, non," Maurice and Jules protested together.

But the adjutant was not listening. He glanced around, then leaned close. "Listen, young citizens, how would the Convention like to know the National Guard password Hanriot designated for this week, eh? It might make things march easier, since the uniforms are alike." He lowered his voice even more. "The password is 'Unicorn,' and the countersign is 'Volcano.' Remember them, and tell the Convention where you got that information, will you?"

"Why can't you go and tell them yourself?" Maurice asked.

The adjutant nervously fingered the hilt of his sword. "They might just fling me into prison beside Hanriot. Robespierre himself has shown that kind of gratitude, if the truth be known, though I admit I used to believe his excuses. Now I'm going to go home and burn this uniform and drink a bottle of wine."

"If you want to go to ground," offered Jules, "you had best leave Paris at once and hide in the country."

The adjutant smiled wryly. "It's too late for that. Haven't you heard? All city gates have been closed, by order of the Paris Commune. *Au 'voir, mes amis!"*

Jules' face went white. "We're trapped—all of us!"

"Claude was right," Maurice said slowly. "The Terror isn't over yet. There's going to be a fight to the death."

The Storm Breaks

XVI Heat dragged over Maurice's shoulders like burning coals as he and Jules ate the cold potato soup Yvette served them and blotted their thirst with mugs of astringent wine.

The little backroom quarters were unbelievably stuffy, and the tiny windows looking out over a cramped backyard admitted little air and less light. Though slanting into evening, the sunlight did not temper its merciless blast. Yvette, moving about her household tasks, paused often to wipe her brow. And Estelle, sewing industriously on clothes she would take to America, pushed back damp locks of hair. Only old Tante, hovering over her cards by candlelight and wrapped in her usual shawls and petticoats, seemed dry as a wrinkled mushroom.

Though these three had had no news whatever all day, Yvette had not allowed talk when Maurice and Jules had arrived but had insisted they eat without delay.

Now that the table was cleared, the youths described the day's happenings. Tante paid no attention to anything beyond her cards, her gnarled fingers weaving a ceaseless pattern as she shuffled, laid out, regrouped, and shuffled again. Estelle was shocked, and Yvette indignant, over the possibility of Deputy Wautier having attempted the betrayal of Claude's secret work through the kidnapping of his young sister.

"That must be taken care of," declared Yvette fiercely, the first time Maurice had seen her angry.

"I'll see about Wautier myself," said Jules determinedly. "Just tell me where he has his quarters."

Yvette gave his address, but added, "This matter must wait, Jules. It is not important enough for attention with the fate of France hanging in the balance of tonight's events."

"The people who were guillotined this evening were also too unimportant to bother with," said Maurice. He could not get those desperate sobs out of his mind. "They died needlessly."

"Maurice," said Yvette, "thousands have died just as needlessly."

Unexpectedly, Tante spoke up without taking her eyes from her cards. "Eh, that blood is on the sergeant's head. The *sot* should have delayed, sent for orders. But he will die." A bony finger tapped a dark card. "Horribly. It is here." She swept the cards into a shuffle, chuckling to herself.

The gloom deepened and Yvette lighted another candle, then brought out a bundle of knitting. Jules stirred restlessly, but Maurice was too hot and sweaty to move. Conversation was sparse until Estelle began asking about life in Boston. This interested everyone, and soon Maurice became absorbed in recalling his home life.

A knock on the door silenced them. Then Yvette nodded. "It is the signal." She unlocked the door to Sebastien, who swept her into his arms with a flood of endearments. He gallantly kissed Estelle's hand and made a teasing reference to when she had played the part of a dirty gamin. Then he greeted Maurice and Jules with hearty blows on each one's shoulder. "Great events march, *mes amis!* You are privileged to be living in such stirring times!"

"Eat, *chéri,*" commanded Yvette, setting a place and touching his bearded cheek with a loving hand.

Sebastien ate with gusto but lingered over a second mug of wine.

Yvette, knitting needles clicking, asked, "Why are you so late, *chéri?* And what of the others? The Convention adjourned over two hours ago."

"*Chut,* my sweet, you speak like a waspish schoolmistress!" chided Sebastien. "Claude kept us working, running here, persuading there, collecting deputies in droves to look over Hugo's papers." He turned to Maurice and Jules. "Ah, that was quick work, *mes petits,* to direct Hugo right to us at the Convention. Claude and the others, they have sent out for a cold supper, but I wanted to see my *chérie's* face and tell her the news myself."

It was true, Sebastien told them, that the Convention had recessed, but the Committee of Public Safety had stayed in session. It had many orders to issue, calling up the Army and the National Guard on behalf of the Convention, forbidding men to arm for the Paris Commune, ordering the arrest of Mayor Fleuriot-Lescot and Government Commissar Payan. Meanwhile there were reports that the Commune, assembled in the Hôtel de Ville, was issuing counter orders. One of them forbade Paris prisons to accept arrested suspects without an order from the Commune. "Robespierre and his four friends were sent off under armed guards," said Sebastien, "but they were turned away from the gates of several prisons. We did not, of course, discover this absurd play-acting until too late to take action."

"You mean," cried Maurice in disbelief, "that prisons

refused to admit them, that their guards could not force the captives behind bars?"

Sebastien nodded. According to eyewitnesses, the arrested company broke up into individual escorts, trooping from prison to prison, the cripple Couthon carried on a plank and Robespierre himself riding in a carriage. At one prison a crowd in the street recognized the Incorruptible and cheered halfheartedly. "And now finally word has come that each villain is housed in a different prison, under restraint at last," said Sebastien. "At seven o'clock the Convention assembled for the evening session. All the guards were still away finding prison space for the arrested men, and no new troops had yet assembled. Suddenly a messenger hurried in, and the presiding officer rose to announce that a detachment of Commune troops had freed Commandant Hanriot in a distant wing of the huge building. At this very moment those same troops were marching against the Convention.

"Silence fell like a stroke. Then the presiding officer cried, 'Let us die at our posts!' The public was ordered out of the gallery, and when the rustle of their departure had died away the hundreds of deputies sat in stillness at their desks among the dancing lights of the candles. I was next to one who began scribbling, and I saw he was writing his last will. Another began a farewell letter to his wife. A few actually continued their work, one composing a speech, another writing to his constituents in the east. Some talked, seriously or made nervous jokes. A few stared out of the windows into the dusk. And all the while, growing in gradual strength, rumbled the wheels of distant artillery, the trotting of horses in unison. I fancied I heard the echo of crisp orders. We sat there in silence, Claude and Guy and Hugo and I and the deputies, all waiting for booted feet to pound up the outer steps."

Sebastien's shadow loomed gauntly on the scabby walls of the stuffy back quarters. Maurice held his breath until it ached. Yvette's needles poised in mid-stitch. "And then?" she whispered.

"The cannon wheels ground louder and louder," said Sebastien, beard jutting like a sword. "Horse hoofs clattered like icicles crashing to the ground. Then suddenly—" he broke off, reliving the scene—"suddenly the groaning of wheels and the clopping of hoofs began to diminish. They grew fainter and fainter until once more we sat in stillness among the flickering candles.

"Suddenly a deputy jumped up. 'I demand that Robespierre and his associates be immediately outlawed!' With a roar of approval, it was so declared. Then the chamber rang with proposals and orders, the Convention truly united in its resolve to crush the Commune's rebellion." Eyes flashing, Sebastien held his dramatic pose for a few moments. "Now, *chérie,* I return to the Convention. Maurice! Jules! I leave these fair ladies in your hands. *Au revoir!*"

As they listened to Sebastien clattering down the stairs, Jules grumbled, "I would like to have gone along!"

Time dragged. And though the last of the day's light drained out of the sky, the heat remained as oppressive as ever. Yvette entertained them with anecdotes of theater life in the old days. Tante hunched over her cards, turning up dark designs and muttering, "Death! Death!" in almost gleeful prediction. Jules prowled in silent agony until Maurice could no longer bear watching him.

"Why don't you go sit on the stoop downstairs, Jules?" he suggested. "There may be a breath of air."

Yvette framed a protest, but surprisingly Tante spoke up. "Let them both go. Great events are in the cards, and they are to be a part of them."

"Bien," agreed Yvette reluctantly. "But go directly to Claude at the Convention. He will watch out for you both."

Outside as they strode along the cobbled street fitfully lighted at wide intervals, Jules said, "I couldn't help feeling caged, Maurice. It was too much like the time we orphans in our hospital waited for things to happen, and when they did . . ."

"You don't believe in Tante's card reading, do you?"

Jules grunted. "That's for amusement, but once in a while Tante is touched with some foreknowledge. *Alors,* let's pass near the Hôtel de Ville. We may come into some news for Claude."

Maurice could never have found his way alone through the twisting maze that formed much of Paris. An occasional candle from inside a modest dwelling augmented the feeble public lighting. Most of the populace seemed to be crowded in their open doorways or leaning against walls. Those in the streets walked hurriedly, either responding to some call of duty or evading it. Once when he and Jules edged past tables crowding the narrow street outside a shoddy café, Maurice overheard tense arguing: "But if the Incorruptible is guilty of all those executions, *mon ami,* then so are we. Did we not cheer every head that fell under the knife?"

"Don' matter," responded the wine-sodden voice of his companion. "Robespierre's wage maximum's drivin' us deeper 'n' deeper in poverty. Scoundrel d'serves t'die!"

As Maurice and Jules neared the Hôtel de Ville a phalanx of soldiers appeared across a well-lighted street and turned them away.

"Rumors of the mayor organizing resistance must be true," said Jules, leading them around the cordoned area to the river. Crossing the brightly lanterned quay behind a solid rank of armed National Guards they slithered down the dirt bank and started making their way in the darkness past the broad avenue and the Hôtel de Ville above them. A nearby noise made them crouch in tense silence.

Two guardsmen climbed down from the quay above, removed their headgear and splashed their faces with water. "It's been stand and sweat for the last five hours," complained one, mopping his wet brow. "It's action I want, or I'll go along home."

"You'll get your action," promised the other. "Saint-Just, Hanriot and most of the others are gathered together, only awaiting the arrival of Robespierre himself to direct the *coup d'état*."

"He might hurry," grumbled the first. "He has but to walk down the quay and across the square to the Hôtel de Ville."

"Perhaps he arrives at this very moment," returned his friend.

They scrambled up the steep dirt bank to their posts.

"They—they've just walked out of their prisons!" whispered Maurice in astonishment.

"The mayor must have ordered them set free," said Jules. "I wonder if Claude knows."

"Let's first see what we're up against," suggested Maurice. Carefully the two pulled themselves up the bank until their eyes were level with the quay.

Maurice blinked in the bright light. The quay and the huge square in front of the Hôtel de Ville were brilliantly illuminated by what seemed to be hundreds of lanterns and candles glowing steadily in the still air, increasing the local temperature of the already sweltering weather. The steady light fell on rank after rank of bayonet-bearing guardsmen; it gleamed on the poised cannons; it moved rhythmically over the muscles of officers' pacing horses.

And the great gray stone of the Hôtel de Ville itself, the administration building of the city government, was fretted by glowing yellow windows. On the first floor above street level, Maurice thought he saw a man's shadow move across the room.

He and Jules slipped back to river level and rapidly made their way downstream. When Jules judged they must be near the Convention building, they pulled themselves up to street level and were immediately seized by two guards. "Spies, Robert!" one shouted in the dark. "Call the Corporal of the Guard."

Maurice twisted in the guard's grip. "We have an important message for Claude Donard, citizen!"

At the guardsmen's derisive snort, Jules added, "He can identify us. We've worked with him."

By the time the Corporal of the Guard arrived the two guards were doubtful about their captives. The three consulted and, under the pleas of Maurice and Jules, at last took them across a spacious garden and into a side door of the huge Convention building. They waited for a long time before Guy arrived. Producing his own identification he vouched for them, then led them through a maze of corridors until they arrived in the small room off the Convention chamber that Claude had been using as his office.

Like Guy, Claude looked very tired. "You should have stayed with Yvette and Estelle," he said reproachfully.

Maurice wasted no time. "Claude, Robespierre is at the Hôtel de Ville with the other outlawed men!"

As he and Jules explained what they had learned, the tiredness of Claude's face set into determined lines. Claude said, "Guy, find Barras at once." And to Maurice he added, "Barras has just been made Commander-in-Chief of all armed forces in Paris."

When Commander Barras arrived, Claude had Maurice

and Jules repeat their story. Barras' lips went tight. "Since the city gates are closed by the Commune I cannot communicate with troops outside the walls. And the men of Paris are responding sluggishly to my call to arms. With every street surrounding the Hôtel de Ville guarded as these youths claim, I would need cavalry to fight through to the conspirators."

"The password!" exclaimed Maurice. "Commander, we know the password being used by the Commune troops. One of Hanriot's adjutants told us!" He described the meeting in the street.

"The password is 'Unicorn,' " said Jules, "and the countersign is 'Volcano.' "

Barras' eyes narrowed thoughtfully, then he nodded. *"Bien,* we will use them to save lives. Yet I would still wait, Citizen Donard, for the declaration of outlawry to take effect throughout the city. Everyone must know that if he lifts a hand to help these outlaws, he himself is subject to instant death." He smiled grimly. "The declaration may also help shake loose a few National Guardsmen from their homes, *n'est-ce-pas?* You lads, stay here. I may have further use for you. Now I must report these latest developments to the Convention."

Maurice and Jules were left to their own devices, for Claude still had a great deal of work to do among the deputies. Guy went off on errands. Occasionally Sebastien or Hugo entered the room on some urgent matter only to slip out again in haste. Deputies came and went, as did ushers with messages and papers to deliver.

Bored, Maurice and Jules wandered through the halls, to be stopped by Hugo and warned not to stray into the unlighted passages and become lost in this huge building whose intricate suites and gilded rooms had once housed the Royal Family. Maurice leaned out of an open chamber window, searching vainly for a breeze. Far off along the night horizon orange flickered amid a wild tangle of clouds. "Storm coming, Jules."

Below, there was movement in the crooked streets of the sparsely lanterned city where people lay sweating in the dark, waiting for sleep, or perhaps for the outcome of this brooding, tense night. A small procession of drummers and four guardsmen with torches leading three deputies on horseback marched briskly down a nearby street and stopped at a corner. Drums snarled, the deputies drew their swords, and one announced in a carrying voice the outlawing of Robespierre and his cohorts, as well as anyone who ventured to help these men. The procession marched to the next street corner, and the ceremony was repeated. In the wake of the proclamation, Maurice saw shadows moving as people darted out of their houses or leaned out of windows to talk over this latest event.

"It'll take all night for Paris to hear the news," Jules complained, looking out over Maurice's shoulder.

"Let's see what the Convention's doing, then."

They sat in the all but deserted visitors' gallery above the floor, but there were no grand speeches, just low tense murmuring and a bustling of men and papers. "How dull it is to rule a country," remarked Jules.

They went back to Claude's room. Maurice sat in a comfortable chair near a window and leaned his head back. . . .

He was awakened by a crash of thunder and a spray of rain on his face. Jumping up he swiftly closed the window next to him just as a gust of wind blew out most of the candles in the room. Claude hurried to relight them as Jules shut the other window. Rain streamed down the dark glass and wind rattled the frames as pink lightning etched patterns against the boiling clouds. Another crack of thunder, louder this time, and it seemed Maurice could feel the great stone building trembling under his feet.

A clock thinly stroked the midnight hour, announcing the start of a new day, the Tenth Thermidor. But Maurice knew he would remember it forever as July 28, 1794.

Commander Barras entered, looking for Maurice and Jules. "As soon as the storm is over, we march against the Hôtel de Ville," he told them. "You lads will come with us to be certain the correct password is given. Report to me in the garden."

The storm lasted half an hour, whipping trees, banging loose shutters, and carrying the dust off the cobbles in muddy streams. Then reluctantly the clouds rolled away, grumbling and forked with yellow flashes, dragging the last sheets of rain with them.

Claude opened the windows, and Maurice and Jules went down to the garden. The vast lawns sparkled wetly under the brilliant starlight except where the shadowed ranks of armed men stood in formation. A corporal took the youths to Commander Barras.

"We're moving in two columns," he told them tersely. "Maurice will come with me. Jules will go with the other. Put on these coats and hats. You're soldiers for tonight. Can you shoot a musket? Never mind, you'll get a pistol each, but you are not to shoot except in defense of your lives."

In a few moments Maurice was standing stiffly in the fore ranks on one side of the huge garden with Jules a wide sweep of lawn away. He fidgeted in his uniform coat with its crossed white belts and the heavy cocked hat. A pistol in a holster weighted one side. The walks were steaming dry and the air hung with sultry heat, for the brief storm had brought no lasting relief.

Barras uttered a sharp command, and the column

swung out of the garden, past the Convention building, and down the broad Rue St. Honoré. A last glimpse showed Maurice that Jules' column was heading down the quay.

They marched in virtual darkness, boots stamping on the cobble, past the shuttered shops of fashion, past the locked Jacobin Club and the darkened house of Duplay, past closed theaters and dead churches, past black-market-victualed cafés patronized by war profiteers where candles were hastily snuffed.

A barrier of uniformed men stopped them. "Password?"

Maurice, just behind Barras, murmured, "Unicorn."

And Barras spoke it aloud.

"Volcano," returned the sentry. "Glad to see more troops. Proceed."

The Convention's troops marched through. Twice more the magic word opened the way. Then the houses crouching on either side fell away. The column swung smartly and entered the great square before the Hôtel de Ville. Most of the brilliant lighting had been extinguished by the sudden storm, and apparently many of the troops had dispersed. In the scattered lantern light cannon barrels shone dimly, and the remaining troops lounged in ragged lines. On the opposite side of the square a smart column marched up from the quay, and as the two armed flanks approached, Maurice saw Jules in the front.

Barras shouted the command to charge.

The ranks split up under subordinate officers, leveling bayonets and running to surround the vast Hôtel de Ville, to seize the unattended cannon, to clash with the remnants of the Commune troops, subduing resisters with shot and thrust.

Maurice found himself running with Jules behind a detachment surging up the Hôtel steps under the other commander. They burst through the doors and flooded into the sprawling corridors. Passages rang with the tattoo of boots on marble and the thud of muskets clubbing down doors. "Where's Robespierre?" cried out the commander.

"Upstairs!" shouted Maurice, remembering that moving shadow across the window. "To the right!"

He leaped along as they stormed up the steps, Jules just behind him. One hallway out of many was lined with candles and down this roared the troops, pausing only to smash open doors. Maurice, dashing along in the commander's wake, caught glimpses of stunned white faces quickly hidden behind a press of soldiers. From a distance, around some corner, a shrill scream burst, echoed, was cut off suddenly. The troops hurtled on amid cries and warning shots.

Another door splintered; the commander plunged in, Maurice and Jules at his heels.

Maximilien Robespierre sat at a desk, a pen in his hand, as soldiers boiled into the room.

"Robespierre, in the name of the Convention, I arrest—" The commander got no further.

Another man in the room, Le Bas, put a pistol to his own head, fired, and slumped to the floor. Robespierre's younger brother vaulted through an open window. The Incorruptible suddenly snatched up a pistol, raised it to his head, and pulled the trigger. The shot seemed an echo to the first, so close had both come.

Robespierre fell to the floor, blood staining the carpet and flecking the beautiful snow-white lace at his throat.

Ride the Tumbrils

XVII

"Is he dead?" asked the citizen in a cautious whisper.

"He still lives," answered Maurice with a glance at the wounded man lying on the table in the office of the Committee of Public Safety. Robespierre had been brought to this room in the Convention building over two hours ago. Guards pushed back the curious citizens crowding in the doorway, but this man had been let through. Maurice asked, "Are you the physician?" He knew one had been sent for.

The man shook his head. "No, young citizen, I'm a deputy."

Maurice studied the timid elected representative. "Tell me," he urged, "all the while Robespierre bloodied the whole of France, what did you accomplish?"

Weariness and relief mingled in the deputy's voice. "Young citizen, I survived."

When the man left, muttering a curse for the fallen dictator, Maurice thought again of that fateful scene in the Hôtel de Ville.

Acrid black smoke had hung like a curtain in the small room as the commander had bent to examine Maximilien Robespierre. "He's breathing!" The pistol ball had shattered the Incorruptible's jaw, leaving him alive but with a horrible wound of gaping flesh and splintered bone. With his own handkerchief the commander had bound the fractured jaw shut, and blood had quickly dyed and later crusted the white linen.

"Fetch a board to carry him on," the commander had ordered. "There, that leaf from the table."

The other man, Le Bas, had been successful in his suicide. The younger Robespierre, who had sprung through the open window, had made his way along the outside ledge and, reaching a corner, had either slipped or jumped and had plunged to the square below. He too still lived, though unconscious from his extensive injuries. The crippled Couthon had been found with a fractured skull at the bottom of a dark staircase, down which he had fallen in an attempt to scuttle away from the invading troops. Saint-Just, Robespierre's golden-haired partner in death, had submitted to arrest without resistance along with the mayor, other Commune officials, and those Section leaders who had made the Incorruptible's cause their own. But Hanriot, the deposed Commandant of the National Guard, had not been found.

The captives had been marched or carried to the Conciergerie prison nearby, except for Maximilien Robespierre. Barras had had him borne to the Convention chamber where the deputies still had been in session. The presiding officer had announced to the assembly, "The coward Robespierre is here. Do you wish him brought in?"

"Non, non!" the representatives had shouted, for fear of the Incorruptible had still gripped them. And one man had cried out, "The place for him and his accomplices is before the sword of the law at the place of execution."

At this, deputies had jumped out of their places, cheering and waving hats and scarves, for the first time realizing their victory.

Robespierre had then been carried to this office, formerly one of Queen Marie-Antoinette's sumptuous apartments.

In the mellow candlelight the painted cherubs on the ceiling smiled, and the gold beading gleamed softly. Robespierre lay as still as a statue, breathing so shallowly that Maurice could hardly detect movement beneath the blood-stained lace-ruffled shirt and sky-blue frock coat. The knee straps of his yellow breeches were loose and his silk stockings sagged over his silver-buckled shoes. His head rested on a tin box, and patches of powder had fallen off his curled and queued hair. A linen cloth held the pieces of his jaw together, and his face was nearly as waxen as the candles burning near it.

A uniformed officer carrying an instrument case shouldered his way into the room. He was the surgeon. Briskly he undid the crude bandage around Robespierre's head and began picking out pieces of bone, cutting away blasted flesh, sponging and suturing. With impersonal efficiency he bound up the wound, then replaced the bloody handkerchief with a clean linen cloth. A little clock struck five times, and through the curtainless window Maurice saw the distant sheen of dawn.

The pressure of citizens against the guards slowly forced them back. And now that the recently departed surgeon had said the scoundrel would live there seemed little reason for the soldiers to deprive the Parisians of their look at the Incorruptible. At first the gawkers spoke in hushed tones, but gradually the voices were raised as citizens pushed and shoved and filed past the green felt-covered table. "Isn't he a fine-looking king now?"

"A bit thin for a sausage," answered another. "But we'll slice him with the National Knife anyway."

The jibes grew more insulting, the crush increased. Maurice wormed his way across the room, intent on getting out. A push carried him against the table for a moment, and his eyes rested briefly on those of Maximilien Robespierre, for the wounded man was fully conscious and following the progress of each face past his pallet.

Then the crowd jostled Maurice away and swept him out of the room.

Guy met him in the corridor. "Maurice, go and eat. There is a cold supper in that room, and the deputies are taking a little refreshment now."

He went to a long room and filled a plate with cold ham and bread and fruit and took a glass of wine, then sat at a table with some deputies and listened to them arguing about removing the maximum wage or not. Stomach full, Maurice felt a sudden wave of fatigue, and put his head down on the table. The deputies had already gone back to the session.

Someone shook his shoulder and Sebastien's voice said, "Arise, young wolfhound. I'll take you home. Jules had the sense to seek his bed there hours ago."

Sleepily, Maurice allowed Sebastien to drag him through the dawn-lighted streets of Paris, only noting that, strange for such an early hour, the foot traffic toward the Convention was very heavy, and that happy voices rang in the broad avenues and crooked alleys.

Sun struck his eyes, flinging him awake. Maurice looked around and discovered he was in the quarters of Sebastien and Yvette.

Estelle came to the door. "Awake, yes? *Bien,* Maurice, will you have lunch or supper?"

He sat up, for he had slept in his clothes. "What time is it?" But the slant of the sun told him. "It must be well after four in the afternoon!" Hunger knifed through him.

"I'm starved!"

Yvette set a huge plateful on the table; mounds of mashed potatoes, some little pickled apples, and—yes, a miracle!—two well-browned sausages. He savored them slowly, making them last. "Where's Jules, Sebastien, all the others?" Even old Tante's corner was empty.

All the men were busy among the deputies at the Convention, which had adjourned at six in the morning, and reconvened three hours later. Many crimes needed investigation, the victims to be compensated, new laws to be propounded, and all this before the representatives-on-mission returned to Paris. These were deputies, Robespierrists all, sent out to the provinces and the army lines to turn up conspiracies, punish rebels, and administer the harshest of the dictator's laws. "Sixty-eight representatives are absent from the Convention," Yvette explained. "That is why the *coup* succeeded last night, why the remaining majority of deputies dared seize this moment to move against the Incorruptible. Perhaps now the Constitution, which has been suspended for many months, will at last be restored, and France can live under genuine law once more."

Estelle added news she knew would interest Maurice. Hanriot, the missing former Commandant of the National Guard, had been dragged out of the Hôtel de Ville's cesspool that morning, having fallen into it last night when he had attempted to hide in a narrow shaft. He and the other outlaws had been taken before the Tribunal that morning and identified. They would be executed in the late afternoon, as soon as Sanson and his helpers had finished erecting the guillotine in its original place near the Convention. The Duplay family had been arrested early that morning, except for the two daughters, one being the widow of the dead Le Bas.

Tante had gone out freely in the streets to visit old

friends. And Jules had left shortly before Maurice awoke to find Wautier, determined to bring this personal enemy to justice.

"Jules will need help in tracking down the scoundrel," said Maurice. "After last night, Wautier would hardly dare stay at home."

Yvette mentioned two or three cafés Wautier had been known to frequent during the time he had been a trusted member of Claude Donard's undercover organization. One was Le Matelot, and Maurice said he would go there first.

The cobbles threw back the heat like a furnace, and the scaling stucco walls reflected the afternoon light blindingly. But what amazed Maurice was the sight of hundreds of gay banners and ribbons in patriotic colors affixed to the houses. And as he went through the crooked streets, he encountered men, women, and children trooping along in groups, making jokes, calling out cheerfully to one another.

At the Café le Matelot, the rickety tables crowding into the narrow street were lively with men celebrating with cheap wine. And to listen to the useless bragging of the ragged customers, everyone had defied Robespierre and had worked against his cruel dictates. Maurice wished it had been true. Then the Terror could not have lasted a single week.

The short fat proprietor denied knowing a Deputy Wautier, and when Maurice reminded him of a meal arranged for three ragged children but two nights before, he said, "*Chut,* everyone is making arrangements! I tell you, little one, a café owner is as put upon as a spinster aunt. I would go mad if I tried to remember all these details. Wautier? Who knows?" He shrugged and started scrubbing a tabletop.

Something furtive in the man's manner made Maurice

positive that he knew Wautier well. It suggested that perhaps the deputy had been accustomed to meeting Félix, the secret policeman, in this district.

Maurice, remembering the address Yvette had given Jules, set out for Wautier's quarters in a better part of the city.

He could not blame the family men, the people responsible for children, for invalids, the aged; they had to bow before the Terror in order to protect their charges. But he despised those who used the Terror to gain personal revenge or to accumulate money, for even death can be made to pay someone. And worst of all were those volunteers, the representatives who worked for election and once in the National Convention sat trembling under Robespierre's universally accusing finger, not challenging his condemnation of entire groups without a genuine court trial. And the men who accepted official positions were often either too lazy or too afraid to assert their vested authority. Pressed, they resigned rather than take a stand and left the way open for Terrorists.

A group of laughing young men pushed past Maurice. They were boldly dressed in the old-fashioned knee breeches and frock coats, white wigs askew on their heads. Heaven only knew where they had gotten these garments they wore to mock the Revolution, for only two days ago mere possession of them would have readily sent a man to the guillotine. Perhaps Yvette was right, that now true law would return to France.

More and more people pushed by, and soon Maurice found himself caught up in a fairly solid moving mass of humans. He let himself be carried along, watching for an alleyway through which to get free. But every street they passed only fed more people into the crowd. They called to friends, laughed or shouted sentiments like "Down with the wage maximum!"

Helplessly Maurice was borne along, and when the street debouched into a broad avenue, he recognized it as the Rue St. Honoré. Here the mobs grew denser. Gay bunting decorated each building, and every window was open and crowded with eager faces. Some landlords, leaning perilously far out from the ledges, hawked yet additional space at so many sous each, and some escaped from the street mob to slip inside, pay the fee, and squeeze even more tightly within the window. A few brave lemonade sellers tinkled their bells, but were so overwhelmed by the masses that they had to retreat. More slowly now, the segment in which Maurice was embedded went past a few wagons whose owners were selling space.

And then from behind there arose such a storm of yelling that people paused to crane their necks. "Here they come! Here comes our fine silken-breeched Incorruptible!"

Maurice stumbled on a box, then quickly jumped up on it to see over the heads of the crowd. The soldiers came first on their horses, swords poised to sweep a path for the four tumbrils behind. Sanson, as usual, sat imperturbably in the leading cart. Armed escort ranged alongside the tumbrils, and the drummers came after, their hands whirring in tattoo, but the sound was completely lost in the howling of the mob. Fists shook, some threw rotten eggs down from the windows, others jumped up on the tumbrils to curse the occupants. The escort tolerated this with rare good humor, only urging the vehicles onward. Slowly the procession neared.

When it drew abreast Maurice, there were yells of, "Which is he?" One of the cavalrymen pointed with his sword and identified the tyrants. Hanriot, covered with blood and filth from his fall in the cesspool, cowered on the floor of the first cart next to the younger Robespierre.

Saint-Just stood upright, immaculate in his vain dress. Robespierre the Incorruptible lay in his cart, eyes closed, bandage once more blood-soaked. Couthon, Dumas of the Tribunal, the mayor, all of them jostled and swayed as the tumbrils struggled through the rejoicing crowds.

A woman sprang onto Robespierre's cart, spat upon the Incorruptible and screamed, "Go to hell with the curses of all wives and mothers!" One of the guards detached her kindly and got the tumbrils moving again.

Maurice was swept from his box and kept in pace with the procession by the pressure of the mob around him forcing itself through the greater crowd stolidly braced against the walls of the fashionable shops and houses. A group of women halted the cortège before the house of Duplay and ringed the tumbrils, dancing and singing insulting lyrics. A butcher's apprentice appeared, grinning, and, having drenched a broom in a pail of ox blood, he swept dripping red swaths across Duplay's fine entrance and handsome shutters. The crowd yelled with laughter and shouted abusive remarks. Maurice overheard someone say, "That old cow, Madame Duplay, hanged herself in prison. I just heard."

When the tumbrils were moving again, Maurice still drifted along in the press of the mob, sticky with sweat, nearly choking from the heat, the closeness of people, and the continual screaming. It seemed to take forever to reach the short street leading into the Place de la Révolution.

This gigantic square at the end of the gardens behind the National Convention was even more closely packed with humans, and yet they found room to give way before the flats of the escort's swords. Maurice fought to keep his footing, and finally grabbed an iron railing before one of the great houses bordering the square. More and more people jammed up next to him until he was actually lifted off the ground, his back scraping up the brick wall. A man yelled down from above, "Come through the door! You got to pay for the view!"

Twisting around, Maurice saw a window above him filled with jostling figures, one angry person demanding several sous. But Maurice's involuntary movement toward that window was halted, and he was pushed against the side of the house, with a decorative ledge to brace himself on above the heads of the mob.

Amid the insulting, fist-shaking, laughing, and yelling crowd, Maurice saw some faces pale from lack of sun. Since no one stayed long in prison under Robespierre, these people must have been in hiding from the Terror, and were now abroad to taste sweet air and sweeter vengeance.

The soldiers and the tumbrils reached the guillotine rising high on its great platform in the center of the vast Place de la Révolution. They had left the Conciergerie prison nearly two hours and one mile ago.

Methodically, Sanson felt along the edge of the triangular blade, rasped a section of it, then signaled to begin. The first one hauled out of the tumbrils was the crippled Couthon.

The noise of the crowd slackened to an eager murmuring and heads strained to see the first tyrant die. The assistant executioners could not straighten out Couthon's warped body; they finally strapped him on his side on the tilting board. They ripped away his collar so the blade would bite cleanly. Drums rattled as they slammed the board down and dropped the wooden neckpiece in place. Sanson tripped the knife.

With a flash of orange in the setting sun's rays, the steel triangle hurtled down and boomed to an echoing halt. Couthon's head flipped into the wicker basket, and a great cheer leaped from thousands of throats. With a broom in his hands and a wilted flower between his teeth, one assistant swept the planks clear of blood as the others pulled out the next criminal, and Sanson wound the blade up on its ratchets.

Twenty times the giant steel knife crashed downward, and twenty times the roar of the crowd applauded the judicial thunder of the blade. The wicker basket was taken away and replaced by an empty one. One of the tumbrils was filled with headless corpses, their blood streaming from between the palings. The guillotine platform was spattered by red blood on red paint, and the steel triangle itself bore a crimson death flower.

Now two men awaited death: Mayor Fleuriot-Lescot and Maximilien Robespierre, who was to be last. To the crowd's surprise, Sanson's men next pulled the Incorruptible to his feet. "Aha," murmured a knowing fellow in the window above Maurice. "They fear he'll die before they can kill him."

Thin, pale, small, the man who had held France in the grip of Terror stumbled up the guillotine steps, his arms bound behind him. The assistants pulled his sky-blue frock coat from his shoulders and ripped away the lace at his throat. Amid the curses screamed by the citizens, Robespierre was strapped to the upright wooden plank. Sanson's knife clicked to the top of the twin posts, and the crowd quickly fell silent but for the continual jostling and shoving. Now the angry snarl of the drums could be heard.

Sanson gestured for the removal of the bandage which was an impediment to the blade. An assistant stepped to the upright plank, reached for the linen around Robespierre's face, and tore it away.

An incredible shriek leaped from the raw gaping hole; a pain-filled scream penetrated to every corner of the vast square, its shrill echo clawing away among the buildings.

The plank slammed into place.

The knife thundered downward.

Boom!

The shattered head dropped into the wicker basket.

A great jubilant bellowing burst from the thousands packed cheek to jowl in the Place de la Révolution. The deafening clamor trumpeted through the streets and rolled among the hills ringing Paris. Scarves and ribbons fluttered madly and plumed hats whirled giddily from every window and along each avenue.

"À bas la tyrannie!"

"Vive la Liberté!"

"Vive! Vive! Vive! Live, live, *live!"*

People embraced, tears streaming down their faces. They danced and waved their arms, and they screamed their joy and relief while windows rattled and the ground pulsed beneath their stamping feet.

Through the din, Maurice heard a woman near him sob happily, "Now no more blood will flow!"

With the triumphant uproar still reverberating, Sanson dropped the knife on Mayor Fleuriot-Lescot.

The man died virtually unnoticed.

Two days later, Maurice, in serviceable clothing bought by Claude, and Estelle, in the garments she had sewn, watched the coachmen strap their valises on top of the Marseille coach.

Claude Donard said, "It's a long hard journey, but you will arrive in time to board Captain Hawthorn's vessel."

Estelle clasped and unclasped her hands. "I want to go to Boston, Claude, but I still feel I should stay here to make a home for you."

He shook his head. "It will take a long time and a great deal of work to rid our country of the last shreds of mob rule."

His words carried a note of grief, for not many hours before Claude had learned of the Companies of the Sun. These were bands of roving men who had sprung up spontaneously throughout France. They had instituted a counter Terror in which they were hunting out, beating, even slaying the Jacobins who had oppressed them. Claude wondered aloud how long it would be before the Companies of the Sun, if unchecked, would begin to massacre those who merely disagreed with them, as did the Jacobins.

Maurice said, "It's true they had suffered under Robespierre, but now they are committing the same crimes. What's the answer, Claude?"

"History gives us no answers, Maurice. These are modern times, and we must devise our own solutions. God grant they are the right ones! I know this: all that stands between man and terror is law, not the dictates of one person or of a mob." He paused in thought, then added, "Now that I am openly publishing a newspaper again, I can work to prove that when you respect the law even while it protects your enemies, the law will in turn protect you against those who wish you harm."

Estelle protested, "You wouldn't want the Jacobins to go unpunished!"

"Of course not! Right now the Convention is busy drawing up arrest warrants to deal lawfully with those whose cruelties overshadowed even Robespierre's," said Claude. "If only the Companies of the Sun turned their backs on the cheap pleasure of revenge, they could accomplish much for our country! Why must they go on killing in the days ahead? There are other wars to be won, and a new

France to be built."

"And for some of us, a new life entirely," said Estelle with a little sigh. "Look, here comes Jules."

Jules Volant, sack over his shoulder, sauntered down the street toward where the coach was loading.

Maurice called to him, "*Bien,* you have changed your mind, then, and will come with us after all."

Jules grinned and shook his head. "*Ah, non, alors!* I would bend my head trying to learn the English tongue. I came to bid you farewell and to start wandering down some lazy valley, perhaps the Rhône."

"Be careful," Claude warned. "There are bands of men—"

"*Oui, oui,* I have heard," replied Jules. "They also say that the very worst of these Jacobins are whining that they only obeyed orders."

Estelle said, "Jules, you went out earlier to continue your search for Wautier. Have you found any trace of him?"

Jules scowled. "No one admits knowing him except his landlady. She is angry, for he packed his things and left hastily, owing her money." Then he shrugged. "*Bien,* it is finished. I won't waste any more thoughts over that type."

The coach driver called out to the group of waiting passengers, "Places, *s'il vous plaît!*"

Maurice and Estelle had earlier taken leave of Yvette, Sebastien, Guy, and the rest of the theater troupe. Now Claude embraced his sister, tweaked her nose, and made her promise to write him. After a round of handclasps and final farewells, Maurice and Estelle crowded into the nearly filled coach.

The driver clicked to his horses. The coach lurched into motion. Estelle waved out of the window until a bend in the street hid Claude and Jules.

Flashing through the city gate, the coach picked up speed and rattled off at a fast pace, bearing Maurice and Estelle toward Marseille, days distant, toward the sea and toward Boston beyond.

Bibliography

Brinton, Clarence Crane, *A Decade of Revolution 1789–1799,* Harper and Bros., New York and London, 1934.

Carlyle, Thomas, *The French Revolution, A History,* Modern Library, New York. Originally appeared in print in 1837.

Castelot, André, *Queen of France: A Biography of Marie-Antoinette,* trans. from the French by Denise Folliot, Harper and Bros., New York, 1957.

Johnson, Clifton, *Along French Byways,* Macmillan, New York, 1925.

Lowell, Edward J., *The Eve of the French Revolution,* Houghton Mifflin, Boston and New York, 1895.

MacLeish, Kenneth, and Conger, Dean, "River of Counts and Kings: the Loire," *The National Geographic Magazine,* Vol. 129, No. 6 (June, 1966), pp. 822–869.

Moffett, Cleveland, *The Reign of Terror in the French Revolution,* Ballantine Books, New York, 1962.

Morris, Gouverneur, *A Diary of the French Revolution,* edited by Beatrix Cary Davenport, 2 vols., Houghton Mifflin, Boston, 1939.

Ogrizek, Dore, editor, *Provinces of France,* McGraw, New York, 1951.

Rude, George, editor, *Robespierre,* Prentice-Hall, Englewood Cliffs, New Jersey, 1967.

Sieburg, Friedrich, *Robespierre: The Incorruptible,* trans. from the German by John Dilke, Robet M. McBride and Co., New York, 1938.

Tschan, F. J., Grimm, H. J., and Squires, J. D., *Western Civilization,* 2 vols., Lippincott, Philadelphia and New York, 1945, Vol. II.

United States Department of State, *The American Passport: Its History and Digest of Laws,* Government Printing Office, Washington, D. C., 1898.